I0738396

CARRY ME HOME

Stories of Horror and Heartbreak

by

Michael Paul
GONZALEZ

CARRY ME HOME: Stories of Horror and Heartbreak
c. 2020 ThunderDome Press
ISBN: 978-0-578-70930-7

Design and Typesetting by Michael Paul Gonzalez

Cover art: "Sweetwater" by George Cotronis (*cotronis.com*)

Interior images:

Throughout YOUR MUTUAL FRIEND: Plate 28. The mandibles (jawbones) and teeth.. Credit: Wellcome Collection. Attribution 4.0 International (CC BY 4.0)

P 24: The identification of the wicked and their descent into hell. Engraving by A. Collaert.. Credit: Wellcome Collection. Attribution 4.0 International (CC BY 4.0)

P 52: The entrails of a horse (?), showing kidneys and bladder. Engraving by R. Gaillard after J. de Seve.. Credit: Wellcome Collection. Attribution 4.0 International (CC BY 4.0)

P 66: Frankenstein observing the first stirrings of his creature.. Credit: Wellcome Collection. Attribution 4.0 International (CC BY 4.0)

P 112: A bear in a rocky landscape, below, its footprints. Etching by J.E. Ridinger.. Credit: Wellcome Collection. Attribution 4.0 International (CC BY 4.0)

P132: Two anatomical oil paintings by D'Agoty. Credit: Wellcome Collection. Attribution 4.0 International (CC BY 4.0)

P148: Skeleton and écorché figure holding placard featuring male and female figures: half-title page to 'Trattato di anatomia pittorica'. Lithograph after C. Squanquerillo, 1839.. Credit: Wellcome Collection. Attribution 4.0 International (CC BY 4.0)

P 112: Bears: Papers of Charles McMoran Wilson, Lord Moran.. Credit: Wellcome Collection. Attribution 4.0 International (CC BY 4.0)

P 178: Newgate prison.. Credit: Wellcome Collection. Attribution 4.0 International (CC BY 4.0)

P 198: Men are fishing for whale in small boats with harpoons; larger sailing ships are in the distance. Aquatint.. Credit: Wellcome Collection. Attribution 4.0 International (CC BY 4.0)

P 202: The phoenix immolating itself on a funeral pyre; representing rebirth and eternity. Engraving by J. Droeshout.. Credit: Wellcome Collection. Attribution 4.0 International (CC BY 4.0)

P 210: Daedalus and Icarus. Engraving by A.G.L. Desnoyers after C.P. Landon.. Credit: Wellcome Collection. Attribution 4.0 International (CC BY 4.0)

P 239: A woman is holding her dying lover; a sword lying at his feet. Engraving after F. Goya, 1812/1888.. Credit: Wellcome Collection. Attribution 4.0 International (CC BY 4.0)

When you're done - For the Good of All Humanity: Take this book and fold it into a bird. We've had our moment, you and I. You picked this up and read it all the way to the end. Or maybe not. Maybe you stopped a few stories in. That's okay, because you've already read this, the important part. Fold this book into a bird. The message you've taken away from this, what you got out of it, it's in your brain. You don't need to read this again. You need to make a bird out of it. A swan. Maybe a dove, if you're crafty enough. Maybe you're reading this electronically. The experiment will still hold. Move this file to an empty folder. Delete it. In its place, save a picture of a bird. Something distinctive, but native to your area. Get exotic. Maybe others will see the same bird. Maybe they'll see it and think it's a different bird. We interpret birds differently. Talk to each other. Don't fight about it. This is for the good of all humanity. After you've released your bird, you must cease thinking of it for a while. Then, in a month or so, when you remember, look to the skies to find a passing shadow and see what's become of us.

-adapted from work originally published in Gather Kindling, a zine that's gone, but still a bird to me

May you find light and hope in dark times.

Hello, and thanks for buying this book. Or picking it up in a store and thinking about buying it. Or looking through it and deciding to get it later from an online corporate behemoth. Thanks, at the very least, for noticing it.

TRIGGER WARNINGS

All of these stories contain some element of horror or loss. There is violence, some of it visceral, some more like a fun B-movie. I might miss a few big-ticket items, but I specifically want to call out a few stories without spoilers:

Your Mutual Friend: violence against children/kidnapping
Worth the Having: extreme violence involving manipulation and abuse
Upper Crust: extreme gore, degradation, misogyny (look, it's an allegory about a certain thin-skinned, power-mad real estate megalomaniac...)

***

THANK YOU

Does everyone read the thanks section, or just people hoping to see their names? If I missed you in here, I really am sorry, and you really are thanked. Deadlines, man. Gotta get this thing finished.

Thanks to: Aleksandra Bienkowska, Kate Jonez, Max Booth III & Lori Michelle, Eugene Johnson, David James Keaton, Gillian Whitaker, Sara Read, Eric Miller, Linda Nagle, Xach Fromson, Lauren Salerno, John Palisano, Kate Maruyama, Amanda Gowin, Berrien Henderson, Hal Bodner, Katarina Leigh Waters, and the entire L.A. Chapter of the HWA. All of you have taken chances on my work or just offered me general encouragement, and I can't thank you enough. Sometimes your reading was the only reason I kept writing.

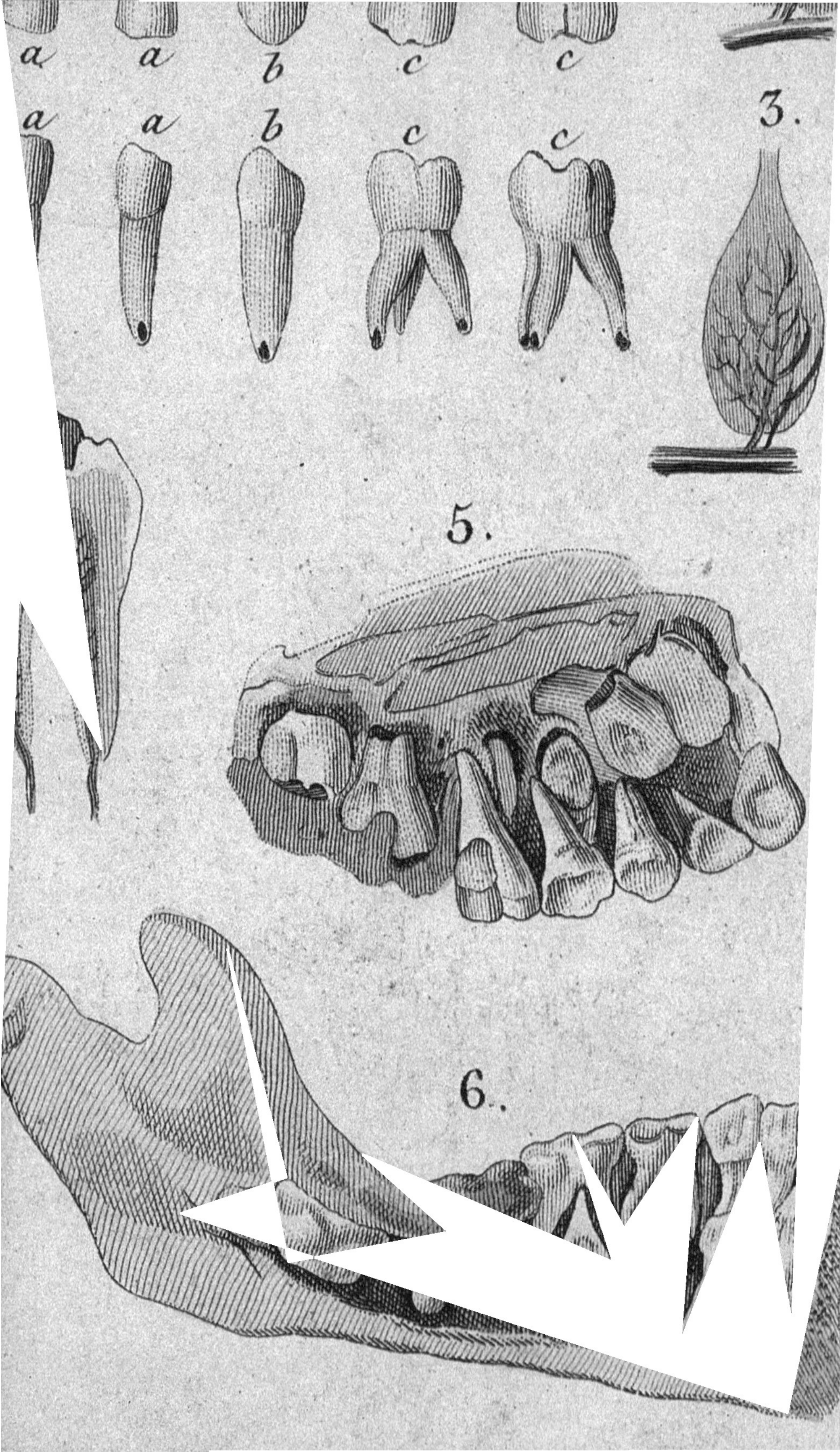
a
a
a
a
b
b
c
c
c
c
3.
5.
6.

YOUR MUTUAL FRIEND

October 31, 1986

There were three constants when it came to Halloween:

The weather would be horrible.

Chris would hate his costume.

It wouldn't matter what his costume was because he'd have to wear a winter jacket over the top of it.

One thing he liked about Halloween, or any holiday really, was that it gave his family an excuse to talk to each other. Most nights, his mom and dad sat silent on the couch watching the news or *M*A*S*H**, barely saying a word. With costume plans or candy sorting, they had something to talk to him about besides school.

When he planned his costumes, his ideas grew too grandiose. They'd listen, sure, but nothing ever panned out. Chris prided himself on accuracy. If he had the chance to dress as a zombie, he'd be the most diseased, shambling mess his classroom had ever seen. If he could be a werewolf, he'd arrive with blood dripping off of his maw and spattering his shredded clothes.

None of that mattered, because his mom wasn't crafty and his dad was always away on duty, so whatever he wore would be coming off the rack at the local grocery store. That meant an uncomfortably hot vinyl jumpsuit that would be horribly inaccurate. Last year, he'd been forced to go as Batman, a suit that came with numerous problems:

You could see his sneakers below the boot tops painted onto the legs of the outfit.

The cape only fell to his waist. Safety be damned, you couldn't threaten a criminal in a cape made for a drum major.

If there was one thing for certain about Batman, it was this: He would never wear an outfit that had a cartoon caricature of his own face next to the word BATMAN™ across the chest.

He was determined to make this year different. Store-bought or no, he would find a way to customize whatever he got, and he would brave the near-zero Wyoming temperatures for some properly costumed trick or treating. Whatever was at the store that night, he'd make it into magic.

As it turned out, his mother had forgotten that tomorrow was Halloween (how could that even be possible? They'd gone over costume options a million times coming home from school!) and after a mad dash to the grocery store they'd returned with the only things they could find: three red-tagged makeup kits and a plastic jack-o'-lantern bucket.

Army man it was, then.

With his dad out in the field "watching the pigs" (an Air Force euphemism for guarding sensitive nuclear sites), Chris had to figure out how to do the camo on his own. He spent the night studying all of his GI Joe comics, looking at his action figures to find the best way to convey *remorseless killing machine* without being so scary that people might hide instead of give him candy. His mother offered to help, but what kind of soldier lets his mom paint on camo?

The big night arrived, and Chris headed out into the dark, bundled up in one of his Dad's field jackets. If there was any saving grace to this whole fiasco, it was that he could go out in a warm jacket and still be authentic to his character. The plan was to meet up with friends at the school nearby and then raid the surrounding blocks until his bucket was too heavy to carry home. His mom stayed behind, warning him to be back in an hour or she'd come looking for him.

He trudged down the silent street out of his cul-de-sac. The neighborhood was quiet enough that their parents could stay at home. It had snowed a few days earlier and most of the ground cover had been blown away by the Wyoming winds. He'd called Steve and Kevin before leaving just to make sure they weren't chickening out, and they assured him everything was still on. They just had to be home by a set time. This wasn't a curfew, no. They were on *a one-hour mission* to snag all the candy they could and return to base.

Too cold to snow was how his dad always described it. The night was quiet, as if most of the kids had decided that it wasn't worth it in this weather. He wondered if it was like this out in the field where his dad was, silent and cold. Chris imagined giant underground silos, steam and cables and super spy gadgetry. He'd been assured numerous times that it was a boring thing, guarding the missiles, just driving fencelines and doing paperwork.

The wind came in waves, leaving a strange quality in the air when it died down, a stillness that amplified every ambient sound on the empty street. A little scary, but Chris spent the first two blocks reminding himself that he was a soldier. Stealthy. Camouflaged. A lethal shadow in the night. If trouble came, he'd be ready to fight or fade into nature and become invisible. He managed to push those thoughts out of his mind as he saw a few other brave souls going door-to-door. He wasn't supposed to start without Steve and Kevin, but a test run surely couldn't hurt. Two houses later, he made the final approach to the rendezvous point with a mouth full of fun-sized Snickers. It wasn't cheating. It was a scout mission to tell his fellow soldiers about rich targets of opportunity.

The elementary school was perched on a hill, with two tall streetlamps throwing sickly yellow light down on the fence surrounding the playground. As he approached, he saw two shapes moving near the fenceline. A hunched demon howled and snarled as it attempted to wrestle a robot warrior to the ground.

"Get off, fart head!" the warrior sprung back and spun the demon against the fence, bringing laughter from both of them.

From fifty feet away, still unnoticed, Chris decided to see how good his costume really was. He removed his dad's dog tags and quietly laid them in the candy bucket. He tucked the bucket into a nearby hedge and slowly skulked along the fenceline inch by painfully slow inch. When he was thirty feet away, headlights pinned him to the spot. A car pulled up next to his friends at the school. With the lights directly in his eyes he couldn't see what kind of car it was. There was only the smell of unfiltered exhaust and the rumble of its engine in his belly.

He didn't hear anyone in the car say anything over the roar of the engine, but Kevin and Steve approached the passenger side. The engine lulled for a minute, then roared as the car skidded down the icy street, high beams clicking on to pin Chris against the wooden fence where he crouched. He leapt to his feet, sprinting down the road, looking for a yard to jump into, screaming out for help, but there was no noise in the night beyond the booming thunder of the V8.

Every corner he turned, the car followed. Out of breath, blocks away from home, he hobbled toward the only house on the street with a light on. He pounded at the door, jackhammered the doorbell so fast only one note rang from inside. The car crawled down the street, revving a growl that brought a quiver to his legs. He ran across the yard, hopping over the short chainlink fence and into the neighbor's yard, screaming. A light popped on across the street and an elderly woman leaned outside. The car rolled to a stop between Chris and that house, a dragon in the river that he had to cross to safety.

The windows were tinted with cheap adhesive plastic that turned them dark purple under the streetlights. It wasn't a cool car, not the kind of thing they showed in those stranger danger films in assembly. One of those big boats from the seventies that his dad used to drive. Two doors. Black. Maybe dark blue. The rear wheel had one of those weird space-saver spare tires on it. It was the kind of car Chris would have mocked in safer circumstances.

He took two large strides diagonally across the yard to the rear of the car, each step bringing a rev from the motor. There was another noise under the engine. Hands slapping at glass. Muffled screams. That brought the old woman all the way out of her house and onto the front step. A face popped up, blurred and distorted. It could have been Kevin or Steve, there was no way to tell.

BANG

The face slammed into the glass as if shoved from behind and the car fell silent.

The driver's door opened.

Chris broke into a full sprint, planting a hand on top of the chainlink fence and vaulting to the sidewalk. It was so smooth, so fluid, that he couldn't help but marvel at it, pumping his legs across concrete, then the little grass median before the curb, then asphalt, and then, black ice.

The world went sideways. Chris was down on the ground before he knew what happened, his head ringing from banging against the blacktop, the hot breath of exhaust in his face. He heard the woman yell, then felt his pants tighten as a large hand lifted him from the ground by his belt. Something hard and flat banged against the back of his head, dazing him.

His body felt far away. He was thrown roughly on top of a lumpy bag of *something* in the backseat, the world outside painted purple through the chipped windows. He managed to sit up and claw at the window. The old lady's eyes grew wide before the world got louder and she grew smaller as the car sped away down the street. He watched everything he knew disappear into blackness through the rear window. Streetlights flashed in the windows as they sped away, every pool of light revealing the nightmare in the backseat. He wasn't on top of a bag. It was a body. Kevin's body. His eyes were wrong. Glassy, far away, and his mouth was all weird and--

"Hey, kid," a voice from the front.

Fire blossomed between his ears and everything went dark.

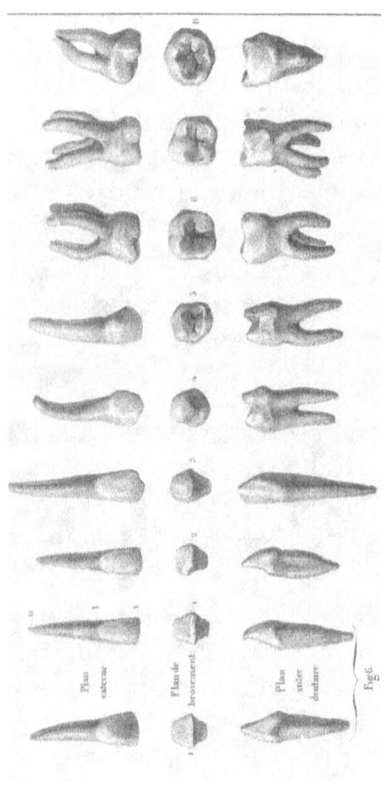

October 31, 1988

There were three constants when it came to Halloween.

The weather would be horrible.

Anna would stand at the front door, lights out in the house, watching for her little soldier boy to return.

She would go to bed in tears.

There were no words for what this night did to her. No phrase that could capture the absolute pit that opened inside of her every year as fall approached. Other parents in the area had formed a support group, and she had tried to attend the first two meetings, but it was too much.

Grief shared should be grief halved, but being in that room with all of those other people only multiplied everything. Where did you start? Where could you start, collectively, in a room of people with one thing in common?

Their sorrow was outlined in cruel mathematics. One single father, two single moms, four couples in various stages of marital decay. Between them, thirteen missing children. That number was all the media could focus on. It was enough to create a distraction, to make people imagine what kind of monster was at work instead of focusing on the faces of the missing and searching for clues.

The national news had descended into southeastern Wyoming with a fury, turning over every stone, chasing every lead hoping for a juicy story.

Not clues. Not leads. A story.

Even the newer cable news stations had sent delegates. They came back the next Halloween for a followup piece, but everyone refused to talk to them. Now, two years later, with no more shocking news to milk, no meat left on the bones, nothing but thirteen empty beds, the story faded from the national conscious until its weight was left to be borne by the families.

Anna could barely manage her sadness, let alone help others, so she quietly retreated to her home. Marco was still seven years away from retirement in the Air Force, and his long weeks in the field allowed her to suffer in peace. His absence may have been the only thing that saved their marriage. They rarely spoke, but they wouldn't let the marriage die. They were the only thing holding each other up. They were the beacon that could guide him home. It was a useful charade.

She moved away from the front door, three steps, before the gravity of hope pulled her back. She knew he wouldn't show up, but she also knew she had to be there to see it when he came back. She felt like an idiot with that faded plastic bucket in her hand, those two-year-old candy bars still inside, the dog tags nestled among them. His favorite stuffed toy in her other hand, a stuffed sheep in denim overalls with a broad-brimmed hat. She remembered the Easter she'd gotten it for him, how he'd hated the thing with a fury for half the day before he decided that flipping the brim of the hat turned the sheep into a certain whip-cracking adventuring archaeologist. Then, they were inseparable.

Inseparable. Oh, how that word stung.

Come home.

Come home.

She cast her thoughts out into the night, staring into the blackness, watching every car that drove by, imagining Chris in every shadow, trailing behind every group of kids that wandered by in their costumes. By nine o'clock, the streets were empty. By ten o'clock, the wine had taken hold, and Anna slept in a heap by the front door, fingers clutched around the stupid stuffed sheep.

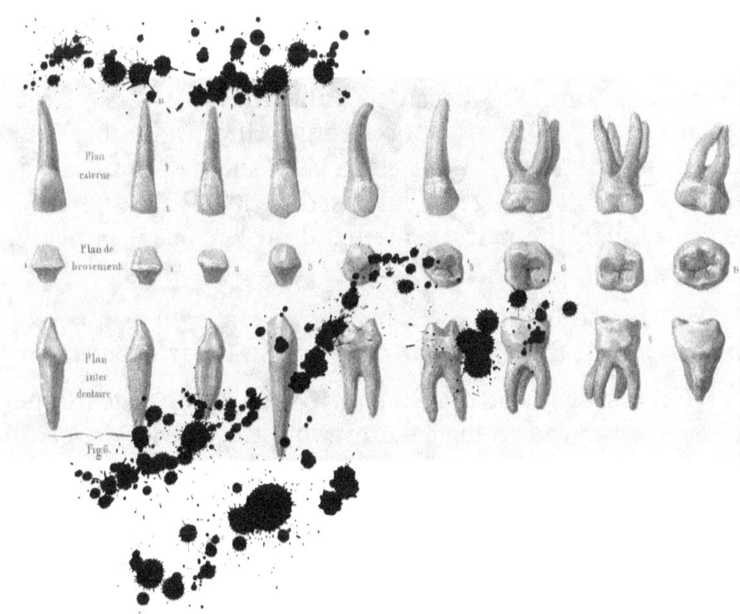

November 1, 1988

Her phone started ringing at seven o'clock that morning and didn't stop until close to midnight.

"Did you get one too?" the first voice asked.

It took her a minute to hear familiarity through the watery panic. Kevin's mother Georgia.

"Did that bastard put one on your porch? Did you get one too?"

Anna dropped the phone and ran to the door, yanking it open to find a sea of reporters being herded toward the street by the local police. Flashbulbs popped, blinding her, and a State Patrolman in a puffy brown jacket approached, hat in hand. He didn't speak, instead put an arm around her shoulder and hustled her toward his car. The reporters exploded into a cacophony of questions, like a flock of birds startled by a gunshot. There were words that kept registering, pelting her across the face like a hard slap.

Son.

Box.

What is in the box?

She was too numb to react, but saw some of the reporters pointing toward the front door, and she turned to look.

How had she missed it? She must have stepped right over it.

A brown cardboard box, crudely taped shut with wrinkled brown packing tape. She began to pull, tried to wrestle free of the patrolman's grasp, but he was too strong. All of the cameras focused on her, each flash, each shutter click, each shouted question sapping the strength from her legs. She collapsed backwards into the back seat of the cruiser, felt the patrolman's hand on her head, protecting her from taking a bump.

Her house looked foreign now. Like an oil painting. Like a nightmare canvas. Empty. Still. And a box on the front step.

"I'm sorry you had to come out to this, ma'am," the trooper said. "As soon as we started seeing a pattern in the calls we were getting, we sent cars to everyone's houses, but I guess… these vultures move faster. I don't know how they do it. Better technology than us, I guess. And this is just the locals and the Colorado crews. Probably going to be more before the day is over. I can drive you to the station. Some of the others are staying down at the Hitching Post in a private--"

A sound escaped her. Her breath came, her lips fluttered, her eyes fogged over as she stared at the patrolman.

"Huh?"

"What is it?" she whispered. "What's happening? Did they find him?"

"I just have to keep you at a safe distance until we can see what's in there. None of the other boxes have had anything dangerous inside, but we can't take any chanc—HEY!"

She was out of the car like a shot, driving her shoulder into his midsection so hard that he tumbled backwards, darting across the lawn before he could find his feet to stop her.

She reached down for the box, fingers brushing the cardboard surface. She nudged it, said a silent prayer that it wasn't him in there, or that it *was* him and this would be it. Her hands shook too fast to get a grip on the cover, but the sound of the patrolman approaching gave her sudden focus. She slipped two fingers under one flap, ignoring the way the corrugated cardboard bit into the webbing between her fingers and drew blood. She tore the flap off the box entirely.

And then she screamed.

She was outside of her own body, howling at the sky until the patrolman wrapped his coat around her and led her into her house.

She made the front page the next morning, there on her lawn, mouth impossibly wide in a scream, on her knees clutching that faded green Air Force field jacket to her chest.

The full report took up the first three pages of the paper. One of the things media loved about big news in small towns was that nobody was equipped to deal with it. Access was lighter, officials were more apt to give information before they realized they should be clamping down. There was the recap of the morning after Halloween in 1986, the night they vanished. The search for clues, the hunt for a suspect. The frustration that they'd spent the better part of two years chasing vapor.

The third page was a detailed list of what was found. Every house had received a box at some point in the night, each containing a single item of a child's Halloween costume. More in the cases of the houses that had lost more than one child. Plastic masks, coats, a tattered cape, mummy wrappings, and in one case an entire vinyl superhero costume, kids' size small. None of the items were bloody or damaged. In the case of the vinyl costume, the legs and sleeves had been cleanly sliced, possibly to make removal easier.

What Anna had missed in the frenzy was the note.

Every box had a note taped to the inside. She'd torn hers in half in her frenzy to open it, but the police were able to fully reconstruct it. It was carefully handwritten in a tight, small script and run through a Ditto machine to obscure identifying characteristics. The deep purple ink so familiar to parents from the worksheets their kids brought home was just another knife to the ribs.

THE NIGHT BELONGS TO THE DEVIL

THE DEMONS HOME TO REST

NO REWARD FOR THE ANGELS

NO DISGUISE FOR SIN

THEY ARE SAFE

SOME ARE QUIET

SOME ARE SILENT

FOREVER MINE

FOREVER YOURS

—YOUR MUTUAL FRIEND.

The Ditto machine was the only solid lead they had. All of the kids attended the same school. It spurred an investigation into every teacher, every aide, every janitor. All of the bus drivers and maintenance men that serviced the area were hauled in for questioning. Promising leads were quickly dispelled and no further evidence presented itself.

The discovery of the boxes was a stain on the rest of the year, casting a pall over Christmas and the New Year, frozen into place by the Wyoming winter. It stayed with everyone in town, making them fearful, sad, withdrawn, and it didn't fade until spring came, when people were able to leave their houses more frequently, get on with their lives, and leave the abandoned parents in their cold stupor.

October 31, 1991

Anna didn't watch from the front porch anymore. She had the first year after the move, even though this house was in another state, over a thousand miles from Wyoming. The Air Force was sorry for her loss (was it a loss? Was he lost? What right did they have to use that language?), but her husband had work to do, and that required being stationed at a new base. There were promises from the other parents, an informal letter writing circle, mostly as a means of allowing them to stay in communication with the each other in case more evidence was discovered.

Marco said it might be for the best, that it could help them. Forgetting wasn't an option, nor was a fresh start. But moving forward might be. He never bothered her in October. He didn't try to distract her, never talked to her about her feelings, because he understood that it wasn't something to be talked out, just endured. He did long to hear her voice again. The Anna that existed before 1986. Well before. He wished he'd paid more attention to that Anna, that she'd heard him, that he'd listened, that they'd never let the heavy blanket of routine fall over them and muffle their love.

Halloween night, here in their new home, was the same as it had been in Wyoming since '86. He strapped his service pistol to his chest, put on a light jacket, and took the dog for a long walk. From the first trick-or-treater until the last kid went home, he walked. The smile that never left his lips didn't quite reach his eyes. He watched people. Cars that drove by. Men on foot that didn't have kids with them.

Inside, he always prayed for trouble. He wanted something, anything to happen. Kidnapping. Rape. Theft. Something he could confront, a forehead he could gift with a bullet. Going home after an uneventful evening left him feeling impotent.

When he came inside, Anna was asleep on the couch. He unleashed the dog, sending it skittering over to her to curl up and sleep. He moved a chair from the kitchen and walked out to the front porch, setting it down quietly and sitting, pulling out his pistol, racking one into the chamber, and staring out into the night until the sun came up.

November 1, 1991

Marco woke up when the phone rang at six AM sharp. He stumbled out of his chair on the porch, unsure of when sleep had taken him. The second ring woke Anna and she began to scream. Marco was through the door, reaching for the phone. The third ring, he picked up, and Anna fell silent.

There was heavy static, a steady rumble in the background. An engine, or possibly a machine of some sort.

And then, "Yeah."

A faint voice.

Marco's mouth moved, tongue battering the back of his teeth, unable to get sound out beyond the first letter of his son's name.

"C-c-c-c-c-c--"

Anna yelped and reached for the phone, but Marco's grip was iron.

"Yeah."

His voice, again. The same. Marco heard the machines running in the background, and then a popping sound, a low rumble, and Chris again.

"Yeah."

A recording. A loop. Then a beep loud enough that he had to move the phone away from his ears, so loud Anna heard it. Marco raised an open palm, pleading with her to be silent.

Two more beeps, then a sharp *POP*, so harsh he feared it was a gunshot. Maybe a tape recorder being stopped.

"Yeah," a whisper.

"Yeaaaaahhhhh," drawn out.

"Yeaaaaaahhh!" rising to a shout.

"They are safe," a rough whisper. "Fewer quiet. More silent."

"Who are you," Marco asked.

"Your mutual friend."

"Bullshit. Tell me who you are. Tell me where you are. No cops, I swear to god. Nobody's gonna know but you and me. You tell me where you are and I will end you."

"No reward for the angels," the voice hissed. "No reward. No reward."

"I still have your letter. Taped to the inside of my gun safe. Burned on the back of my eyelids. Motherfucker tell me where you are and--"

Another pop and the voice changed, deepened.

"Why did you leave Wyoming? It's almost done. They're running out of words. Words hold secrets. One by one I take them out."

Marco heard the phone creaking and cracking under his grip. He wanted to bolt out the door. He could be in Cheyenne by that afternoon. AWOL was the least of his concern.

Another pop and the voice changed again.

"The demons home to rest. The demons home to rest on Halloween."

Marco was left grasping for words.

"Who are you?" Anna shouted.

"Your mutual--"

"I just want my boy. Give me back my boy. What did you do? Where is he?"

"Forever mine. Forever mine! FOREVER MINE!" The voice raised to an inhuman shriek, distorting over the phone line to a garble that would be incomprehensible if Marco and Anna hadn't learned the words three years ago.

"HOME TO REST. HOME TO REST. THE DEMONS. THE ANGELS. HOME TO REST. FOREVER MINE. FRIEND. FRIEND. FRIEND. FRIEEEEENNNNND!"

The line went dead.

Marco and Anna collapsed into each other, silent on the floor, crushing each other.

Twenty minutes later, the phone rang again.

Anna slapped Marco when he grabbed it, ripping the receiver from his hand and screaming into the mouthpiece. Again and again, slamming the phone against the floor until it shattered, until her hand started bleeding.

Minutes later, their front door was kicked in and Marco placed into handcuffs. The police had gotten an urgent call from a federal investigator that they needed to reach out to Marco and Anna. The other parents had all gotten the same call simultaneously. When they'd called shortly after that to hear Anna's screams, they feared she was being attacked. Police arrived to find Marco clutching her, the blood from her hand spattered around the living room. A tense hour passed while they sorted out the pieces, and eventually Marco was uncuffed.

They were getting closer to catching a suspect. They said he'd been sloppy this time. It had been a recording. Autodialed from an untraceable source. Everyone had been there to pick up their phone except for one person, whose answering machine had grabbed part of the call before running out of tape. It didn't give them much, but they had audio to analyze. Marco mentioned the pops he'd heard, how the call had started with a loop of Chris's voice, something the police took great interest in. Nobody else had recognized the child's voice at the beginning of the call.

"His old voice. His voice. You know, from when… from the year he was… I mean…"

When Marco mentioned the middle of the call, how the voice had changed and asked why he left Wyoming, the policeman blanched. Nobody else's call had gone that way. Some of the other parents had also received a letter in the mail, self-addressed. Inside of a tiny white envelope was a copy of the original message they'd received in 1988, certain words circled in thick red marker.

NIGHT. DEVIL. HOME. YOURS.

Scrawled at the bottom in the same tight, block lettering, the word HALLOWEEN. The paper was ringed with smiley faces, wide open, friendly grins like you'd see on a cereal box mascot. Toothless, tongues lolling, eyes wide, hyper-excited. Nine of them in total. Police begged them not to speculate on the meaning, as numbers seemed to be so important to everything surrounding the case.

Marco and Anna never received a letter. Other parents had, some more than one. Nine letters for nine children.

October 31, 1992

Marco sat on the porch all night long. Inside, in his living room, two police officers waited. On the roof of the house across the street, a sniper took up position and scanned the streets all night. Trick-or-treating was encouraged to continue under heavy supervision. They needed everything to look normal. Their words.

For the first time in years, Marco kept the porch light on at his house, but nobody approached. When the streetlights turned off in the morning, Marco stood and went inside. He returned to the porch moments later and smashed the chair he'd been sitting on, kicking the shattered remains into the street, spinning like a wild animal and braying into the wind.

The police eventually escorted him back into his house.

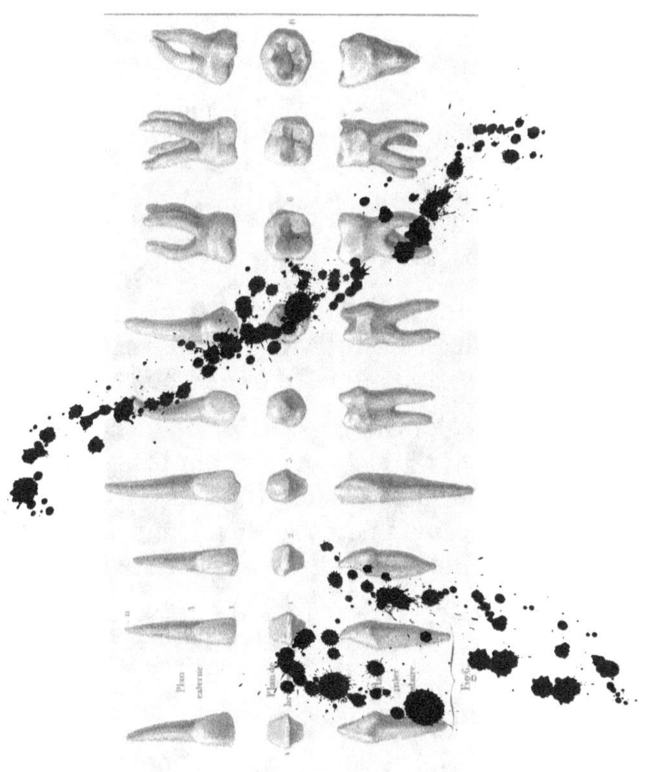

October 31, 1994

Anna walked by the bookshelf in her living room and squeezed the dusty hoof of the stuffed sheep. She picked up a roll of painters tape and two dayglo yellow signs and went outside. She taped one to her mailbox and the other to the screen door.

NO CANDY

Her therapist had suggested leaving town on Halloween, getting out of the country, going somewhere where she wouldn't have to fear every shadow or wonder what's lurking.

"There is no such place," she told him.

She and Marco had come to terms with everything at this point. They'd try to spend a quiet evening at home. Nothing ever happened on Halloween night. Not since 1986. At the urging of police, they'd had their home phone rerouted to a local dispatch office. Any calls that came in would be traced immediately.

As expected, it was an uneventful night. A few kids had approached their house, heedless of the sign and determined to find candy. Anna stood in the living room, staring at them through the window curtain as they jostled each other and giggled, but she never opened the door.

"I can see someone," one of the kids said.

"The sign says no candy, I told you guys…"

After a beat, they all clomped away. Anna didn't realize she'd been holding her breath until it all rushed out of her. She opened another bottle of wine and retreated to the couch.

At ten o'clock, long after the trick-or-treaters had gone home, there was another knock. Light at first, but insistent. Three taps and then three more. Anna approached the door and stared through the window. Marco came up behind her. Under the dull glow of the porchlight, through the haze of the white curtain on the door, stood a horned figure. It was too late and the kid was too tall to be a trick-or-treater. Probably just some damn high school kid looking for leftover candy.

Marco yanked the door open.

The demon had a slight frame. He looked like someone had draped a filthy white sheet over a lab skeleton and put a rubber mask on top. It was a horrible thing, a three-dollar special, shoddily painted with synthetic fur tufts for eyebrows and a lolling tongue. Somehow the bargain-bin nature of it only increased the disgusting quality of the costume. The mask sat askew, so they couldn't see the person's eyes. One hand was behind his back, and the other held a plastic candy bucket shaped like a black cat's head.

"Read the sign, kid. No candy. You're way too old for this shit anyway. Get out of here."

When the kid didn't move, Marco continued, "Someone put you up to this? You know whose house this is, right? This a dare? You wanna wear a damn demon mask to my house? Got something to say?"

There was a trembling noise, a low vibration from the candy bucket like pebbles rattling. The kid slowly raised the bucket and held it forward, hand shaking, until the bowl was buzzing like a rattlesnake.

A car outside revved its engine and the kid's head snapped back toward the street before looking back to Marco again.

"Last warning. I don't want trouble but I will kick your ass back to your friends in the street if--"

THUNK

The noise came suddenly, and it took a minute for Marco to register that the kid had dropped something. He was shaking like a leaf, the noise from the bucket a cacophony of buzzing stones. Marco looked down at his porch, saw a wet spot forming on the front of the kid's sheet, and then caught sight of the barrel of a snub-nosed revolver at his bare feet.

"What the--"

The car in the street roared to life. The lights were off, but the driver peeled out down the block. Marco froze for a second, feeling at his hip for a sidearm. Instinct took over and he blew by the kid, full sprint across the lawn, over the fence, off the sidewalk and down the street after the car.

The driver locked his rear wheels and tried to slide around the corner but couldn't control it. The vehicle fishtailed wildly, striking a parked car and caroming off of it to jump the sidewalk and slam into a light pole. Marco was closing in, unsure of what to do next or why he was even out here, when Anna screamed. He slid to a stop, caught in a pool of yellow light between the monstrous Caprice crashed at the T-intersection at the end of the block and his wife, alone with that strange demon kid.

"Call 911," Marco screamed to anyone, to everyone. "Call for help!"

He chanted it at the top of his lungs as he turned back for the house, ignoring the burning pain in his side, the strange stinging in his bare foot. What had initially felt like a three-hundred yard dash toward the car had actually only carried him a few houses down the street, and he was back to the curb in no time.

The strange kid in the blanket was nowhere in sight. Anna was on the porch clutching the cat head candy bucket. When Marco approached she cried out to him, holding the bowl like a church offering, begging him for answers.

"What are these? What are these?"

He looked over the lip at the white stones inside. Some were clean, others were dirty, brown and yellow and irregular and then he realized that they weren't stones at all, but teeth.

Children's teeth.

Marco barged into the living room, where he found the strange kid kneeling on the floor, curled into a ball, clutching something to his chest. Marco slapped at the kid twice, bringing strange muffled yelps.

"Who are you? What do you want?! Where's Chris? What did you do with Chris? Why are you doing this to us?!"

Marco seized him by the shoulders and hoisted him to his feet. When the kid wouldn't uncurl, Marco slammed him against the wall twice until he went limp, dropping the stuffed sheep to the floor and howling a strange muffled noise. Marco yanked the mask from his head.

He was gaunt, skinny, sickly yellow. Eyes sunken into deep sockets, cheekbones so sharp they could cut glass. His entire lower face was coated in layer after layer of duct tape, wrapped around his head, clinging to his stringy brown hair.

Marco still couldn't put it together, didn't understand any of this, until he heard Anna behind him, a whisper barely audible over his animalistic panting.

"Chris?"

The kid locked eyes with her, afraid, as if she'd whispered a decades-old secret. His legs went limp and he collapsed. Marco stepped over him, rushing to the bedroom. He charged back out seconds later, gun in hand, kicking the screen door so hard it shot off of its hinges and tumbled into the yard.

The car was still there at the end of the street. The doors were closed and the windows rolled up, but there was someone inside, trying to start the engine. Marco broke into a run when the car finally turned over and skidded back from the curb. The car lurched forward, then stalled. From the way the front tire was leaning, Marco guessed the ball joint had busted going over the curb. He wasn't going anywhere. Marco changed his mind with every step on whether to open the door or open fire and kill the man inside. The other families deserved a trial. The man didn't deserve to live.

Marco's training took over as he closed in. He stopped and leveled his gun at the car, slowly advancing.

There were voices in the car, an argument. Marco couldn't see through the bad tint job, but it sounded like a man and a woman fighting. The woman's tone was fear and pleading, and the man's was rage. Marco grasped the door handle and steadied his aim. He popped it and stepped back, and the shouting stopped. The driver's seat was empty.

In the passenger seat, a short, doughy, balding man sat. He wore a filthy satin coat that couldn't contain his ample belly, which itself was only half covered by a black T-shirt. His ankle was stuck in the between the driver's seat and the transmission hump, a ruined escape attempt out the passenger door. His face was covered in five days' growth of salt-and-pepper beard, his nose an odd shade of purple and coated in broken capillaries. The bags under his eyes jostled as he snapped his head toward Marco. He opened his mouth, a gaping smile that sent a wash of blood over his lips. His lower teeth were missing, as were half of the uppers.

"No more," he said through foaming pink saliva. "No more." His voice was high-pitched, frightened. His left hand pawed at the driver's seat, where a small pile of freshly-pulled teeth jittered.

"They're all silent now," he spoke, a woman's voice. "All silent except the angel. The angel was supposed to claim you. The angel was supposed to claim you and failed! Now the demons need more." Then his face contorted into a gruesome mask and his voice shot down several octaves. "MORE," he shouted. "MORE MORE MORE."

Marco watched this in dumb fascination until the man raised his right hand suddenly, something shiny and silver there.

The world turned into platinum light and thunder as Marco emptied his revolver into the car. The first two shots struck the man in his shoulder and torso. The rest, somehow, missed.

Sirens in the distance. The man in the car sucked air and groaned, a strange gurgling noise. He locked eyes with Marco and tried to say something in that strange high voice, but no words came. His left hand lay in the driver's seat, two of the teeth he'd pulled from his own head stuck to the back. His right hand lay in his lap, still clutching a shiny pair of dental pliers coated in blood.

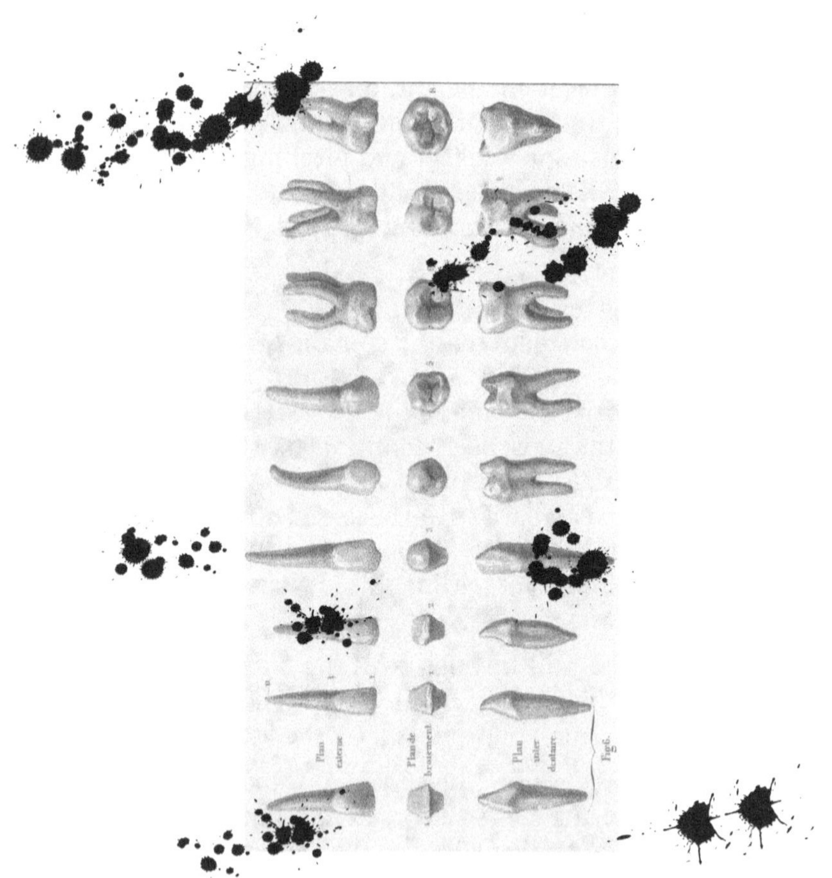

November 1, 1994

The fitful sleep Marco caught that night was haunted by dreams of teeth, hailing down, piling in great drifts in front of his house. The sky filled with the faces of giant, toothless, screaming children, their blood and saliva making rivers in the streets, currents that carried splintered incisors, filthy molars, canines that trailed long strings of nerve and gristle until they clattered down the drains in the gutters.

The following day, the investigation began in earnest. The man's name was Arthur Kenneth Beach, because people like him always had three names. He'd lived his entire life in Wyoming in a house at the dead end of Four Mile Road. That, perhaps, had been the hardest pill to swallow. Numbers had always been so critical to this case. Thirteen children abducted. Nine murdered with more remains to be identified. One survivor. Eight years gone. All of it contained in an old ramshackle two bedroom with a couple of big barns for a car restoration business just outside of town, two and a half miles from the school as the crow flies.

There were teeth to sort and identify, biological debris in the man's trunk. When they examined Beach at the hospital, x-rays revealed strange masses in his stomach that turned out to be condoms stuffed with baby teeth. The barns where he worked on cars were neatly organized into sections. Two bright red rolling toolboxes, neatly organized. One full of sockets, bolts, drillbits, and sawblades. The other would be pored over for months. Dozens of tiny drawers, neatly labeled in small, tight lettering. Some had the children's names. Others had archaic symbols and seemingly random numbers.

There were boxes in the trunk of the car full of clay plates where he'd made impressions of handprints and footprints, and in some cases an ear or nose or face. There were two photo albums that meticulously detailed four of the children, bound in a faded beige leather. The investigator that found those two books had passed out after her fingers brushed over a raised bump on the back cover that turned out to be a nipple.

Beach fired his attorney a week before the trial and represented himself. He pled not guilty, his opening statement a rambling affair about angels and demons, sin, guilt, and the true meaning of innocence. He insisted that a being named Raziel should be the one in court, that this was entirely its doing, that he was merely a vessel and a pawn. Beach opened every day of the trial by invoking Raziel, imploring it to manifest through brief prayer. He left a small empty cup in front of the empty chair to his left as an invitation.

The trial became his final work, a drawn-out torture session where he was able to call the parents of some of the children to the stand for questioning. Every child was catalogued, presented into evidence, their final days, months, or in some cases years laid out until the jury was numb. One by one, they all found the answers to their questions. Twelve children dead, some quickly, others not so lucky. Beach spoke of the victims in glowing terms, called them beautiful, wonderful children. He thanked the parents for the job they'd done raising them, and never once apologized for his actions.

Beach did not call Anna or Chris to the stand, and neither did the prosecution. Marco was barred from all proceedings after attempting to bring weapons into the courtroom. Beach's closing statements were cut short when he shuddered and collapsed on the floor, crying out in the woman's voice that the angels wouldn't stop talking, that there was one more, one more, one more…

Arthur Kenneth Beach was found guilty of twelve counts of kidnapping, child cruelty, and a laundry list of every minor offense the judge could find to throw at him. The lesser charges resulted in twelve consecutive life sentences without parole, followed by twenty years for each count of kidnapping. He was found guilty of one count of premeditated murder. The state wanted to leave the other eleven charges on the table should he successfully appeal the first. Wyoming rarely sentenced criminals to death, and this was probably the cleanest and fastest order for lethal injection in state history.

Chris hadn't spoken through any of it. The first few days back at home, he'd found the family Bible and spent his days cross legged on the floor in the corner, holding the book open at arm's length without reading it. When Anna tried to move him, he'd yelp and cower, curling into a ball. They removed the book from their house.

Anna didn't try to pressure Chris. She would sit in the room with him, holding his favorite stuffed sheep on the floor in front of her, sometimes puppeting it to raise a hand to wave at him. That had been enough to crack him. He smiled and cried, rushing to her and curling protectively around the sheep. She didn't try to hold him them, only rested a hand on his back, feeling his ribs rise and fall as he breathed, trying not to read into the braille of the scars and divots that decorated his back.

Marco and Anna finally heard his voice again on Halloween the following year. They thought he had his radio on at first from the exchange of different voices in his room. Marco was going to barge in, but Anna stopped him so they could listen. It was Chris's voice, unmistakably, some of the rasp from his childhood still there, the odd lisp. He said a few words that they couldn't make out, and after a moment of silence, an answer came, a woman's voice.

They rushed in to find him alone, the windows open wide. He was naked on his bed, streaks of blood on his chest. The black plastic candy bucket was in his lap, rattling with his Halloween treasure. He cried as he presented it to them, the only words he could manage were "I helped."

Over and over.

I helped.

I helped.

I helped.

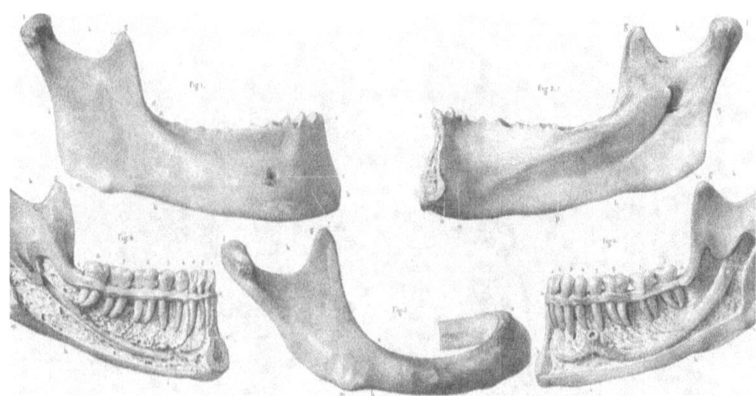

WORTH THE HAVING

How does it feel?

It asks this as it cuts deep into the inner thigh, flesh and fat zippering apart, its tongue probing into the fresh wound.

How are you doing?

The thing wouldn't want an answer even if there was one. It only wants screams.

This is going to be worth it. You're going to love next year. This will make it worth the having.

I used to wonder what could be worth this. The heat of its palms pushing legs apart. The cold, slow rivulets of saliva dripping down like icy syrup, washed away with slowing pulses of hot blood. That single tooth in its lower jaw, barbed and curved. That awful, knowing smile from the puckered sphincter of its mouth. This year, I finally understand that phrase, *worth the having*. This year, the final year of our horrible agreement—the thing still uses that word, *agreement*, as if I wanted any of this—I understand it all.

Twenty-two years ago, I cut across the backyard of Mikey Slater's dad's house. This was the night before Halloween; the night, I'd later learn, that the thing would stretch its legs and go for a walk. The thing was the reason for the season, the whole tradition of Halloween had started because of it. Masks, costumes, disguises, none of it for fun.

All of it primal camouflage to help the prey hide from the predator.

Nobody remembers that part of the tradition anymore. Not even the thing itself. It just knows to walk the night before Halloween. And it walks to me. I don't ask where it goes when it leaves me or what it does on Halloween night. I'm just glad it's gone.

Anyway, Mikey Slater. His parents had been divorced a few years, and I treated our hangout like a second home. The other bonus was that it was a quick end-around the neighborhood when I needed to get home fast. I was on my way home from checking out Mikey's Halloween costume at his mom's house and had about two minutes to get home before dinner was cold and my ass would get spanked.

We'd made a pact to dress as characters from this cartoon about interstellar knights. We had some great things rigged to our costumes, lights and fake swords, the whole works. We expected that tomorrow night, we'd barely be able to do any trick or treating since we'd be mobbed by admirers wondering how we obtained these amazing costumes.

I vaulted the six foot wooden, slatted fence, landed soft in the garden, not caring if my presence was announced or not, since Mikey's dad never cared if I cut through.

And then I saw Mr. Slater lying in the grass near the back door, naked. Another person straddled him, pinning his arms down. Pale skin, soft curves, it looked like a woman. The back did, anyway. The head was too small, and bald with a Mohawk of downy feathers. This thing, this silhouette dipped down, the head bobbing just above Mr. Slater's crotch. I was young, but not so young that I didn't have a small clue about what I might be seeing.

I heard a whisper, Almost done, almost done. Next year is going to be fantastic. This will all be worth it.

And Mr. Slater replied, "No, no, no. No more. There's nothing I want. Everything I want is gone…" Occasionally he hissed, his breath, stifling a scream.

Pleasure wasn't part of this.

"No more! No more, please!"

You must want something. It's you and I forever. If you don't want anything…

And here the thing yanked a hand back from Mr. Slater's thigh, and that's when I noticed the blood, and the flap of flayed skin that I'd initially mistaken for underwear pulled down.

I tried to turn around, grabbed the fence to bail out. I wanted to get out of there, wanted to be home.

You…want?

It whipped its head around at me, and I felt its voice in my head more than I heard it.

"Take him! Take him!" Mr. Slater cried out, pointing at me.

I can't explain any of what happened next. Can't explain the face I saw when I locked eyes with the thing. Can't explain the speed with which it moved. It crossed the yard in three hitching strides, seizing my ankle as I tried to get away. I flopped my upper body over the fence and struggled for anything to grab, to pull, to get free.

I heard a whisper…no, felt it.

Mine.

One quick bite on my ankle. A burning pain, searing, electric.

Make a wish before you go to bed. Think about what you want next year more than anything. We have an agreement now.

It wasn't a question or an offer.

It released me and I dropped to the ground in the alley behind the fence.

I reached to my ankle. There was a fading flash of pain and burning, but no blood. No cut.

Mikey's dad came stumbling around the corner clutching a handgun. His leg was soaked in blood, that angry red flap of skin jiggling from beneath the leg of his shorts, bare chest heaving, a strange, wet, three-fingered handprint blazing red on his stomach. "Is it still here? Is it?"

I said nothing. What could I say? What the hell was happening?

"My God, if you hadn't shown up… I'd…I'm free." He smiled at me and turned away. There was a flash in his eyes, a moment where he was teetering between life and death, that gun the fulcrum between finishing something very bad or starting something new. His hand rose slowly.

"But, don't, Mikey…" Those were the only three words in the mess behind my lips that could break through. It was enough. His hand swung free and heavy.

"I'm sorry. I'm so sorry. Try to… just… try to think of good things for yourself." He looked at the gun again. "Heh. What the hell was I gonna do with this thing? Don't ever think about trying to kill it, whatever you do. Just think of good things for yourself and then take what you have coming."

I barely remembered getting home. By the time I was through my front door, the details were hazy. My ankle was fine. No cut, no scab, not even a scratch. I slid into bed, trying to remember the thing, the face, the hands, anything, but it was all gone. Mist. My gaze drifted over the shelves around my room, the random toys scattered around, the baseball bat leaning against the corner. I hopped out of bed and brought it close by, feeling like it would keep me safe, not knowing from what. As I drifted off that night, my last thought was about Little League and my wish that I wasn't too damn fat to play shortstop.

That's good enough. A whisper, shot through the center of my brain.

Cold sweat broke over my upper lip, then calmness, then sleep.

When I woke up the next morning, I'd forgotten the previous night completely. I was full of energy, light on my feet. I felt ready to take on the world. Things felt a little darker in the afternoon as I walked by Mr. Slater's house on my way to Mikey's, but I couldn't quite peg why. I saw him sitting on his porch, a strange smile on his face. I kept moving, and that night was a Halloween much like any other.

The following year I dropped a lot of weight. Got faster. Made the team. Didn't think of how or why, just attributed it to hard work and eating right.

Then early October came and I found a postcard on my pillow when I got home from school. I'd like to say I got cold chills when I picked it up, or that it felt like flesh or leathery hide, but no, just plain, cheap cardboard. Typed in a neat white font on one side, it read:

Halloween is almost here. Did you have a good year? What do you want next year? Think hard! Make it worth the having.

I wanted to show the card to my mom, but by the time she

got home from work, it was gone. Every time anyone brought up Halloween, this icicle of dread dribbled down my spine, then disappeared in thoughts of candy and costumes, an itch at the back of my mind that I couldn't quite scratch.

The night before Halloween, laying my costume out before going to bed, my only thoughts were on candy and sneaking around in the dark. It was two in the morning when I woke to a great weight on top of me, pushing the blankets down tight and cocooning me inside. I opened my eyes to see a silhouette, slight shoulders that were a bit too sharp, full breasts that seemed too round, slender arms that pinned me down. It was too dark to see details. I tried to cry out for my parents, but the thing lifted a hand to my mouth, three cold boneless fingers clamping down. The palm spread like cold jelly as the thing drew its hand back, forcing one, then two fingers into my mouth. There was a texture to the bottom of them, something between a snake's belly and octopus suction pads.

Shhhhh…

The whisper in my brain.

Have you thought on it?

Thought on what?

The postcard I sent. What you want for next year.

Who are you?

It doesn't matter who I am. It matters who you are. You are mine.

How did you—

Just as you hear me in your mind, I hear you in mine. You are mine.

What does that mean?

It means you are mine.

I felt the thing rock down with its pelvis, grind into my stomach.

The agreement is not without benefit to you.

I didn't agree to anything.

Does a fish agree to feed a shark? Does a tree agree to be struck by lightning? You are mine.

The thing drew closer, and I squeezed my eyes shut. Everything grew bright, until I could make out shapes, then colors. Then I could see it in front of me.

You don't need your ears to hear me, nor your eyes to see. You are mine. You will look at me. You will watch everything.

It was mottled and grey. The torso was curved and sensuous, but the head, that too-small head. The puckered sphincter of a mouth that prolapsed in and out, exposing that single jagged tooth. The two giant eyes, bulbous and red, shot with veins but no pupils, the two smaller green eyes in between. No ears. No nose. The tuft of white feathers in a stripe over the shining bald skull. Squeezing my eyes shut tighter only seemed to draw out more clarity.

You need to understand how this works. I will show you. Think of a woman you desire.

I couldn't. I was twelve. There wasn't desire yet, only a strange fascination. An occasional stirring if I saw a woman on TV in a swimsuit or that time I sneaked a peek at my dad's private magazine collection—

The thing on top of me changed. Hair grew. The head filled in. The face melted and morphed into the perfectly sculpted features of that lady from Beach Patrol who had just done the cover shoot for Playboy. Bronze skin. Swaying breasts. A sculpted collarbone. Skin coated in a sheen of sweat, just as I'd seen her in the centerfold.

Better?

It hadn't changed the feeling of the fingers in my mouth, cold like snails, twitching and probing around my tongue.

Every year on this night, I'm going to find you. I must feed. In exchange, you will tell me something you want, and over the course of the next year, you shall have it.

But I don't want—

*You are—*and the fingers extended slowly, pushing against the back of my throat, gagging me *–mine. Understand it. Tell me your desire. Make it worth the having.*

I want you to leave.

Not part of the bargain. Not your place to ask. You are mine.

The fingers pushed deeper still until I felt them sliding into my throat. I couldn't breathe. Instinct kicked in and I began to thrash. I needed to escape. I bit down hard on the fingers, breaking the skin, cold peppery ichor oozing into my mouth.

The thing didn't draw back. It moaned. Reached up its other hand and caressed itself.

More.

It pushed hard on my mouth, wanting me to bite. I let my jaw go slack. It sighed, the kind of sigh I was too young to understand as sexual frustration, and its fingers pulled back.

I sucked in air, certain I was going to die. Thoughts of school. Thoughts of family trips I'd never get to take. I'd never get to see Disney World—

Is that something you desire?

I nodded in spite of myself, tears spilling down my cheeks. The thing on top of me slowly morphed back to its original form, spinning around on my body so I could only see its back. It pulled at the sheets covering my feet.

I want you to think harder next year. Make it good. Make it worth the having. This is scarcely worth a toe, let alone two.

"What, what—"

A cold hand clamped down on my ankle while other fingers slithered between my toes, constricting them, spreading them apart.

"No. Nononono please don't—"

Next year you will remember this and understand what it means when I say make it worth the having.

Its head lowered and its lips wrapped around my big toe. It sucked once, twice, then clamped down with a force I can't describe. That single tooth razored into the meat of my toe and flicked, cutting, tearing. I screamed. I had to have screamed, but there was no sound. I could feel the blood pumping out of my toe, the vibration of serrated tooth on bone; clamping, twisting, pulling, until it was all electricity and cold air. The thing turned to me and pursed its lips. It showed me my toe, sucking it so it bobbed in and out of its mouth before tipping its head back and swallowing. The opening between its legs pulsed and shuddered, cold slime pooling onto my sheets. It sighed.

One more.

This time I did get a scream out, a small yelp as it latched onto my second toe and began chewing again. Its leg cracked and bent around at an impossible angle until its foot was over my mouth, spreading like taffy, covering my nose and lips so that no sound could escape, no breath could enter. There was no smell, just electric pain, vibrant agony.

A crack, a tear, and more cold air. The second toe went much easier than the first. The creature arched its back and swallowed, ripples shivering down its flanks as it came again. It spun, bringing its face close to mine. I squeezed my eyes shut to no effect.

Enjoy your trip. Next year, think harder.

Without moving its torso, it raised one leg, stretched it toward my window sill. Gripping hard, it pulled itself up and out into the night.

I stared down over my soaked sheets at my foot. The silhouette in the dark room danced through the purple lightning of pain. There was no blood, just intense pain. Weren't you supposed to pass out from intense pain? When I tried to count my toes and had to stop at three, the room went grey, then black.

I awoke screaming. Someone was shaking my shoulder. Unbidden, I saw that face, round and leathery and purple, hovering inches from mine.

"Honey, it's okay!"

When I opened my eyes I saw my mother's face.

"Are you feeling okay? Your bed is soaked. Did you wet the bed?"

I burst into tears, kicking at the sheets until they came free. I could feel the burning sensation in my toes still, the raw wound scraping at the fabric.

"No!" I shouted. "Look what it did! Look what it did!"

I held my foot up. Five toes. Had I not already been crying, I might have started then. Or possibly even wet the bed out of sheer joy. I wiggled my toes. Jumped out of bed.

"What's gotten into you?"

My big toe was a bit red. My second toe had a definite hard ridge beneath the skin like a scar, but they were there. They were back. I was whole. My toes were—

Mine.

Mine.

"Did you stub your toe last night?" My mom grabbed my foot, poking at my toes.

No pain.

"No, I'm...Ow!"

There was a scab on the underside of my big toe. Damp sheets. No blood. Five toes.

"You need to get up! And be more careful. You get a cut like that, you show me, okay? Otherwise it could get infected and you might lose your toes. You wouldn't want that, would you?"

I blanched.

"You need to get up. It's Halloween! Big breakfast to fuel up for a big night, right?"

Her hand sank into the dampness on my sheet, the essence that the creature had left behind in its ecstasy. Her eyes became vacant, distant, as she pulled the sheet off and bunched them on the floor.

"Well. I'll wash these later. You go run along." She absently licked at her fingers as she left, moaning softly.

By the time I made it downstairs for breakfast, I'd forgotten about my aching toes. By the time I was out the door, my sheets were in the wash and my mind was on Halloween.

The events of the evening never returned to traumatize me. I don't remember much of the school year that followed, but I remember our vacation. The best time we'd ever had as a family. I remember years later, my parents telling me that trip had been a new beginning for them, bringing them out of a rough patch that I had been blissfully unaware of.

The next year when Halloween drew close, I got another card, this time in my lunchbox at school.

Matte black, bearing only the reminder: *MAKE IT WORTH THE HAVING.*

Those words sent a spasm of pain through my foot and up my spine. I couldn't see the creature in mind, but it was omnipresent, that assault, that pain, and the reward it brought.

The night before Halloween that year, I asked if I could sleep in my parent's room. And as soon as the question left my mouth, a whisper buzzed through my brain—

Oh no, don't make them watch. Why would you do that to them?

So I didn't. I slept in my closet that year, thinking it might not find me, but I was wrong.

I could explain this. Break it down year by year and tell what happened, but that's not what this is about. That phrase, *Make It Worth the Having,* I just need someone to understand.

That second time, it stood at the door of my closet, towering over me, taking on features it must have thought looked friendly, the face shifting from Santa Claus to Jesus to cartoon mice and rabbits.

I don't want you to go through this for nothing. Think big.

Please stop.

I'll stop when I'm full and finished and I'll still come back next year. Don't wish for toys. Don't wish for things for other people. Think of yourself. Remember our meeting last year, and know what's about to happen will be far worse than a few toes. Don't let this happen for nothing. Make it worth the--

I screamed hard, muffled by the gelatinous glob of fingers it had forced into my mouth again. I just wanted it to shut up. I never wanted to hear that phrase again, but I knew I would. I knew this, all of this, would be happening again, and again.

That's a big burden to put on the shoulders of a child, right? Have almost anything you want, in exchange for giving the thing what it wants. That's not accurate. In exchange for the thing *taking* what it wants. I mean, what can a child think of that would be worth that? The second year, all I could think of was sports cars. It made me try again—why ask for something I couldn't legally use? Millions of dollars? Same thing. It had to be personal. So the second year, I wished to be the fastest, strongest kid in my school.

Done.

And in exchange for that, for the next sixty minutes, the creature flayed my arms and legs with that horrible tooth, peeled back my skin and chose three strands of exposed muscle from each limb, snapping them near one tendon and pulling them out like spaghetti, lifting it as high as it would go before placing the strand in its mouth and sucking it down greedily, biting off the other end at the tendon. It held its gelatinous foot over my mouth the whole time, tiny suctioned footpads inhaling the screams that never made it into the night. Blood everywhere. The terror of endless suffocation. Pain like I'd never felt.

It finished and left me wide open like a biology class project pinned to a tray, trying to sleep and failing miserably. I could raise my head enough to see the insides of my biceps, my skin curled into rolls just like Mr. Slater's thigh. I passed out at some point and woke up in the morning, mildly sore but fully intact, testing out my newfound strength on my dad's weight bench by the end of the day. By the end of the week, I was running home from school without breaking a sweat. By the end of the school year, I was medaling in every sport I chose.

When October rolled around, and the black postcard fell out a library book I pulled from the shelf, the sinking dread in my stomach was almost matched by the excitement of the next thing I planned to ask for.

That night, it ate half of one my kidneys. Once it managed to pull the organ free it wasn't so bad, but getting there was sheer hell. Fourteen years old, I made the wish any hormonally rampaging boy would, and that year I got every girl I was interested in. Was it worth it? Hard to say. But that year I came to understand that I was addicted. That I understood what *worth the having* meant, and that my life was going to improve.

I thought I had it all figured out. I had to try something new, and something new, despite seeing the thing lick its lips, despite seeing the horrible tongue dance over that single stupid tooth in the puckered maw it called a mouth, something new was too enticing to resist. Year by year, piece by piece, I was going to become a better man.

Everything that's happened in my life is a bit of a blur, but not those nights. Those, I have perfect clarity on.

I got better-than-perfect eyesight the year it spent hours working my eyeballs free from the sockets after using one jagged nail to cut my eyelids off. More length and girth downstairs (it was my first year in college, after all), that year was sheer torture. It changed its shape to a calendar girl, arousing me, bringing me to climax orally in spite of myself, the soft supple features of the woman's body betrayed by the cold, slimy oatmeal feeling of the thing's mouth and throat. And then came the pain, my member first peeled like a raw potato with that single hooked tooth, then the soft tissue torn free, then the tongue probing into the open wound at my crotch until my testes were pulled free from my body and eaten—no, nibbled, held daintily between thumb and forefinger with pinky extended—until they were gone. Then it kissed me, deeply, forcing the entire meal back into my mouth, some long proboscis pushing it past my tongue, own my throat, deep into my stomach.

That night I was on a camping trip, so the thing didn't even need to muffle my screams when it pulled back, and I obliged it until I was choking on my own vomit - it could only rise so high, then it would sink back into my gut, burning my lungs and throat raw. Physically, I was fine the next day, but it took me a few weeks to get the feeling of it out of my mind. The taste of my own organs. The weight of it never seeming to leave my stomach despite the newly developed replacement. I quickly developed a reputation as *Big Man on Campus* in every way imaginable. By the end of the year, every man and woman worth having knew my number.

After college, I became career-oriented. Real estate. Stock market. Passive income. I wanted to be rich while dedicating all of my free time to learning how to finish this thing. Mikey's Dad, all those years ago, had simply begged the creature to stop, and when it saw me, it did. I had everything I thought I could want. I asked it one year if I could do the same thing as Mr. Slater. It only replied, *You are mine.*

I researched through college and beyond, and when I had enough money to hire people, they researched it too. I couldn't be very specific with them about my reasons, of course, but I could offer grants to religious studies students, hire paranormal investigators, demonologists. Six solid years of research yielded nothing. Not a damn thing. Every ancient society, every dead culture I could study I did, end to end, to the extent that there was some buzz that I'd be nominated for a MacArthur genius grant for advancing the studies so far. It was a ghost of a ghost.

At one point, I realized I hadn't tried the simplest approach: I went back to ask Mr. Slater about it, how he'd encountered it, how many years it had followed him. His life wasn't so great. What if that was the first night he'd encountered it? What if the thing had been with him for years and was on a downswing, taking things away instead of granting them? I'd never know. He looked at me blankly the entire time I explained it, occasionally offering a knowing or supportive nod. After I'd unburdened myself, he looked at me and smiled, asking me when I'd gotten there. Offered me a drink and a snack. Reset the entire visit.

I was thirty five, with another Halloween approaching, a wife I loved and my first child on the way. And that was the final straw. I couldn't have this thing in my life with a child in the house. This year I would demand an exit.

I received something worse than a black postcard in the mail. The afternoon of what I'd come to think of as Visitation Night, we had to rush to the hospital. Complications. Our baby was lost. It made no sense. My wife was perfectly healthy, and everything had been going fine. But there was no heartbeat, no sign of life. My wife was inconsolable. She had to be sedated, and even as they were putting the IV into her, she was crying out, asking: *Will this hurt the baby? You can't give me these drugs. It'll cause complications…*

My wife refused treatment, insisted that they were mistaken. We went home, the doctor pulling me aside to suggest that we let her rest a few days, then discuss inducing labor to finish the procedure.

Finish the procedure. Just like that, our baby had somehow changed from human being to benign growth. A mole to be scraped off. A boil to be lanced. All of those cardboard pumpkins hanging on the wall, smiling, calm. That stupid friendly skeleton on the door. They were the only witnesses.

That night, it came. Slow, silent, and sad-eyed. It sat at the foot of the couch where I was sleeping. My wife wanted to be alone, and I didn't know what to do. I didn't notice that I'd drifted off, but one minute it wasn't there and then it was, laying a hand on my calf. I didn't feel fear. I only felt empty.

I am ready—

Just take something and go, I said.

I am ready to end our bargain.

I was speechless. It felt strange, another gut-punch, another loss, another branch pruned from the tree of my life. I wanted to dictate terms. I wanted a safe exit, but once the baby was gone… I wanted it back. I wanted it to continue. I needed it, this thing, this surety.

I will give you your child.

What?

I will give you your child. I will take it. I will be the surrogate. Tomorrow, you will be a father.

It wasn't a question or an offer.

"But my wife can't—"

She will remember nothing.

"I don't want this. You can't have it—my child. You can't. It's done."

Have I ever asked your permission for anything? It ends because I say it ends, and this is how. You are mine. Your body, no matter how far from your body. Cells of your cells. Heart of your heart. Tomorrow you will be a father.

It led me to the bedroom. Made me open the door. Made sure my wife… I can't describe the look I saw on her face, how she instinctively curled her arms over her stomach, how her feral glare burned through me until *it* came into the room. Then she froze, and softened, and looked at me, her lower jaw working, trying to get out a question, to ask me what was happening.

It mounted her, stretched its arms out and wrapped those rubbery, cold fingers around her wrists, pinned her legs down, didn't bother to cover her mouth, because there was nobody to disturb with her screams. All I could do was watch. I knew what it felt like. I knew *exactly* what she was going through. I chuckled in spite of myself that she'd never be able to hold the pain of this childbirth over my head.

That single tooth tore her nightshirt open. That sphincter mouth traced kisses down her collarbone, between her breasts, suckling at her nipples until milk started to flow. Then it moved lower, elbows and shoulders dislocating so that it could keep her pinned down. Not that she was fighting at this point, only staring at me with wide eyes, panting for air until the thing's mouth reached her thighs.

How does it feel?

It asks this as it cuts deep into the inner thigh, flesh and fat zippering apart, its tongue probing into the fresh wound.

How are you doing?

The thing wouldn't want an answer even if there was one. It only wants screams.

This is going to be worth it. You're going to love next year. This will make it worth the having.

Its head stretched thin, narrowing impossibly at the mouth, the entire face a tubular beak, a hard proboscis that poked at her vulva until it found its way inside. She screamed then, my wife.

I could do nothing but watch it root, its palms pushing her legs apart. The cold, slow rivulets of saliva dripping down her sides like icy syrup, washed away with the regular and slowing pulses of her hot blood.

That single tooth in its lower jaw, barbed and curved, that awful knowing smile from the pucker of its mouth as it comes up for air, slowly retracting its head to stare at me, neck bent round the wrong way, slime coating its face, it made that hideous ring-mouth into an imitation of a smile.

It's a boy.

It hammered its beak into her stomach, slicing through skin, and fat, and muscle, splaying her open. Cold, grey slime oozed down her love handles, mixing and pooling with her blood. That ringing, that ringing in my ears isn't ringing. It's her screaming. Screaming for the baby, screaming *no*, screaming my name, cursing me, damning me. Cursing the thing, even as it lowered its face to her flayed abdomen and forced its head inside.

Its back lurched up once, twice, as if taking great gulping swallows, and then it came, orgasmic shudders rippling through its spine as it straightened and stood up from the bed, staring at me, one hand cupping its swollen belly. It caressed my cheek, pushed a finger inside my mouth, pressed until my knees buckled. It lowered me onto the bed beside my wife. Tears streamed from her eyes, her organs warm and wet against my stomach. I reached out to her, stupidly, tried to cradle her in my arms.

The thing stood above us and arched its back, convulsing, straining, eyes swelling until the veins that laced them burst and bloody tears flowed. It straddled her, crouching lower and lower until it positioned its vagina above my wife's open torso. It pushed, pushed until it came…until…a child came. A membranous sac, slid out of its dilated opening and landed inside my wife. I saw through the pale pink membrane a face, calm and serene, sleeping.

Sleeping.

I woke to her screams, my wife clutching my arm, saying, "It's time! Holy shit it's time. They were wrong! My water broke! Do you feel it?"

I climbed from the bed, soaked not in her blood, but amniotic fluid. Aside from that, the sheets were clean in a way my memory could never be.

We drove to the hospital, and I strode through the doors like a champion, pushing her wheelchair through the throng gathered there. I stared at the confused faces of the nurses and doctors and told them it was time.

They checked signs. They double checked charts. They made me sign waivers promising not to sue over all of this stillbirth confusion. "These things happen sometimes. We will of course be paying you for your pain and suffering in exchange for—"

I told them to shut the fuck up and do their job. We could discuss it later. There would be a later. There would be a rest of our lives. That's all that mattered.

You are all that mattered. Our son. My son. Mine.

I'm telling you all of this now before you can understand, because I never want you to hear it again. I never want you to know about any of this. It's gone. It's gone and it won't come back. It always keeps its promises. You're in my arms, with your perfect eyes, your ruddy cheeks, and I love you. More than anything. More than everything. I'm laughing at your gurgles, your tiny nose twitching, your perfect little ruby lips when they stretch into that smile, that same kind of goofy smile your mother gets. Your happy little gummy mouth that looks perfect. Perfect and normal except for that one thing. That single, smooth tiny tooth breaking through your lower gums. Doctors say this isn't unusual, they call them natal teeth. I know better. You yawn wide, showing me that tiny ivory blade, and you stare at me placidly, and I can only think,

Worth the having.

THE SEAS OF HELL
IN A LITTLE GLASS BOTTLE

Mr. Bloom meets me at the entrance with a curt nod and we make our way up the staircase. The door whispers closed behind us, shutting out the haze, the street vendors, even the clatter of horse and carriage. The stairwell is dim, ivory walls and brass banisters that convey us to a long hallway lined with doors. Save for the builders, nobody is sure of the true size of this place, or the exact amount of rooms it holds. Mr. Bloom (this time a stout older man, silent as always) turns smartly at a door ten feet from the stairs and clicks his heels. He motions me inside with another nod. I place a few coins into his palm for thanks and enter.

A room, no larger than a closet with a single chair. A glass screen dominates the wall, surrounded by buttons, lights, levers, and of course, the omnipresent Dictaphone. A selection of masks lines the wall, all molded from the same austere face, each displaying a different emotion. In the Chattertorium, it is illegal to reveal your identity. I slip on a neutral mask, situate myself properly, and pull the lever. The incandescent lights above me fade away, swallowed up by the prismatic globe of the Refractrix mounted on the ceiling. It is rumored that Mr. Tesla stumbled upon this device in a fever dream, and the feeling it evokes as its light pulses and synchronizes with the eyes is always unsettling. Duopresence: the demon light, some street preachers have called it. They say we're ensnared in a web of sloth, lust, and gluttony, a web that Mr. Tesla will weave around the entire world! I say Mr. Tesla is only aiding in speeding the opening of our eyes to the truths around us.

The close quarters feel as though I've come to give confession, a sensation enhanced all the more when a window scrapes open next to me. "State alias and gender, please." The Facilitator. The things they must hear as they monitor our comings and goings.

"H.P.L., Male."

A brief shuffling of papers, followed by a low buzz. "Accepted," the voice drones.

"Messages?"

"You've received an offer from a most honorable Prince Najeel Makumba regarding an inheritance—"

"Thank you, no," I cut him off. "What else?"

"Tate Publishing has declined your latest manuscript, citing its macabre nature. No market for such things."

"We are the market, my friend. Each and every one of us in this building," I mutter. "I'm ready to browse."

"Where shall we go today, sir?"

I inhale and draw the small scrap of paper from the hidden compartment in the brim of my hat. I read aloud the Harlowe/Tesla Matching Link coordinates couriered to me this morning. My passport to The Muse Factory. A blue light blinks three times on the console.

"Ready, sir." The voice drones. "Thank you for attending the Chattertorium, your connection is good for forty more minutes."

I push the button and dry my palms on my trouser legs. From my valise, I withdraw a small notebook and fountain pen. The LumiereScreen before me changes, a warm glow that creeps in so subtly it's difficult to tell if I'm looking at something taking place hundreds of miles away or merely peering through a window to the room next door. From my pocket I produce a flask of Nepenthe and take a deep drink.

A light rises on a young woman sitting in a chair. A small placard behind her, inscribed with her name: Delphi. She's chosen a very neutral mask this evening, stark white, smooth, unpainted. It's difficult to tell what the mouth conveys; it could be a secret smile or a pout of dissatisfaction. I've worked with this woman on several occasions and she never fails to inspire.

She gives a small curtsy, meaning, "Good evening to you sir,"

"And to you, Miss," I reply with a mild doff of my hat.

I lean toward the Dictaphone. "Inspire me. Dance for me as I dance with the cosmos." I shake my flask at her. "The Grim Fairy! The Publishers tell me there are great truths to be writ down. Articles about politicians. Romances. Happy endings. Facades!"

"Shall we try, then?" She rises and prepares to dance.

"Delphi. The written word is worthless to me if it's hollow. This, these moments, the act of writing is the gateway to discovery. To a greater understanding of what hides beneath the veneer of society, and you! Only you understand."

I sigh, slapping my notebook against my leg. I can nearly feel the Nepenthe slosh and tumble in my cranium, carrying my mind on an unsteady tide, the shores of inspiration somewhere over a distant horizon, not drawing any closer. "Alas, I have bills to pay. A family. The worst truth of all. To survive, I must give Tate what they want. Bare yourself to me." I feel shame at asking, again, to see her body. I've described her smooth white skin dozens of times in my tawdry romance books (published under a nom de plume, thank the Gods!). There are only so many ways to paint the roundness of her hips, her soft neck, the gentle curve of her earlobe. "Delphi, the most merciful thing in the world is the inability of the human mind to… correlate all its contents."

"It's not a mercy," she says.

"I beg your pardon?" Her silhouette widens and warps briefly, then she snaps back into perfect form. The Nepenthe.

"This is no mercy."

She tips her mask up, revealing full lips, unpainted. Her upper lip is swollen and cracked. She hesitates for a moment, then turns away and removes her mask. This is a breach of protocol that could bring our session to an instant halt if a monitor notices us. She turns back to me, pushing the hair from her face. Her left eye is blackened.

"What happened? Who did this to you?"

She holds up an ornate drawing of a heart, a black valentine on a sepia card. "This was all I got for my troubles." She pulls down the top of her dress, revealing a line of bruises and welts tattooed across her breasts and stomach. "I'm a dancer." A tear spills from her good eye. Her hair begins to float and swim in the air, and I know I'm at the mercy of the elixir. "I'm a good dancer…" she cries softly and pulls a small knife from her boot. She traces it over the skin of her arms, then cuts a harsh line across the top of her hand.

"Please! Wait!" I shout. She hesitates for a moment, her face twisted in a snarl of defiance. "Let me write this." I tell her, "Dance."

And she does. An intricate, violent, bloody tarantella, her body twisted, contorted, sliced raw. A blur of motion and shining metal, her tongue darts out occasionally to lick at the blood coursing down her forehead. She has become something…other, a gateway of sorts, and my hand scrambles to capture what I've seen. Her steps reach a pounding crescendo, such that the very walls of the room pulse like a living skin holding back a tide of blood and ichor. She collapses, spattered in her own sweat and blood, her hair soaked and dangling in her face.

In the silence, a halo of shadow forms around her, pulsing, beating like a heart, expanding. The Nepenthe is trailing away and clarity is seizing firm hold. I hear in the back of my head a voice, insistent, cold, oozing its way from the far reaches of my psyche, sinking claws icy and deep into my mind.

Ph'nglui mglw'nafh Cthulhu R'lyeh wgah'nagl fhtagn.

I repeat it out loud.

"Has the drink set you ill, sir?" Delphi pants.

I ignore her and translate as best I can. "*In his house at R'lyeh dead Cthulhu waits dreaming.*"

Delphi looks up from the floor, panting, smiling. "We've made something?"

"Yes. God help me, I'll never be able to sleep again, but yes!"

In that moment, I clutching my pen, she her knife, we two are damned. Doomed. And happy.

***

I cannot sleep. I long for a return to the Chattertorium. I long to see my Delphi again, but she has fled away to parts unknown. I had, perhaps, imbibed too much of her as of late, and too much Nepenthe as well, for it has caused some ill in my personal life. My wife stopped speaking to me the first night I came home *inspired*. She claimed I was half-mad like a demon, and perhaps I was.

I locked myself in my writing closet for hours, hammering at the keys, the only light from the faint glow of the lumikeys and the green text on the viviScreen. I took no food, no water, the Grim Fairy in the flask my only companion. Every draft from that bottle burned the image of Delphi into my eyes, opened pathways into my mind for horrors unspeakable and visions insistent.

I wrote until the sun came up and went down again, I wrote even as my wife beat on the other side of the door, tearfully announcing that she was taking the children away to her family until my senses returned. My senses had never been sharper. This was an urgent missive from somewhere beyond the pillars of creation, an historical announcement and a warning to all of humanity and I, only I, could be its conduit.

The bottle ran dry.

I chased it. Spent every last credit until I was nigh-destitute. Nepenthe became my addiction and Delphi was the promise of reward at the end. I had not been back to see her. I cannot, not until I can present her with the sum total of my work. To see her face when she realizes that she was the threshold to the realm of the Gods, that she could inspire such a journey...

I am a man on the run. To return home is to admit defeat. I remain on the streets, hiding, running from shadow to shadow, determined to find what I crave. I sleep where I can, in alleys, in bars, in houses of ill-repute.

When I close my eyes, I dream of a continent. Long-deserted, desolate, stone buildings and pillars in the Greek style scattered about its rolling hills. The sky is a strange, swirling eddy of blues and purples, and it is only after some study that I realize the whole landscape is submerged. Fish move between skeletal houses, hovering at windows, skirting pillars. Strange, tiny, shelled things reclaim the land from long-vanished settlers.

I drift through clouds of silt until I come to a clearing, and I find her. She lays in perfect repose, a thin white shift billowing around her frame, hair woven with strands of kelp. Her skin is pale as the bellies of the fish that pass overhead, hands clasped across her breast clutching half of the mask she wore the last night I laid eyes on her.

The bruise surrounding her eye is gone, replaced by an anemone that has burst from the socket, flowering into a breathtaking pink flower that reaches strands into the water to snatch at tiny krill. Between her lips is a tiny golden key. I pull it free and the ground trembles. Fish scatter, and sand fills the currents in front of me until I am blind. A great pressure builds, pushing against my feet until I am cast upwards, through endless fathoms, suddenly breaking through the foam and sailing into the air!

I ascend until I can see for miles. The very curvature of the earth stretches below me. A great chasm has formed in the waters. The island is rising, but it is not land at all. It is a creature! A vast and terrifying thing that stretches limbs that have lain still for eons. Great buildings still cling to its arms and shoulders. How tall it must be that even here, in the middle of the vast and endless sea, the waters break at its waist! It faces away from me, fissures forming on its back until the rock and sand accrued there explode, sending a shower of debris into the waters as titanic wings extend, blacking out the sky.

I reach the zenith of my ascent, impossibly high, and the thing turns its gaze on me. Its eyes are strange windows containing hellish light. I float, the beast below me and the stars above. She is there in the heavens, deep in the recesses of the constellations, Delphi, her face restored, her skin aglow.

She whispers, "That is not dead which can eternal lie..."

The beast roars.

I wake.

***

I have no pen and my words must scream.

I am distraught. Cast out. Alone.

My pockets are as threadbare and thin as my stomach. I stumble from place to place, desperate for her. Collapsed from hunger, unable to feel my legs beneath me, I lean back against a fountain in the City Center. The rush of water behind my head diminishes all other sound. I lean my head back and look to the stars. The lights from the surrounding buildings erase the night. The sky is a still black sea, and I am drowning at its bottom.

Great zeppelins and personal gas-gliders float silently above, lights blinking, tailfins swishing as they cut through the night. The spires of the surrounding skyscrapers reach up like man-made kelp, clawing into the night to snare god-knows-what – the hopes and dreams of all of the dull, brainwashed masses down here on the ocean floor?

I slump further, curling onto my side, unable to seek the infinite, all hope of seeing her face lost. My world becomes a frenzy of passing legs and dresses and petticoats, dancing in the night air like sea grass. I long for the great beast beneath this city to awake, to stretch its limbs and cast off the pall of humanity.

The night is cold, and near sleep she comes to me. Bare feet on the pavement in front of my face. I look up to see her, Delphi, clad in golden robes and a brilliant mask resembling a bird of paradise.

"You," I say dumbly. "You have destroyed me."

"No."

"I have destroyed myself searching for you. Are you an illusion?"

"No."

Her golden dress brings warmth to my blood. Supplicant at her feet, I realize she has thin sandals on, delicate silver chains weave between her toes and around her ankles. Her shawl is painted with brilliant feathers. Were she to spread her arms I fear she might fly away.

"Where have you gone?"

"Somewhere else. Somewhere better."

"I cannot create without you. You haunt my thoughts, my minutes, my hours."

"I do not belong to you. I owe you nothing."

She looks away from me across the square as an airship comes in low over the buildings, rippling the air with the rumble of impellers. The profile of her jaw and the bird mask are indescribably beautiful. I follow her gaze toward a throng of people gathered near the Governor's Ballroom, all of them in costume, masked and resplendent.

"We made magic…together, we…"

"You used me."

"I would never."

"What was I to you? A conduit? I bared myself to you, nearly destroyed. You told me to dance." She draws her shawl closer and moves away into the crowd, shimmering blue and green feathers flitting across a forest of tuxedos and dresses.

I don't recall climbing to my feet. I don't recall walking across the square. My mind is jostled. My synapses fire in fits and starts.

I am on the ground speaking to her.

I am walking through the crowd trying to find her after she walked away.

I am in an alley behind the ballroom, choking a patron with his own scarf.

I am walking through the front door in an ill-fitting suit, hoping nobody notices the hairline fractures in the mask, the slight spill of blood on the dress shirt.

Two large men at the door admitting guests. Not knowing where my quarry stored his tickets, I pat myself down absentmindedly until one of them jabs a thick finger into my chest pocket. I follow his eyes to the gloves sticking out. I remove them and notice nothing special beyond a faint design stitched into the top in a slightly darker shade of ivory.

I watch another guest move past me and insert his hand into a brass reader by the door. It bathes his glove in indigo light, revealing an intricate piece of art. The light changes from blue to green, the doormen nod him in.

I smile and slide the gloves on, putting my hand into the reader. The back of the glove is beautifully embroidered with an octopus, its tentacles reaching down the fingers. The light turns green and the design darkens on my glove, becoming permanently visible. The doorman doesn't trust me, but I've met the requirements for entry.

The hallway is resplendent. Gaslamps circle the room on a clever conveyance of gears and tracks, casting shadowshow creatures onto the ceiling. To walk into the foyer is to enter a mystic jungle. Acrobats hang from vines on the ceiling, scantily clad men and women cavorting and contorting to steady drums.

I move to the grand staircase, hoping to have a better vantage point. The men are a swirling eddy of tuxedos and top hats, flitting among them are the lithe and slender forms of young ingénues in shimmering gowns and great, proud matrons in broad and shining hoop skirts and layered dresses. Among the blues and greens and violets and crimsons, I spot her, moving like quicksilver, following a path unknown behind a line of similarly attired women.

The house lights pulse and a voice emanates from a speaker cleverly disguised as a conch shell above the grand stairs.

The ceremony begins in five minutes. Please take your places.

A ceremony. Places. That implies I—or my victim—had an assigned role in tonight's festivities. Not knowing my duty, I follow the crowd, noting how the men and women separate into different lines. The younger women line the outer wall. The older women move off to the left of the stairs. Men in top hats ascend the stairs. My victim had no hat. I follow the line of masked men to the right of the stairs.

The ballroom is a grand thing, a circular arena theater accessible from four sides. We proceed down the hallway and enter the amber-lit theater under a large ornate arch. The line of older women comes in through the opposite arch. The men in hats circle the upper mezzanine. My line falls into ranks on the outer perimeter of the ballroom floor.

A low horn sounds and the room goes dark. Faint footlights begin to glow, limestone and flame. A rustling of fabric and the lights rise. The young women approach a giant circular cistern rising from the center of the immense floor. They circle round it, then, with a great effort, they slide the heavy metal lid back.

A light green glow fills the space.

I know what's in the container. I recognize the smell. My cheeks and tongue are suddenly dry, my eyes watering. My skin crawls with lines of unseen insects, thousands of them racing over my spine and chest. Hands shaking, I struggle to remain upright. I must not allow the others gathered to notice my state.

The women dip their arms into the cistern, withdrawing chalices. Nepenthe.

My heart leaps, filling my chest with lightning. It is warm, like seeing a loved one long missing. No! It is a desperate thing, a thorny nest full of hungry baby birds screaming into the morning for mother's food.

They circle the ballroom and present the chalices, first to the older women, and then to my line. It is a shared experience. A communion. After each person drinks, the woman holding the chalice wipes the rim clean and moves to the next supplicant.

She is before me, a woman in a sterling silver gown, her mask like a jungle panther, her burnished skin like copper. I seize the chalice, drinking so deeply that the Nepenthe spills down my shirt, tilting my head back so far that my mask goes askew. Liquid fire torches my gullet, I feel its heat in my nose and ears. My eyes water, blurring my vision. Nepenthe assaults me.

The women circling begin to change, masks fusing with flesh, until they are half-formed beasts. The older women in their large dresses merge together until they are a mass of writhing humanity. They look like women lost at sea, their dresses threatening to submerge and suffocate them. The men on the mezzanine have removed their masks, and I know them all. My critics, my contemporaries.

Words surge from the bottom of my gut, rattling through the dusty hallway of my windpipe, cracking and splitting my innards until they ring from my mouth like a trumpet. It is a call, a language I do not understand that is gifted to me from the other side of a veil unseen. At its speaking, everyone in the room turns back to gaze in fear at the cistern. The Nepenthe has turned a deeper shade of green, roiling and spilling out onto the floor.

A hand erupts from the liquid, massive and clawed, buckling the floor as it pushes higher and higher. The cistern collapses inward, leaving us clinging to small remnants of floor ringing a deep sea of swirling chaotic liquid. There is no bottom to this ocean. What looks like a mountain submerged is a living creature, a thing rising, the ruler of that great and terrible hand that even now searches in the empty air for purchase. Its twin erupts from the green sea, clinging to the opposite wall. Then another hand, and another, and finally the crown of the thing's head, like great, shattered jade boulders. It rises, two eyes set deep in crevices that weep green tears. It has no mouth, but a mass of writhing tentacles that wave and slap at the walls.

It sees me.

It sees only me.

One arm extends, palm open, and I step forward. I am broken

and I am whole. The gate is open, and there is no technology, no weapon, no force in nature that can withstand the fury of what I've unleashed.

Not God, but Gods.

In the abyss, I see more of them emerging, struggling to breathe the air of our realm. The one that carries me punches up with a rocky fist, shattering the ceiling of the ballroom. I step to the edge of its finger, looking down on the scene of destruction below.

I tell myself that this is real, even as I see myself below, my body broken and lifeless next to the fountain in the square. A young woman kneels before it, hand on its shoulder rocking it – me – trying to rouse me, but I am lost. The Nepenthe has me, it has taken me across the veil.

Have I opened a gate for another dimension to come to our world, or have I crossed into theirs? The beast that holds me reaches its full height. Black clouds wreath its head as its wings spread wide to blot out the stars. When it howls, I answer in kind.

The sky cracks, the ground shatters, and I am lost to the darkness.

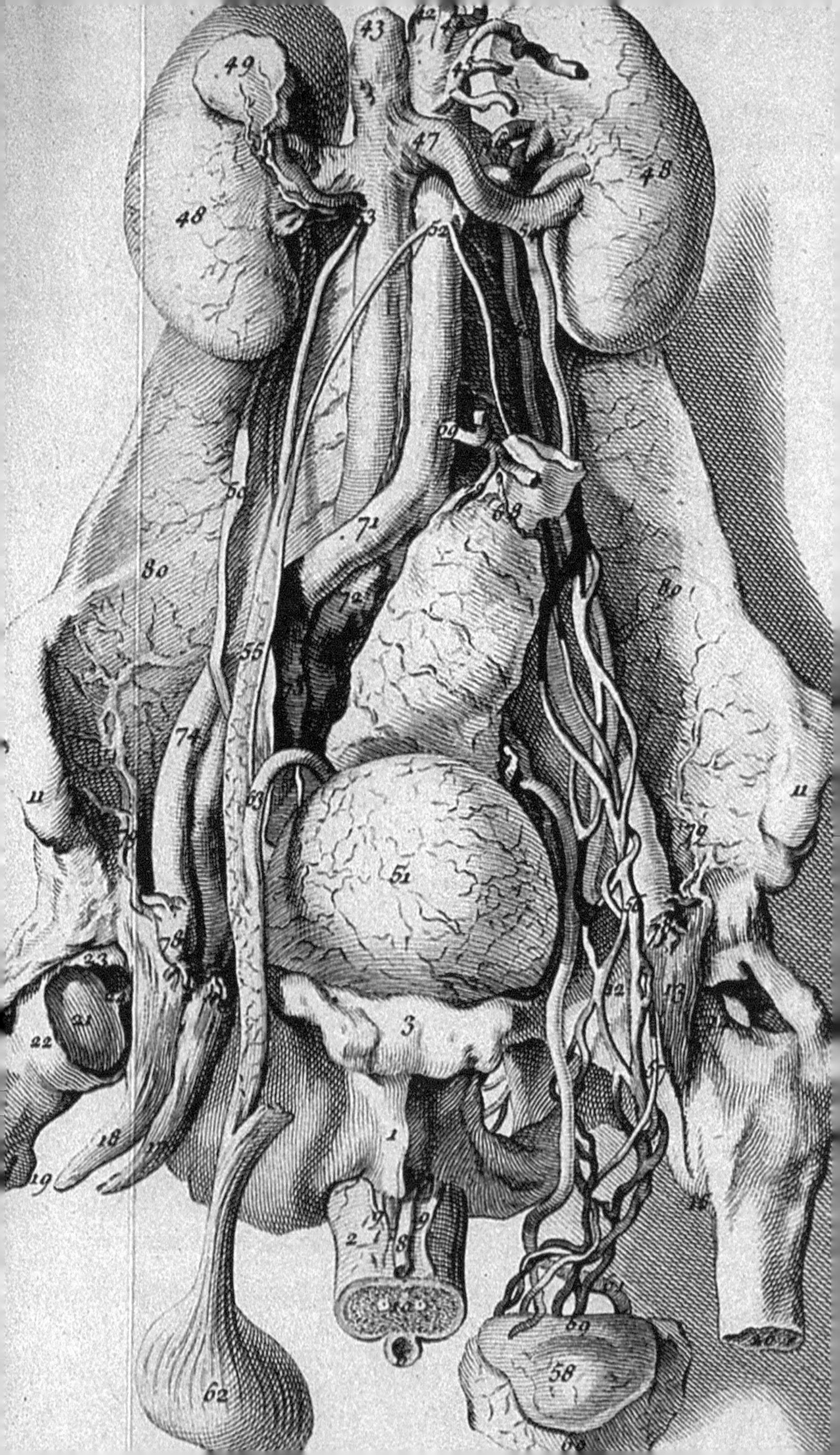

UPPER CRUST

Back in college, I ran in some good circles. Not the best. I always wanted to be in the best. *Now*, I'm in the—I was looking for a fraternity, because you know it's who you know that gets you ahead in the world. I wanted to know the important people. Only the best. My father, when he sent me off to Wharton, he told me, I don't give a shit what you learn or what your grades are. I care who you meet. That's where the important lessons are. Know who to know, and what you know becomes second place.

One night, I'm at a rush party for Delta Kappa Epsilon. Lot of good people in that—Gerald Ford, the Bush Family, you see where I'm going—but this is obviously before any of them were president. I'm at this party looking at a goddamn oil painting of my great grandfather, he pledged so many years—but even legacies have to earn their spot. Out of nowhere, I feel something slide into my pocket. I look down, and there's this hand—silk glove, red silk, sexy as hell and—good party when someone's reaching into your pants before you've finished your first drink, right?

I turn, and there's this woman behind me, just *painted* into this silk dress. Everything red. Hugging every—I mean everything, the curves and her nipples—she just smiles at me, extends her hand, and says, "Ursula Dupree." Just like that. So I kiss her hand, and she flicks a finger toward my pocket, turns, and walks away.

In my pocket there's a little engraved business card. Gold.

Sharp as a razor. Still got it here somewhere. You can see the stains from our meal on the—we'll get to that.

TANNER STEED – YOU ARE CALLED

SEPTEMBER 14, 1964

10PM

FULCRUM

ANWEALD · FEOH · WEALDAN

FOLLOW YOUR GAZELLE

Gazelles! That's what they called them… anyway. And you've seen the Fulcrum logo on my desk. That's usually covered by the first dollar I ever "made," nobody gets to see—but I have to show it to you tonight. And you've seen it, so now you have to — my father sent me there to meet people. Fucking is meeting, right? You don't pass up opportunities.

So, I followed her to this big ballroom, and everyone's eating dinner. We sit, she says, "Don't eat, you'll be eating later tonight," and she slides a finger up her thigh and gives this little shudder, and I'm— well, you get the idea. But she eats! Seven courses. Clam chowder, oysters Rockefeller, escargot, poi and sashimi, mustard potatoes, lamb with mint sauce and jelly, and a pineapple upside-down cake for dessert. I remember all seven, it comes back later. I'm just supposed to watch her eat? But the way she did it was—she could do things with that mouth, and—so we're talking, small talk, and then the last course comes, the waiter sets this little silver dish down, lifts the lid, and nothing's there.

Ursula stands up, and I swear, I don't know how they cut this dress, but it slides open across her thighs, and there, eye level, *pow*, her pussy, right in my face. Just a long enough flash that I can see how neatly trimmed, and she says, "Dinner was delightful. Are you ready for dessert?"

You're thinking what I'm thinking, right? She walks away. Up this spiral staircase in the corner of the room. There's these two guys standing right at the top of the stairs, like big stone—these were, one of them was probably Samoan, I mean huge—and the guy just looks at me and says, "Card." Just, *card*.

And the other guy has his hand out, gentle on my shoulder, but like a granite—so I give them the card, right? I pull it out from on top of my money clip. Back then I was like you, stupid, thinking that power came with showing wealth—anyway, showed them the little card she gave me, and they melt. Big, soft teddy bears. They step aside, backs to the wall, but like I said, big guys, so I still have to squeeze between, and then this door slides open a few feet away.

Maybe she's a prostitute, right? That's what I'm thinking, these were her body guards, they saw the money, they thought I—anyway, I step inside, thinking it's a bedroom, but it's an elevator. The door closes. She's not there. Small elevator. Red lights. And I can't even feel it moving, I'm just waiting for five minutes to move and—the doors open, and I'm on another floor. Basement. Way down. Didn't know it at the time.

I step into this waiting room. Two benches, one along each wall, look like they were from a museum. Like they'd been there since the 1700s, and that's because *they were*. Immaculate condition because people only sat on them once every four years. That's how lucky I was to—anyway, one wall, four ladies sitting. Four silk dresses. Red, purple, blue, and green. Other wall. Three guys. Not even college guys like me. One of them was my age, the other two were older and—they don't matter.

I stood by them. Here's a little secret. If everyone's sitting, you stand. If everyone's standing, you sit.

The walls are covered, floor to ceiling in these small oil paintings, little two-foot-tall portraits of men, great men. Didn't know it at the time. That's another secret—most of the truly powerful men, you never know their names, because there are positions. Roles. Some people are behind the scenes, some people, like me, are destined for the stage. So. We're just looking at these ladies, and they're not talking, just sitting there looking as hot as—and then these two big double doors open.

And the ladies stand, and this is where it gets good. This guy, this little butler, comes out wheeling a cart. On top of the cart, four leather collars, each attached to a chain. Without a word, the ladies stand up, unzip their dresses, and slide them off. You've never seen anything like—I mean, they all had underwear on, same color scheme, red—I guess Ursula had just put them on—and blue, green, purple, somehow that was even sexier than if they'd been naked—each one puts on a collar, walks over to us, hands us the leash. The butler gestures us through the big doors.

Inside, there's a—I'm not supposed to talk about the room, but you're going to see it soon enough, so I'm not really spoiling anything—like a courtroom fucked a brothel. Best way I can—there's a big, tall judge's stand. Big podium, three chairs way up high. On one side, a jury box. Sits twelve people. On the other wall, nothing. Well, almost nothing. Two little iron loops that I didn't notice when we—I'll get to that.

In the middle of the room, where the lawyers would normally go—a small table, like we're here to play poker. I don't know what the hell's going on, I just know I have Ursula's hot blonde ass on a chain. I'm up for anything. The butler claps, and the ladies lead us to a chair. High-backed, satin cushions, and the cushions match our ladies' clothes. My chair's red, guy next to me is blue, the—you get it. You understand. The ladies pull out the chairs, we sit, and they stand just behind us.

The butler claps again and says, "Judges." Two more doors open. Twelve guys in robes file into the jury booth. Then the butler rings this little bell. And it gets quiet. A door opens behind the podium, three men walk in, and they have full hoods on. Can't see their faces. They sit up high. The Triumvirate. You'd know their names. You've read about them in history books. They have done great things—that's a history you only get to learn if you pass tonight.

They sit, and I figure this is it, we're being hazed into the fraternity, right? Couldn't be more wrong. The Triumvirate, as one, they raise gavels and tap three times. The one in the middle says, "Dinner is served."

The butler leaves and comes back, with—get this—a pizza. A fuckin' pizza margherita. The most boring—cheese, tomato slices, some marinara. Smelled good, but I mean, *this* is what you dragged us down to—and nobody else reaches for a piece, so I don't either. I don't know where this is going.

"Gentlemen," the butler says. "This is the gathering of the Fulcrum. You've been carefully selected to begin the process of advancement to an echelon of society known to your fathers and their fathers. Every four years, we open our chambers around the world so that men can prove themselves worthy of joining the ranks of the Fulcrum. Is the Triumvirate prepared?"

The guys behind the podium gavel in turn. They go in order, left to right, saying Secundus, Primus, Tertius.

And Primus bangs his—god I wish I was allowed to tell you his name, you'd die, you wouldn't believe—anyway, he bangs the thing and gives us this speech.

"We are the playwrights of society. We control the stagecraft of the world. This is not an honor, it is the highest achievement a man can strive for. In the Fulcrum, there are no individuals. Behind these doors, we are many. In the world, we are one. If one of us succeeds, it is shared victory. If one of us is slighted, we are all wounded. This is your opportunity to join us. *Sacrifice* is a word greatly misunderstood. *Power* is a word greatly misused. *Fortune* is a word whose meaning few people truly grasp. Tonight, you will sacrifice. You will understand what is required to obtain fortune. With fortune comes power, responsibility, money, and no need to sacrifice again. To show your willingness to move to the next phase, you must break bread together. *La Festa dei Burattinai.* Will you take a bite of the food before you to show you are willing?"

That's all they wanted? I check the competition. They each grab a slice. Me? I do it big time. Slide a knife under a piece, guide it up to my plate with my fork. Cut a slice, the right size, not too big. I pick the guy across the table, the first to grab a slice. Unbroken eye contact while I chew. I look at the next guy, same thing, keep chewing until he looks away. I swallowed before I had a chance to look at the third guy, but he got the idea. It wasn't the best pizza I've ever—and then, after one bite, the butler whisks it all away and another guy brings in a different pizza. This one has sausage. Hot peppers. Like really hot, the ghost kind, we don't know from—and then the Primus says, "The world presents resistance. Can you push through hesitation, work through discomfort, withstand the heat of the forge?"

This time, maybe they're on to me, they're really testing my resolve, because all the cutlery goes away. I have to pick up the slice with my bare hands like these other chimps. We take a bite, and it's hot, really fuckin'—I mean, we need water, and we're laughing at this point, because we can see this coming. Spicy food, gross food, whatever, we're pledging, getting hazed. Same drill again, one bite, butler goes out, new guy comes in with a new pizza. This one is covered in black crickets and live earthworms.

"The world is rife with poor, simple creatures. The mechanisms of society are infested. You must consume them. Their bodies exist to nourish and sustain you."

And here, of course–I mean, fried crickets, yeah, that's

disgusting, but live worms? But then again, it's fraternity life, right? So one of us, not me, I'm not ashamed to admit, goes first, big bite, and then we all dive in. Not as disgusting as I thought. Tastes like dirt. Cold and soft, though. Like a dead lady's lips. I figure once they stopped squirming it would be–but they never really stopped. I could feel them moving in my stomach for–probably a lesson in there somewhere.

"People are the salt of the earth. Though it may turn your stomach to mingle with them, you can, and must. Farm them, nourish them, consume them." Right as the Primus says this, the butler's back in with another pizza, plain tomato and cheese. Big slices. And behind him, another guy's pushing a cart with small cardboard boxes.

We hear this scratching. Pecking. *Peeping*. Our ladies open the boxes and pull out these fuzzy chicks. Little baby chickens. Without a hitch, they take the chicks, and *krick-krick-krick-krick*, break their tiny legs. They set them on a slice, and these little birds are… not fluttering, vibrating. The wings are moving so fast and their eyes squint from the pain and—and the Primus says, "Sacrifices will always need to be made. Vermin and pets alike. You consume them all, those you revile and those you adore. Increase their suffering or end it, but the suffering is not the matter. Our nourishment is. The door awaits."

We stare at each other. Hazing is one thing, but this was… and Ursula leans down and whispers–and I can still feel her juicy lips brushing my ear when I think of this, gives me goosebumps—she says, "Do it. For me." I don't know what the other ladies were saying, and I didn't care, because this time I was first. If only one of us was going to win this game, it had to be me. I rolled the little bird up in the pizza slice, cradled it with the head pointing at my mouth, because I figure, you break the neck and then—and it was a clean bite, I have strong jaws thank god, and it was… it didn't taste like I thought. Crunched like… and the beak just felt like an unpopped popcorn kernel, if it was stuck in a cottonball soaked in blood, and… I saw the other guys going for it too. And the butler, thank god, tells us, "You may spit."

The ladies give us a chalice, and we spit out the mess, and just stare at each other. It was the act, not the eating, you understand? Ursula gestured to me. I had this little piece of gristle and a tiny feather stuck to my lip.

The Primus says, "The game begins. Woman. The ultimate tool of resistance and persuasion. Her fortitude is incomparable. Her service to you is irreplaceable. Her greed will push you to greatness. Her guile will bring down those who would seek to hurt you. Uncontrolled, her fury will consume you. Choose your tools wisely."

The butler brings out the next pizza. A plain ham and cheese. Each woman rotates to the next man at the table. Now I've got blue next to me. They plant their hands on the table and snort. I mean, big, phlegmy… and they start spitting on the pizza. Just greaser after greaser. Big, green shiny… coating the whole thing. Then they fold their arms and stare at us.

After the birds, this seemed like nothing to me, so I grabbed a slice and took a bite. I mean, I had plans to bury my tongue in Ursula's asshole, what's a little spit? We all take a bite. The women rotate again. They put our slices on the floor. The butler gives them sneakers. Each one announces where they walked from to get there. "I took the train from Shitburgh to blah blah blah," you get the idea. They made it clear, these shoes had been through spook neighborhoods, or immigrant shitholes, whatever piss-stained, dog-shit-encrusted sidewalk you could think of. And they stood on the slice. Really smeared their foot in there. Then, without lifting the shoe up, they took it off, carefully slid a hand underneath, flip it, and served the piece to us, like the shoe was a plate.

This one made me hesitate. You know me and germs. Eventually the other guys ate, so I had to.

The Primus says, "Four courses: The women will weed out the weak. They will serve until two remain. This will comprise the end of the second chapter. If all four pledges remain, the women are deemed to have failed. Fortune does not accept failure."

A new pizza comes in. Cheese only, nothing else.

The Primus says, "Sauce."

And two of the ladies squat over it and piss all over the–soaked it–and this was where things got weird.

The Primus says, "Toppings."

You know how sick a woman can—the lady in blue says, "I'm menstruating." Drew out the word like it's supposed to scare us. Reaches into her underwear and pulls out this fat, brown piece of cotton.

The butler comes over with a silver tray and she sets it down, gets out a scalpel, and carefully cuts it into little pepperoni slices, putting them on the pizza. She says, "Who wants a fresh one?"

I figured if I got it while it was still warm, I could—and you know, it tasted—have you ever had a bloody nose? Sort of like that. I meant the cotton was… it wasn't easy to chew. But thank god, the butler clapped again and we were allowed to spit that into the chalice too. So far, we're all in.

Ursula though, what a bitch, brings out this small plastic box with a picture of her dog on it. And she says, "This is Mopsie. She's a purebred Pomeranian." I hated that dog, by the way, so glad when it died. Little worm-infested—always chewed up my—anyway, she opens the box. "Mopsie eats only the finest cuts of meat and pure vegetables. Mopsie made this for all of you."

She takes tongs and sets down one perfect little roll of Mopsie shit on each piece and stares at us. Like little tootsie rolls with rice noodles embedded in—dead worms, you see? And win or lose, eating this means a trip to the doctor's office. You can't succeed without eating a little shit. That's what my father always told me.

It was too much for the guy across from me. He pushes the plate away. The first failure. He starts to curse the Triumvirate, ask them what the hell they thought they were doing, if they knew who he was, who his father was, and in come the Samoans, you know, dragged him out and things got quiet.

The Tertius stands at the podium, and points a finger at the guy's lady. She's dressed in the blue, right? And he says, "NAME?" nice and loud, and I swear I saw a little squirt of piss shoot down her leg. And she says, "Savannah".

"Expendable."

The Samoans are back. One grabs her arms, handcuffs her. The other puts this ball gag in her mouth, and then they chain her neck to the iron loop on the empty wall. Put a big spotlight on her.

"That's a sight," I say. Got the Primus to smile at that. Always try to make friends. Read the room.

"Three remain," the Primus says. "Crimson has proven her breeding. One woman can be a worthy ally and a fierce adversary. A group of women can be insurmountable. Where Crimson leads, the others will follow. Present the next challenge."

And I'm thinking, wow, I got the good one, right? She won, she gets to go again. And the other two women look nervous. Like maybe they're all playing a game too, and Ursula's on the brink of winning their end or something?

"Dinner tonight was splendid," Ursula says. "Seven delicious courses." The butler brings out another pizza, this one just bread. Nothing else on it. But it's deep dish style, right? It looks like a giant bread bowl almost. Our women move back to us and sit in our laps. And even with everything we'd been through, feeling that ass in those silky panties on my—anyway, they sit.

"Our compliments to the chef," Ursula says, and she sticks two fingers down her throat, and everything she ate earlier that night comes back. Chowder, some pineapple cake chunks, the oysters Rockefeller, escargot—whole fuckin' snails, the poi thing, man, the smell of that, and sauce, wine, she stops and pumps her stomach again—like a cat with a hairball— I mean this was Chicago-Style. Just *gallons* sloshing and—I'm just feeling her ass clench every time she retches and watching her ribs expand and lurch as she pours it all out. And it was almost sexy. Almost. I think she's done, but no! The potatoes, more wine, the lamb with mint sauce and jelly like green chunky toothpaste, and all of it's in this perfect cone on the pizza, and then to top it off— how did she do—a perfectly whole pineapple ring from the cake. Like she saved it just, *bam* on top.

And the smell?

The Primus looked at me and said, "You shall begin. The next man to eat may allow his woman to add to the feast. The game continues."

Ursula looks at me, just… the other women, they're all over their guys, right? Rubbing thighs, shoulders, nuzzling their ears—I mean, they all got a shot of mouthwash first, but—they look like they're pleading for their lives. Not Ursula. She's got this gaze of steel, just looks at me and says "Do this. You will do this now." Her eyes are wet and wild, like she's somewhere between crying and orgasm, her crotch is like a dripping furnace sitting there on my thigh, and she's just *animal* and I dove in. I can't explain it, and I know she looks a little tough now after all the surgeries, and who cares, you don't worry how the car you sold twenty years ago looks now—I mean, back then, she was *something*. I don't know how to—and I mean, it's just food. That's all I thought. It's all just food.

I swallowed. Tried not to chew. Terrible. It was like chili. The bile made it taste like old sausage—but the other two guys, it took them another five minutes to even start. I thought I won, for the longest time, I thought, this is it, Steed, you win. But then another guy, the guy across from me, chows through a bite. So his woman gets to puke on the pizza too, and now it's down to the third man. That's all they ever wanted us to do, right, just a bite. That's the big thing. The hesitation. They want you to get over the—but the last guy, he couldn't do it. He went to push the plate away, got some of puke on his fingers, and then *he* puked, everywhere. *Bam*, in come the Samoans, *boom* out he goes.

"NAME," the Secundus, this time, stands up. And the woman, this is the lady in purple, she says, "Posey." And she looks so sad, like a pale little flower. That was the first time I felt sad that night. She's crying right, because same thing, here comes the Samoans, the handcuffs, then they force a piece of puke pizza into *her* mouth, then the ballgag, and *bam*, chained to the wall.

"The game continues," the Primus says. "When your competitor falls, it is up to you to utilize his assets."

I don't know why it was worse to know a man's puke was part of this soup now, but Ursula did this thing with her palm, like cupping my—you know—and instant, I mean instant, like Viagra has nothing on—and so I took a bite. Unbroken eye contact until I swallowed. And the other guy whispered, called me an asshole, and he took a bite too.

It's just me and him. Eyes watering, trying not to lose it. Ursula in red. His woman in green.

The Primus smiles. "Blood and money are the finalists. Names?"

"Ursula," Ursula says.

"Amalie," the lady in green says. Pretty name, I'd never heard it before. Usually you hear AHM-uhlee, but she was AM-alee. Cute girl. Great ass.

"Tanner Steed," I said, offering the other guy my hand. I guess I can tell you, it was Colton Northcutt. Remember him, ran for president a few years ago? Anyway, he goes to shake, and I did this thing, you know my trick, pump twice, and pull them in. Got his whole forearm in that puke pizza. He knew who was in control. You have to break them.

The Primus says, "Loyalty and Ambition will provide *il corso principale*."

The big guys come in, real careful, and take that table out. Didn't spill a drop out of that puke-soup pie. They bring in a new table. White marble, unfinished. That's when I noticed the walls for the first time. Same white marble. Like big tiles, all with these abstract color designs on them. Reds and browns. A year inscribed at the bottom of each one. Little plaque with a name—a woman's name, I would later learn. You see where this is—Ursula in red and Amalie in green sit at the table, staring at each other. The butler sets two empty wine glasses next to a new empty pizza. New pizza, new table. Thin crust. No toppings. No plates. Not even a pan under the pie.

"The gentlemen will pour," the Primus says.

The butler hands us these knives, like little syringes. Or funnels. Like big tubes of… and we couldn't figure out what to do with them, but the Samoans come back, and they unchain the two ladies from the wall. Savannah and Posey. Bend them over the table, yank back on their hair, their necks are just hovering above the wine glasses. They're panting through those ballgags, just frothing and moaning and crying. And the veins on their necks jump up and, just coated in sweat, and you know they're in their little underwear, and this whole thing is kind of sexy until the one Samoan holding Savannah looks at me and his eyes go to the weird knife-funnel thing, and he says, "Sir, will you pour?"

He tapped a finger on the vein in her neck.

I looked at Colton across the table. Looked at Amalie and Ursula, but they only had their eyes on each other. I push the needle into the side of Savannah's neck and—have you ever popped champagne on New Year's? You know? Just… everywhere! Sprayed everywhere! Everything's red, Ursula and Amalie in their little underwear, just soaked and the Samoan is kind of helping me, right, guiding my hand, keeping the funnel pressed in so that I fill up one wine glass with Savannah.

And Colton, in for a penny, in for a pound. They didn't—and see, this is the thing with power, they didn't even have to explain to us exactly what we were playing for here, it just made sense—so Colton pops Posey's neck, and she—maybe she's dehydrated, she's not a squirter like the other one, and she pours out, one glass, and the Samoans grab the ladies by the nape of the neck, haul them out of the room, like meat. Empty boxes. I thought they were taking them out back to ditch the bodies, but—can you believe it—I actually saw Posey at a function a few years later. She couldn't really look me in the eye.

Fucks like a rabbit though, little—anyway—they're gone, right? Now, it's the big deal. Colton and I toast each other and take a sip.

The Triumvirate stands. The butler announces, "The game will conclude!"

The jury stands, and shit, I'd forgotten they were there this whole time. The judges have their hoods off. And they all start saying their names, full names, names you'd know! Cereal companies, newspaper barons, cattlemen, oil magnates, you name it. Fortune. They said their name followed by a woman's name. Not the women they married. Not a woman I'd ever heard of. You'll see in a minute.

"Appetizers have finished. Each woman has hidden a gold ring. The game concludes when an entrée is prepared and served and the ring is found," The Primus says. God I wish I was allowed to tell you his name, it's gonna blow your—anyway.

The butler lays a sword on the table. A real, god-damned ancient... I mean not like a big broad—just like a little curved—an Egyptian dagger thing. I'm standing on one side of the table, Colton's on the other. Ursula to my left. Amalie to my right. The big Samoans are holding them with a short leash. All of this in an eyeblink, mind you, I see their stomachs, bare skin, I see the veins in their necks, smell the sweat, and I just get it. Dinner. It's my job to serve.

So I go to grab the sword, and Colton realizes it too, but I'm faster. All he can do is watch. I swing for the fences, just *hi-yah!* right into Amalie's midsection. Cut it wide open in one—like a piñata! But instead of a bunch of little spic kids running around grabbing candy, it's just me and Colton watching Amalie *literally* spill her guts onto the table. And the Samoans help. White glove service. They're just delicately guiding her large intestine out onto the blank pizza pie, piling it like spaghetti, and it's just—you can see what she ate *moving* in there, right? Even after the puking! Still so much food left. Pulsing and squeezing, and they just keep feeding organs out. Liver, kidney, spleen, stomach and this is a *mess* I tell you.

"The ring is presented!" the Tertius shouts. "Claim your prize."

And the ring—they said she hid one, remember? Way down in her intestine, I see this hard little outline, kind of round on one side, flat on the top. She swallowed it this little film canister thing, see? The ring has the seal of—well, you see it here on my finger. I can't tell when Amalie died. Maybe it was fast. Probably. I mean, her head was rolling back and forth, mouth open, eyes like glass. You get disemboweled, you can't really scream. It was like bad opera. Embarrassing. That was the—I can't describe it. I saw her soul leave, and whatever was left was staring at me, and all I thought—and I said this out loud—was, *I deserve this.*

"Will you serve?" the Primus asked.

I took the sword and cut a piece of pizza. I don't know when they led Colton out of the room, but it's just me at the table with Ursula, chewing this other woman's guts. Ursula had to eat too. They all ate. All of the jury, the Triumvirate, they all came down and took a bite, like this is the best buffet they've ever—And they're all applauding us, and Ursula's crying like Miss Fucking America, covered in blood, and shit, and filth, and she takes my hand, and I'm—I mean normally I'd tell them to take this bitch out and give her a bath, but this was a *moment*, you understand?

I took her hand, and I looked her in the eye, and I kissed her. And I swear if the challenge would have gone further, I would have sat her bare ass in that pile of guts on that pizza and fucked her, right there, that's how happy I was. Because I understood everything.

But it didn't come to that. I don't want you to think I actually— Anyway. That was my dinner that night. That was my entrée into fortune. *The Festa dei Burattinai.* These days, they make fun of me in the press for eating bland food. Steak and ketchup. Simple things. They have people working at restaurants. They test you. They slip in little pieces of things sometimes. And if you're eating fancy food, you might miss it. I want the flavor to stand out. The sacred organs. Liver. Kidney. Hearts. Guts. It reminds me who I am and what I'm capable of. The flavor of life.

You have to meet the right people. And you have to eat a little shit. I told you it takes guts. Didn't say whose. Your job, your only job tonight, is to come back here with my daughter on your arm. Full, and happy, and content. Fortune favors the bold.

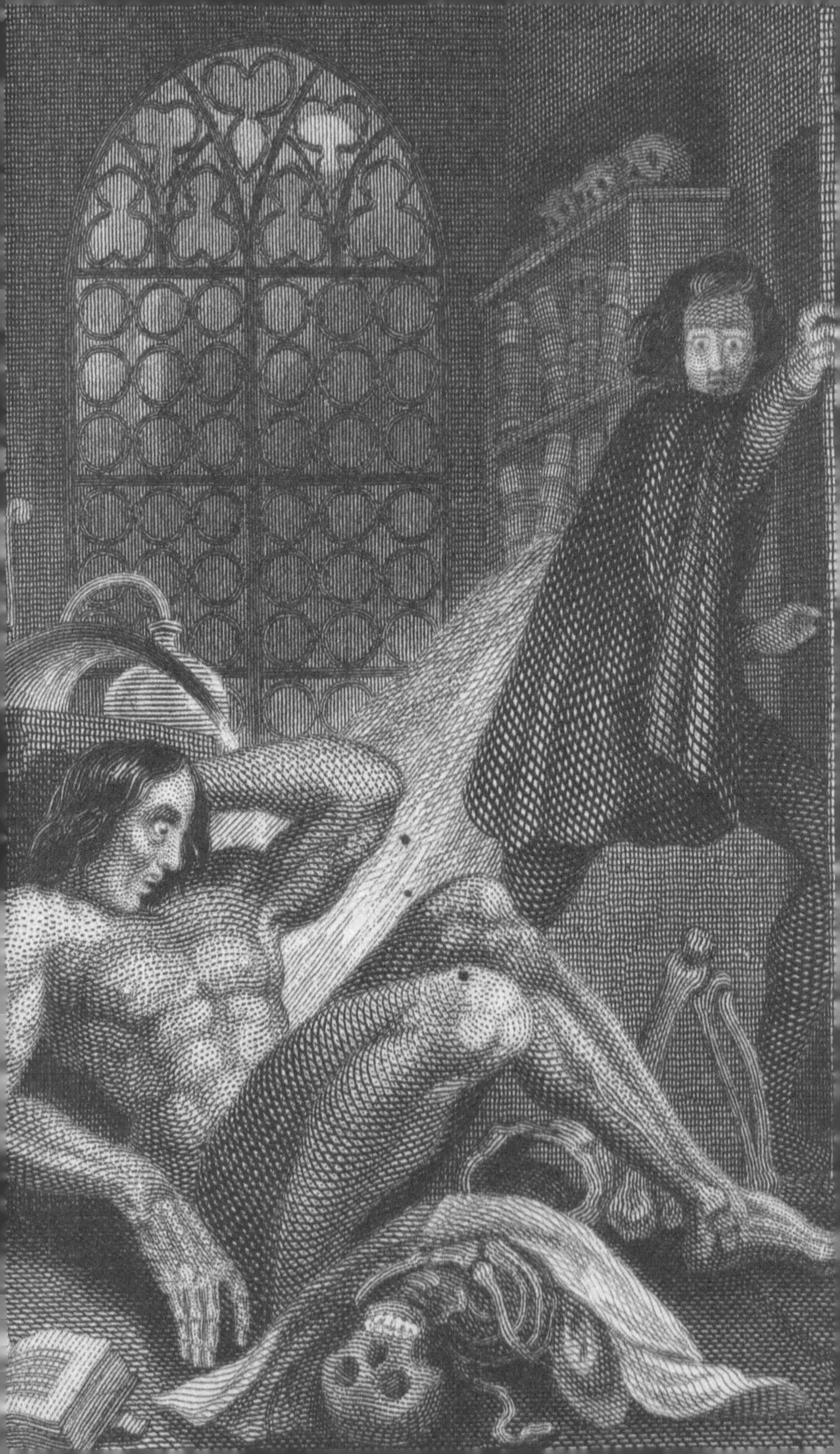

𝕭loodsuckers

(three monologues)

FRANK

We were on top of the world, and now you only come when one of us dies. So the Rag-Man went off and drank himself to death. I don't blame him, you know? All the stuff they made based on us, and what did we get? Not a damn thing. The Coogan rule, sure, that's for kids. But people like us? Especially in those bad years when the hippies took over. They cut us off so fast. No more productions. Said they're out of money, we're not playing so well in the Midwest. And we're not going to get dime one in royalties. Kubrick wanted a shot at my story, but have you seen his stuff? I don't want people thinking Frankenstein was some kind of freak. But even that might have been better than what I got. That's the first lesson Hollywood taught me kids! Don't whore out your life story for the promise of a future and a ten-dollar scotch at a fancy restaurant.

They didn't even get it right. Not one detail. Look at me. Do I have bolts coming out of my neck? Is my head square? No! Well, not so much. My story is gender identity. Those villagers with flames and pitchforks? Does Hollywood even get metaphor?

I wanted Vivien Leigh to play me. If not her, Marlene Dietrich. And who do they get? Boris Fucking Karloff. They tell me, hey it's all right, he's great, he's a master of disguise…blah, blah, blah. Just sign here, sign your life, your pain, your torment away right here on the X, and we'll make something that people can eat popcorn to. And they call *me* the monster.

Did you ever hear my original pitch? I'm born, right? Stitched into a shape that society finds acceptable, but what they can't see is how I feel inside. The first shocking moment, that jolt of electricity? That was supposed to represent me realizing that I was something more. Right? On the table, it's just grunts and groans, whatever I think the good doctor wants to hear. Then the big shock hits, and there was supposed to be this scene, right? Me breaking my shackles, and you'd see me feeling my own body, realizing, glorying in what I was, all of my skins, all of my parts, all of my being.

Then: tragedy! The Doctor calls me a monster! Am I a monster? I run! I hide! I try to make friends. That's the part with the little girl. And in my version, she accepts me, and then her parents find us being friends, and they throw me in the water. Right? Because they want to protect her from what I am. Then, the angry mob, *that was society*, closing in, frightening me, telling me: conform, conform, conform. Act three was me fleeing for my life, trying to hide, tearing myself apart, piece by piece. Literally! Just... do they not want me to have eleven fingers? Fine, I'll tear one off? Do they perceive me as a man? How much of a man? I'll tear off a breast, maybe two, maybe all of them!

I keep trying and changing, changing and trying, and somewhere in there, the girl comes back, that little innocent angel, and asks me why I'm hurting myself? Why am I throwing out what makes me *me*? She finds a mirror, and tells me to see myself, really see myself, all of those pieces stitched together. Then, I understand I am *me*, just me, whole and happy. Some of the yokels would accept it, but others would try to burn me down, so I had to keep running, right? But now, I know where I'm going and who I want to be.

Then, y'know, I had ideas for sequels, like *Lone Wolf and Cub-*style, where I wander the lands with the little girl and we solve crimes and stuff. But that was putting the cart before the horse.

But it had everything! Tension: How can a multi-gendered, multi-species being integrate into "normal" society? Drama: The racial tension in my body! There was a dream sequence where my African kidneys led a revolt against my oppressive white lower intestine. And then some ripped-from-the-headlines stuff, because they like that: Which restroom do I go to? Boys? Girls? Of the four penises on my body, only one is human. And ladies, don't get me started about what my ears are made of. You want to talk about cramps once a month?

You have no idea.

I kid. But the heart of it - how do I identify? How do you? I'm stolen. I'm used parts. But part of me isn't, right? Something in me is more than all the other parts. I don't know... I just don't know if my heart lived in someone who identified as man or woman. I don't know which part of me used to be gay or straight or trans or ace or... it wasn't about that. What people see when they see me? This? All this? But not what's in here, in my heart, and it is *my* heart. I have come to understand that I am the sum of my parts, the good, the bad, the pain, the pleasure, all of it.

I did some test readings of my version, and it pissed the audience off. I think they were afraid. Well, I *know* they were afraid. That's the gateway to ignorance, right? I was everything they didn't want to deal with. I am women, I am gay, I am straight, there's part of a horse and I won't tell you where, I'm made of men, made of pigs...Same thing right? Am I right? Is this thing on? Where was I, some of me was a religious zealot, I am ethnic minorities, persecutors and oppressors, persecuted and oppressed: they're all me, all represented right here. I'm America and that's why they can't stand the sight of me.

You think anybody was ready for that back in the thirties? The whole thing caved in. I was literally a hundred years ahead of my time. They let their trained script chimpanzees get a hold of it and all of a sudden it boils down to two things:

Monster kills people.

Fire bad.

Fire bad.

But the Rag-Man, Rolf, Drac, all of them... they accepted me, no questions asked. Raggy didn't deserve to go out that way.

But you never come knocking on our doors until one of us dies. That's Hollywood, right?

ROLF

So they came up to me yesterday, and they tell me the Mummy died. And I said, "Joan Rivers is dead?"

No? Nothing?

Well, that joke used to kill before she *actually* died. I don't even know who to substitute now. Is Abe Vigoda still alive? Was he ever?

Anyway.

Seriously though, Raggy, that's what we used to call him, really knew how to make an exit. He always told us he wanted to be the brightest star. He must have been awfully bright running down Melrose in flames at four in the morning. Crazy kid…

I don't let it get me down. The other guys love it when shit like this happens. Like a bunch of washed up child actors, they use these tragedies to try to snag a book deal, or maybe get that one last made for TV movie. Not me. I always told 'em when we'd get together and they'd start complaining, I'd say "You know what's wrong with this group? Too many victims, and not enough *victims.*" You know what I mean? We're *supposed* to be the scary killers! We're supposed to scare the holy shit out of John Q. Public.

When our act started going downhill, you know, just before the breakup, Frank kept doing all of these political bits about gender and praxis. What the fuck is praxis? I'll tell you! Fucking *death* onstage. We lost more casino gigs because Frank "found" himself. Themselves. I mean, I get it now. I'm sensitive to all of that stuff. Live and let live and whatever, right? We all… I admit, I was probably the last to come around to Frank being Frank, but after all the shit we went through in this town? Knowing how they stayed true to themself? Nothing but respect.

Anyway, Frank always had these pamphlets, these stupid fucking things to hand out trying to raise awareness about our "plight". Like we all had a unified cause. You know how I used to raise awareness? Full moon comes, I go tear some throats out, leave some bodies piled in the streets, *that's* awareness. That's a statement. But then everyone's too chicken shit to have me as a spokesman. Even the NRA said no. Said I'm too extremist. Fuck 'em. I got acquitted of all of those so-called crimes. "Not Guilty by reason of Feral Bestial Nature." Who needs endorsement deals? I got every disaffected youth in the country clamoring to buy my T-shirts, the poetry I used to write after a full moon, paintings of my victims…

I don't kill anymore of course. I did my time. Not going back. No. Besides, all of the smog in LA, I haven't been able to catch a good full moon in decades. I still go out to the country every once in a while for a cattle mutilation or two. Vegas is just for when the party animal comes out! Then I'm eating something else all night, right? Am I right? *You* know.

No? Nothing, huh…

The Fang Gang. Those were the days. I was the leader. I was like Frankie. *Frankie*-Frankie, not our Frank. And Drac was our Dean-o. And our Frank was like, I dunno, Sammy and Liza mashed up. Frank's beautiful, you know? And Raggy. Imhotep. Our Johnny… or is it Joey… you know the one whose name nobody remembers? Frankie, Dean, Sammy, and that other guy Joey. That was just like us. Rolf, Drac, Frank, and Imhotep. The Rat Pack had Vegas and we had Hollywood.

Am I sad he's gone? Yeah.

He owed me fifty bucks!

No? Tough crowd.

I'm still gonna use that one in my show this weekend. I'm playing the MGM Grand. I've got the nickel slot room booked from Friday Night to Sunday. Yeah, I got the bug to start singing again. There's this great big finish with a simulated full moon, I do a transformation, "slay" a couple of the leggy showgirls…it's something. Balding werewolf conquers Vegas! There's your headline.

Survival of the fittest.

That's showbiz, baby.

DRACULA

Bela Lugosi ruined my life. Absolutely threw it down the shitter. Oh man, don't get me started. You know how hard it is to convince people who you are when they've got that image in their mind? "Where's your cape? Where's your coffin?" *Fuck you*, that's where my cape is, right off the coast of *Bite-My-Ass*, which is where my coffin is housed. These people.

You know who had his shit together? F.W. Murnau. Filmed the classic *Nosferatu*. Talk about dead-on. I consulted Murnau through the whole film. And it was art! But newfound fame made my life a little hard in Europe, so I decided to relocate here, and *voila*! I discover that America makes movies too. I'm expecting big things, but nobody wants to talk to me. Yeah, I was living a little differently back then. Didn't have a house, had a couple of…cosmetic issues happening.

I wanted a way to be seen but nobody wanted to look at me. I meet Frank, and Frank tells me about reconstructive surgery. Trimmed my nails, put some bronzer on, new hair, new eyes, new nose…reborn upon arrival. But there was something stuck in me. Surgery helped me look like everyone else, but inside, I knew I needed to find my people. I also knew that I had to keep my habit going. And what better way to do that than a nightclub? So I use my connections to start something. Don't let Rolf fool you with his stories. I know who ran the Fang Gang. Rolf tries to come off like he was Frankie? I was Frankie. I was *so* Frankie. I alays said it should be called Drac's Pack. I had fangs, and Rolf, sure, but Frank? Raggy? makes no sense. Name it after the leader. Me. We were like the Jackson Five. I was Michael, carrying two Titos and a Jermaine. That math adds up if you count all of Frank.

We'd bring in an audience, get onstage, knock 'em dead and then…really knock 'em dead! I would finish the night by taking the youngest, freshest girls from the audience, serenade 'em, and then take 'em backstage, where they could repay me properly for my performance. I used to do this number…

My heart is my song, and it bleeds for you. Now bleed for me…

That lasted clear through the sixties, where we'd set up these love-ins, and the hippies would come and give themselves to us for… higher consciousness or some shit. Then came the seventies, and the lawsuits, you know the rest. But while it was working…it was magic.

It was rough sometimes, working with all of those personalities. You ever try working with a Mummy onstage? Can't dance worth a damn. Always sliding around, unraveling. And they're really small, I don't care what the movies show you. You try singing a number from Guys and Dolls with a dusty little bandaged horse jockey next to you, see how long your career lasts. Yeah. Imhotep. Raggy. He would always stay in it until the end though. Never gave up, never broke character. Took a lot of crap, but we wouldn't have been the same without him.

He got tied up for a while with Barry. You know, the Invisible Guy? Now there was a lucky guy. Barry actually got to play himself in a couple of scenes in his movie. You know the ones where you don't see the fishing line holding shit up? That got him commercial work, all sorts of TV stuff. You remember the Oscar Meyer campaign with the floating hot dogs? All Barry. Where did that get him? He couldn't handle his money or his blow. Ended up working kids' parties at the end for ten bucks an hour just to support his habit. And he'd show up for these birthdays with a stuffed animal strapped to his crotch, and the kids would go nuts. *"Ooh! Look at the floating monkey! Dance for us, floating monkey!"* Barry, that pervert, would put on a little ventriloquist show. That was some messed up shit. Pretty good show, though. But of course, the kids would pet the puppets, and then with the lawsuits, and a few weeks later he went on the mother of all benders. All they found was a hash pipe, a puddle of blood on a sofa, and a bullet floating in midair, right where his head would be.

Raggy was never one to be outdone. Turned himself into a friggin' Molotov cocktail. I kind of like that. See, you get famous, and then people forget you, and it's just like becoming invisible. Raggy asked me one night how he could make a comeback. I told him, light a fire, make them see you. But Raggy never understood metaphor. Sparklers would have worked, but oh no, nothing small for Raggy. He buys some kind of Chinese New Year Extravaganza, and the sparks hit his arms, and all of the booze had soaked through, and he becomes a giant wick. Running down the middle of Melrose for the Paramount gates, flames around him four feet high, screaming *"Do you see me now?"* Never broke character. Never gave up.

Now he's a legend, right? Now he's famous. Not when he was working. That was a waste of time. Singing songs, putting on faces for people. When he was giving his soul out, nobody cared. You couldn't pay people to watch.

What will people remember most about him?

The same thing they remember about every legend in Hollywood. The one thing Marilyn, James Dean, Dietrich, River

Phoenix, and yes, even Barry, all have in common.

They're dead.

Leave it at that.

His corpse has bled enough, and you're not sucking any more blood out of me. I enjoy my invisibility. I get up every morning and I look at that Hollywood sign and it makes me feel a little better.

I see it and I know. I ain't the vampire.

I ain't the vampire.

THE IRON BULLDOGGE

Rook was digging into the worst apple pie he'd ever encountered when the kid sidled up to his table. He'd seen the type before, hitchhikers, college dropouts starting a misguided romantic journey across the states. This skinny kid couldn't have been more than a week into his trip. Clean blonde hair, light stubble, didn't stink and his cheeks weren't sucked in yet. Rook always wanted to tell them what life on the road was really like. When it's in your bones and in your blood. When you're on the road, you can't wait to get home. You get home for a few days and then you're burning to get back on the road. Instead, he just cut to the chase.

"Where ya headed?"

The kid shuffled his feet, surprised that he didn't need to go into a sales pitch. "West?"

"You don't have to be so specific," Rook kicked out the chair on the other side of the table. "Siddown and let me finish this slop, then we'll get going. What's your name?"

"Oh, you can call me--"

"Not what I can *call* you. Shit, you hippies with your damn names. Not moonbeam, or supertramp, what's it say on your birth certificate?"

The kid looked down at the plate of pie. "Didn't think it was that big of a deal."

"It's probably not. I'm eighteen hours into a run that was supposed to wrap up hours ago, so forgive my *brusqueness*." Rook loved throwing five dollar words at the hippies. "How far west are you going?"

"Gotta get to the ocean. I've never seen the Pacific."

"You ever see the Atlantic?"

"Yeah, that's where I start--"

"Looks the same, just reversed."

"Look, if you don't want to give me a ride, I get it. I can ask around."

"Nah," Rook laughed. "Nah, I'm just giving you a hard time. Wanted to see if you had a sense of humor. Guess we'll keep things quiet. I can get you as far as Salt Lake City, then you're on your own. Word of advice? When we get there, buy a thicker jacket. You're gonna freeze."

"I'll get by. You mind if I grab a quick bite before we head out?"

Rook shrugged. "Don't try the pie."

"You can call me Sticks."

"Nope, see, what did I just say?" Rook shook his head. "Your mama call you Sticks? Then I ain't gonna either."

A waitress arrived in a cloud of scent that was somewhere between knockoff perfume and nicotine addiction. "What'll it be, hon?"

"The steak special."

"Outta steak."

"Ribs with no sauce?"

"We make 'em how they ship 'em. You want ribs, you get sauce."

Sticks sighed. "Just a hamburger patty."

The waitress raised an eyebrow. "Gotta charge you the same either way. You're getting the blue plate special, do whatever you want with the stuff you don't eat." She pivoted and hustled away to the kitchen.

"Come for the atmosphere, stay for the service," Rook muttered. "You got a gluten allergy or something?"

The kid smiled. "Nah, it's just… I'm a meat-eater, you know? It's all I can eat. Don't like it when it has the tinge of other stuff on it."

"Interesting," Rook said.

"It's a long story. It's part of the journey. I'm on a dare of sorts, I guess. Took a job delivering something cross-country. Big payoff. Lotta rules."

"Well, if it's drugs or contraband, you're gonna have to find another ride."

"No, it's nothing like that." Sticks checked over his shoulders and leaned in with the shiniest *trust-me* grin that Rook had seen this side of a used car dealership. "You ever hear of fringe archaeology?"

Rook struggled not to roll his eyes. One of *those* guys. "The study of imaginary bullshit totems and trinkets?"

"You've heard of it then? I know it's easy to scoff, but I believe, man. The world is full of objects that want to remain undiscovered. Things that people want to keep hidden by any means necessary. It's cool shit, man!"

Rook exhaled a fine spray of pie crumbs and laughter.

Sticks leaned back. "Most people feel like you, but I could show you something that would change your mind."

"You know, usually people wait until we're actually rolling down the road to start talking about looney bullshit, but I gotta say, thanks for saving me some time." Rook started to slide out of his seat, but Sticks laid a hand on the table.

"You a vet?" Sticks asked. When Rook glanced over at him, Sticks jutted his chin at the tattoo wrapping around Rook's forearm. It was his namesake, a crow wreathed in black flame, rising from his wrist and up his forearm. Floating just above the beak was a simple black chess piece, the rook, eternally just out of reach.

"Yeah, I guess you could say that. I've seen action in a lot of places. Not exactly *on the books*, if you catch my drift."

"What's it mean?"

"Guess you didn't catch my drift. Let's just say delivering freedom isn't about hopes and dreams and flowery shit. It's a dirty business." Rook scratched at the dark stubble on his chin.

"You're a soldier though. I can show you something that'll blow your mind." Sticks rummaged through his backpack. "Anyone ever tell you that you kinda look like a younger version of Lemmy from Motorhead?"

"Nobody that wanted to keep their teeth." Rook fixed a steely glare on him.

"It was supposed to be a compliment. Rugged badass. You know? Anyway, soldier boy, this is going to slay you. Check it out." Sticks pulled a long, thin black box from his backpack and set it on the table, sliding it toward Rook.

Rook stared at the box. It was smooth and featureless, just a small seam that ran around the top edge. It had the dull sheen of fresh asphalt, and even though it looked like cardboard, Rook knew that it would be cold to the touch.

"Open it!" Sticks laughed. "It ain't gonna bite ya, don't worry."

Rook folded his arms and stared at Sticks. The young man broke, laughing and sliding the box back toward himself. "Fine. Big tough soldier guy scared of a little box." Sticks pushed a dirty thumbnail into the seam and pried the lid from the box.

A small whisper escaped, probably just cardboard scraping cardboard, but Rook swore it sounded like the thing hissed his birth name. Inside the box, laying in neatly piled hay, was a metal blade, about eight inches long. It was chipped and dull. Covered in rust, except for the tip which was bright polished silver. It looked like someone was trying to restore the thing and just gave up about two inches into the job.

"And?" Rook asked.

"Guess what it is," Sticks smiled.

"You have any idea how many miles I have left to go tonight?" Rook asked.

"All right, all right," Sticks leaned in closer, checking over his shoulders again to make sure there were no snooping ears. "The legend is, this is the tip of a spear."

"Certainly shaped that way," Rook rolled his eyes. "You gonna tell me it's magical?"

Sticks danced his fingers along the edge of the box, looking at the spear, then back at Rook. "A Roman spear. Probably the most famous spear in history. That shiny part, that was used to hold a sponge once. And also used to deliver the final insulting wound to--"

"Jesus Christ," Rook muttered, sliding out of the booth and standing up. "Word of advice, kid. You want a ride cross-country, save your batshit crazy talk for whoever's waiting for you at the end of the line. Tell the next guy you see that you're taking a break from college to find yourself. Try to--"

Rook swallowed his next thought as Sticks picked up the spear tip and jammed it through his forearm. He held his arm high, the blade jutting out at an odd angle, the flesh around it puckering.

"No blood," Sticks said. "By his wounds," and he drew the blade out of his arm, "we are healed."

Rook turned on his heel and hustled out to the parking lot, yanking on his battered leather jacket. He heard a chair slide out behind him, Sticks's heavy steps following. Besides one disinterested waitress and two fat guys sleeping in separate booths, the truck stop was all but abandoned this evening.

Outside, the air was congealing into a cold, wet fog that had no business on a Wyoming highway. Rook jogged out to the far end of the lot where his truck, *The Iron Bulldogge* lurked in the shadows.

"Hey!" Sticks's voice called through the fog. "Why are you running?! Come on, man, it's all just shades and shadows. Illusion! Scaredy-cat!"

Rook fumbled in his pocket for his keys. His fingers wrapped around them just as Sticks's cold hand wrapped around his bicep, spinning him around. His fingers were cold, even through Rook's jacket. The target in Rook's pocket had shifted from keys to folding knife. If he couldn't get that one out, he had a few others concealed on standby.

"You know what I am. You've known since I sat down," Sticks said.

"Who sent you?" Rook asked.

"A mutual friend. We know what you're carrying in there," Sticks tipped his chin at the truck, letting out a low whistle. "What has this thing been through, man? Where'd you drive, Hell and back?" he laughed.

Rook remained silent.

The Iron Bulldogge had definitely seen better days, and was usually scary enough on the outside to keep people from asking for a lift. The cab was scorched and burned, pocked with holes and slashes in the doors and fenders. The trailer was a short twenty-footer that looked like it had just been dredged from a swamp.

"What's your real name?" Rook asked.

Sticks stared at Rook, a brief glimmer of red flashing through his eye. "If you want to have a chance of rolling out of this parking lot, I just need to have a look inside your trailer."

"Not happening."

"You picked up a package in Shreveport, right? Last week. Little box, about a foot square. About big enough to hold a human head. Sound familiar?"

Rook shrugged.

Sticks flicked the spear tip out, holding it low and ready. "This is the key. You have the lock on the truck. We want it back. It wasn't yours to take."

"Never said it was mine. I'm just the delivery guy."

"Open the trailer."

"Whatever you say. Put your little shiv away before you bring the wrong kind of attention on us."

Rook slowly pulled his keys from his pocket. He lifted the lock on the latch of the trailer, tapping it precisely four times against the door. He slid the flat of his palm up the metal and rubbed a dusty circle on the truck before slapping the center.

"Gotta clear the hex first," he said, sliding the key into the lock and unlatching the door. "Might want to stand back."

The doors slowly creaked open, a dull purple glow emanating

from inside the trailer. It was impossibly large, a museum on wheels, cavernous. The walls extended back into the darkness, the ceiling was nowhere in sight. The floor was decorated in elaborate marble tile.

"How far does it go?" Sticks asked.

"How far can you walk?" Rook asked.

Sticks shook his head. "Just give me the box."

"Go get it," Rook said. "Just tap the edge of the trailer four times--" and Rook slapped the floor hard four times, "—and hop in. Just…four…times…" Rook slapped the floor hard and kicked at the dirt, muttering "Dammit, Coogles…"

"There's no hex, is there?" Sticks said. "You're trying to trick me."

"No hex. Just a good for nothing lazy-ass Nightshade named Coogles who seems to have forgotten our secret distress call. Fiercest guardian you'll ever know, they told me. More like a flying puppy that eats everything in sight."

"Enough chit-chat. Give me the box. And no tricks."

"Tricks? Nah, I don't do tricks. Just get by on my charm and grace."

Rook hopped up into the trailer. It was no use fighting. Wouldn't be the first delivery he failed to make, probably not the last either. This one would've paid pretty damn good though. And he'd have a lot of explaining to do to the witch's sister in Portland who was expecting this package.

The box wasn't too far back. It was sitting on a low shelf near the collection of shrunken heads and Atlantean statues in the antechamber near the door. Rook tucked it under his arm and headed back to the door. He hopped down to the ground, squinting to see Sticks through the gathering gloom. The fog was thick now, tendrils of orange and blue witchfire dancing in the air around them.

"Dusted it off for you and everything." Rook started to thrust the box into Sticks' chest, then drew it back. "Who are you working for?"

"Doesn't matter."

"Matters to me. I let you have this, you do whatever you want with it, but someone's paying me for my time, trouble, and gas."

"You don't want to go down that road."

"Mister, you don't want to know about the roads I've been down. Gimme a name."

"Or you'll do what, exactly?" Sticks reached a palm out for the box. "Give me the box before I surgically remove your charm and grace."

"I'll follow you until I figure it out."

"Horrible plan."

"I've had worse ideas," Rook scowled. He realized that he wasn't going to stare his way out of the situation and decided to hand the box over while he thought of Plan B.

No! No! A sharp voice barked from inside the trailer. *No give to bad thing! Bad, bad thing!*

A clumsy fluttering grew louder inside the trailer, a noise like a fuzzy sack of potatoes being thrown down a long hallway. A giant blur of white rocketed from inside the trailer, slamming into Sticks and knocking him back. It settled on the ground, a stout creature that was somewhere between a bat and a medium-sized dog.

"Is this your Nightshade?" Sticks groaned from the ground, pulling himself up.

"Yeah, this is him. It's all right, Coogles. We're letting this one go."

No! Bad thing! Not box! Box is bad! Thing is bad! No box!

"He talks?" Sticks said.

"Something like that," Rook laid a hand on Coogles' head.

I love you! Coogles barked, licking Rook's hand. *Not you bad thing! Bad! Go!*

Sticks scrambled to his feet, brandishing the spear tip again. "Well, let's have the box now or I'm going to put this bad thing through his head."

"Was it Azazel? He put you up to this?"

Sticks swiped the spear at Coogles, who skittered backwards and hid behind Rook's legs, clutching at his pantleg with long fingers.

Bad!

Rook dropped the box on the ground and stepped back.

Sticks crawled forward, kneeling and slicing at the lid. "The blade is the key, the head is the lock. The secrets inside unleash the end. You had no idea what you were carrying back here…"

"I never look inside of customer's packages. Union rules."

Sticks reached a hand into the box and lifted his prize out. A desiccated human head, the lower jaw dangling slack, the skin loose and yellow. "The traitor. The interrupter. Judas the liar."

The head spun freely by the lock of hair clutched in Sticks' hand, the dull eyes looking through him.

"Inside," Rook whispered to Coogles. The Nightshade needed no further coaxing, flapping up into the truck.

"Do you know this man?" Sticks asked Rook.

"Well, you just told me his name was--"

"Do you know him?"

"Doesn't everyone?" Rook asked.

"Cursed to roam the earth forever. He tried so many times to end it. Hung himself the day that he killed the prophet, woke up the next morning and went on his way. Same thing happened to Cain. Can you imagine the eternal torment? Living forever?"

"I have a good imagination. So… you know, I never really ask people what they're doing with the stuff they give me. Point A to point B, that's good enough for me. But since this has turned into armed theft, I feel like I oughtta know what the big deal is with a dried-up skull."

"He has work to do. Many people to see, many tales to tell. So much knowledge locked in that brain. So many secrets, so much power. He's been known by so many names through history. The Great Khan. The Impaler. Rasputin. He couldn't bring death to himself so he walked through history and brought it to others. It's why they eventually cut his head off."

"And what's your job? You gonna carry a dried up head across the country and beat people to death with it?"

"My job is almost done. His is just about to begin again. By his wounds--" and Sticks raised the spear, driving it into the side of his own neck, "--we are healed…"

He rested the rotten skull on his shoulder as he proceeded to saw his own head off with the spear. There was no blood. No gore. Just a clean, wet slicing, like watermelon on a hot summer day. Sticks slid the head of Judas the betrayer on top of his neck just as his own head fell to the ground. He dropped the spear and stared at Rook with lifeless eyes, the color slowly returning to ancient cheeks as the wound on his neck knitted itself closed.

Judas shuffled forward and coughed twice, then drew in a sharp breath. He glanced around, taking in the thick fog that was slowly dissipating.

"*I gcás ina? где я?* Where?"

"America," Rook said seizing on the first English word, quickly swinging one door to his trailer closed.

"America. Long time," Judas growled. His face had grown whole, his features unassuming. He had thick dark hair and round cheeks, a chin that would be better hidden by a beard, and solid black eyes. The faint pink scar on Sticks's neck was a line of demarcation between a road tan and pale skin that hadn't seen the sun for generations. "What in carriage?"

"Don't worry about it. Food in there," Rook pointed to the truck stop, "Warmth too. Me, I have to be moving on."

"You will give me your carriage."

"There's plenty to choose from over there. Besides, you wouldn't know how to drive--"

"You have things I need. In there. Then you will take me. To Ocean." Judas pointed a finger toward the trailer.

"Not going that far," Rook said, slowly walking backward toward the cab of his truck.

Judas slowly crouched down and picked up the spear. He raised it above his head and spoke three syllables, an ancient language that this continent hadn't heard since its founding. The fog in the air grew thick again, coalescing around the spear tip.

"I'm afraid I must insist. Years ago, I lost something in a river in Russia. A strange object, you'd call it. I need to destroy it. I am not strong enough to do it. Two things I need. You have them," Judas gestured toward the trailer again. "You will give them to me and deliver me to the ocean, or I will remove your head and take what I need, and leave your body here as food for the beasts."

"Museum's closed," Rook muttered. He slapped the side of the trailer twice and grabbed a strap hanging on the inside wall. "Gun it, Coogles!"

The Iron Bulldogge roared to life, rolling forward. Rook scrambled inside the trailer and rose to his feet, anxious to see Judas recede from his sight. Instead, the man walked behind the truck, keeping pace, arms outstretched as if to ask *really*?

Rook scratched behind his ear. "Coogles can drive, but sometimes he forgets what this ol' bucket can do."

Drive drive drive! Came a faint bark from the cab.

"Flip the red lever, furbag!" Rook yelled, bracing himself.

Judas took two jogging steps and leapt inside, striking hard with his palm against Rook's chest, sending him skidding further backwards into the truck.

Red lever! Red Red Red! Coogles barked.

"No no no no wait! He's inside the--" Rook shouted, but it was no use. Gears ground together and an explosive rumble bucked through the trailer. The truck accelerated from a slow walk to an all-out sprint, sending Rook sliding across the floor toward the open trailer door. As his feet flew out into the cold night air, he managed to hook a hand around Judas's ankle. The temporary brake allowed him to brace his other hand around the closed door. Pulling himself in wasn't an option because of the acceleration.

Judas regained his balance enough to throw a kick. Rook rolled sideways, taking the impact on his shoulder but managing to stay in place. "Brakes! Brakes, Coogles!"

Race Race Race! Came the bark from the cabin.

"I really need a human sidekick," Rook grumbled. He inched

further into the truck and took another kick to the head from Judas. Ears ringing, Rook slid slowly backward, further into the darkness outside, the roar of the wind and engine deafening. The truck came to a curve in the road, shifting both men against the side and buffeting them back as the road straightened. They were on the interstate now.

Judas stood in front of a large rack of shelves. Rook knew that beyond that shelf, the magic that made the trailer into the cavernous space it was took hold, and the room had its own sense of gravity. Fortunately, Judas hadn't figured that out yet. The truck was holding a steady speed, too fast for Rook to overcome. His grip was fading and he couldn't feel his fingers from the cold. One finger slipped free from the door, then another. If there was a God who received their prayers as a litany of curses, Rook was their devoted supplicant. His hand slipped, and his body slid backward, a sickening feeling in his stomach. He closed his eyes and prepared for the pain.

The only pain he felt was in his wrist. He looked up to see Judas gripping him, pulling him back up into the truck. Judas shifted back and threw Rook into the trailer as if he was a spare pillow.

"Your companion is a horrible carriage driver," Judas grumbled. "I need a reliable driver. You may continue to live. You will take me to the things I need."

Rook coughed, slowly climbing to his feet. He risked a glance over his shoulder, watching the asphalt roar by beneath the truck.

"How did you come to own this magnificent machine carriage?" Judas asked.

"Years of hard work. Saved up my money. Union benefits. You know how it goes."

"Your cavalier attitude is wearing thin," Judas said.

"Charm and grace, like I said," Rook answered.

"Personality quirks only get you so far," Judas muttered.

Rook spun on his heel. "Quirks? Nah. Charm is a great thing." Rook pulled a necklace from behind his shirt, displaying a beaten coin encased in glass. "This one has traveled with me for longer than I care to remember. Hell, really longer than I could possibly remember. This charm was with me when Pompeii was on fire. I held it as I watched the Huns pass over the mountains and level everything in their path. I carried it at Gettysburg, had in my pocket in Dallas in '63, and it helped me crawl from the rubble in New York a few years ago. What I'm trying to say is this: if you're trying to scare me with a pig-sticker that's incapable of drawing blood, you're going to have to step up your game."

Rook stared at Judas, watching the glow in his eyes vibrate as his gaze darted from Rook's eyes to the charm, and back to the spear in his hands.

"I recognize the coin. You were there. You were there when I betrayed…" Judas's eyes welled with tears, then hardened. "You will give it to me. The spear may not draw blood, but it can remove your head from your filthy body."

Rook smiled and shook his head. He kicked at some imaginary dirt and turned slightly away from Judas. "You're not touching it. Drop the spear and get lost in the fog if you know what's good for you." Rook extended his arm, holding the coin in front of him like a ward to push Judas back. For a moment, it seemed to be working, as the demon inched closer to the opening in the truck. Rook rested his hand on the shelf near the door and raised an eyebrow.

"You expect me to retreat from a charm?" Judas growled.

"Nah," Rook shrugged. "Charm is the distraction. When the situation falls apart like this, I let Grace do the talking."

The interior of the trailer lit up with a blinding light as Rook emptied both barrels of his riot gun into Judas's head. Gore sprayed the walls as Judas frantically grabbed at the back of his skull, which was considerably more open than it had been a minute ago. Judas looked at Rook with his remaining eye, what was left of his jaw was struggling to make a sentence.

Rook seized the spear from Judas's floundering hand and swiped a clean slice across his neck, liberating the head from Stick's body. The skull clattered to the floor with a wet thud. Rook reared back and drove a hard kick into the sternum of Stick's dancing headless corpse, sending it out into the night.

"Shut it down, Coogles!" Rook shouted.

Down down down down! Came the barking reply, lost in the growl of downshifting.

Rook lifted up the skull. The eyes were lifeless again, the skin dry and desiccated. His cargo had a giant hole in it and considerable damage, but all things considered, a delivery was a delivery. The recipients could try to file an insurance claim. Most likely they'd try to take it out of his hide, but when those complaints came, Rook always handled them with Grace.

He wandered through the hallways of his trailer toward the front of the truck, pausing to hang Grace back in her wall holster beneath a fading tintype photo of a young woman with steel-grey eyes and a mouth set in a firm line. Rook kissed his fingers and touched them lightly to the photo.

"Thanks, Annie." He closed his eyes, letting his mind drift back to the day she gave him the gun as she lay dying, imploring him to abide by the creed inscribed in the handle: *Deal with people in love and kindness. Deal with all else in sacred silver and lead.*

He opened the door to the cab and slid into the driver's seat, accepting a few over-excited licks and nips from Coogles in the passenger seat.

Ready for break. Break break break.

"We can't get off the road yet, buddy. Long way to go and a lot of packages to drop."

Want break! Hunt and fly! Fly fly fly.

"You can take a flight when I stop to pick up more bullets, right? Maybe we'll stop at Chef Ray's. You can have a shrimp po' boy while he blesses my ammo, huh?"

Poboypoboy!

"That's the spirit," Rook sighed. "You think we'll ever get proper thanks for saving the world so many times?"

No! No no! I love you!

"Go to sleep, Coogles."

The furry white beast curled up in the passenger foot well and muttered *sleep-sleep.*

Rook started the truck up and turned on the lights, watching the remaining fog burn away into the night. He almost wished he could have kept Judas around. It would have been nice to talk to someone around his age.

"Fellas. That's the moon. The god-damned moon!"

"You keep saying that, Buzz."

"You're not impressed? You landed on a bigger moon you didn't tell me about, Neil?"

"When my wife bends over to fold the laundry," Armstrong retorted, bringing a nervous chuckle out of Collins.

"You're only saying that because she can't hear you right now," Aldrin giggled.

"You got that right."

"Just for that, I'm going first. We're all switching seats."

Collins spared a glance from his instrument panels out the side of the lunar orbiter.

"What do you think, Collins? You want to go down there, let me fly this thing around the moon instead?" After an uneasy silence, Aldrin asked. "What's gotten into you anyway? You've been pretty quiet."

"This is a special mission of national and international importance," Collins said, almost robotically.

"We know," Armstrong laughed. "Space rocks. Research. Good

of humanity. We're going down there to become god-damned legends."

"First men on the moon!" Aldrin shouted, slapping his thigh.

Collins let out a sigh. "No, it's…I'm supposed to wait until we're in lunar orbit to tell you this. There's no easy way to it, so I'll just say it. Aside from President Nixon and a handful of higher-ups in agencies that don't officially exist, you'll be the only ones with the knowledge I'm about to share. I'm supposed to swear you to secrecy, but I won't. Time's wasting and there's nobody in the world who will believe what I'm about to tell you." Collins locked in his trajectory and flipped down two switches, turning to face them. "Exploring the moon is not your primary objective. You're going down there to go hunting."

"Beg your pardon?" Armstrong said, sharing a glance with Aldrin.

"You won't be… you aren't the first men down there."

"Mike, come on…"

"Buzz, there are men down there. Sort of. Your job is to make sure you're the only men that come back. Gentlemen, your primary mission from this point forward is to locate and terminate three Soviet operatives. Cosmonauts." Collins paused and swallowed. "Werewolves."

Aldrin barked a short laugh, then choked it off, looking at Armstrong.

"You feeling okay, Mike?"

"We're on a controlled entry here, fellas. We have little time for explanation and no time for debate."

Collins reached under his seat and popped open a small panel, pulling out a metal box. "This mission was compartmentalized. Need-to-know. Until now, you didn't need to know. You each have one of these boxes under your seat. Pull it out."

Collins opened his box to reveal a large metal wrist brace. Mounted to one side was a long barrel with a large cartridge box behind it.

"What the hell is that supposed to be?" Aldrin asked.

"What's it look like to you?" Collins replied.

"It looks like that prototype bolt driver they had us working with in case anything broke while we were down there."

"The very same. And now it's driven by a big pressurized gas canister. Brace your feet. Wait for your target to charge you. Let 'er rip," Collins stared at the two other men. "It's a gun."

"You're serious about—now just what in the deep blue hell is--" Armstrong's brow creased, his eyes meeting Collins' in the eerie silence. He flicked on the radio.

"Houston, Eagle. How do you read now?"

"Roger. Five by, Neil."

"Houston, we might have a situation on the CSM here. Collins is saying--"

"Collins, you started early?"

"Roger that, Houston."

"This was supposed to wait until dark side, Collins, and--"

"Pardon my French, Houston, but this is a lot of shit to dump on a couple of guys before they go to walk on the god-damned moon, and I need to get it done so I can get busy helping them land on said god-damned moon, and if you have a problem with the way I'm running the mission at this point, feel free to fire me and send up a replacement."

A long silence, punctuated by the occasional click and ping of metal.

"Copy that. Aldrin. Armstrong. Collins has command. You don't have to like this situation. You don't have to believe a word of what he tells you. But you *will* do as he tells you. Copy?"

Armstrong and Aldrin looked at each other.

"Houston," Aldrin's voice cracked. "Houston—Jesus I hope this is off the national record -- Collins is claiming there are… werewolves on the moon. Can you confirm--"

"Collins is incorrect. There's no such thing as werewolves. These are Soviet agents."

Aldrin sighed and looked at Armstrong. Houston broke in again.

"More accurately, these are Soviet Lupine Lunar Mutations."

"Is it April first?" Armstrong muttered.

"Handy of them to wait until after we did the TV shot to drop this on us," Aldrin said.

Collins flipped a switch and killed the radio. He opened a small panel in the box on his lap, withdrawing two slim pamphlets.

"We've got about twenty minutes until you need to go strap in the lander. My recommendations are to take ten of those minutes to read through those pamphlets, take the next five minutes to familiarize yourself with the guns, and take the last five minutes to pray to whatever god you hold dear."

Armstrong unbuckled from his seat and drifted down toward the lunar lander module. Aldrin followed suit.

"You're staying up here to wait for us, right?" Armstrong asked.

"Of course."

"Why do you have a gun? You supposed to kill us if we say no?"

"If you don't come back, I don't come back," Collins said.

"You'd kill yourself if--"

"They'd change my course. I'd suffocate and die somewhere between here and Venus. I'd rather not have a slow death. I'd rather not hear the broadcasts they'd send up letting me know the ramifications of mission failure. I'd rather not hear my wife and your wife on the news crying over us. Neil," Collins said. "Get this done. Please."

Armstrong drifted down the hatch into the Eagle lander. Collins replaced the storage box below his seat and flicked on the internal comms.

"You copy this?"

"Yeah," Armstrong muttered.

"Fuck off, Mike," Aldrin said.

"Copy that," Collins said. "Everything you need to know is in that book, but I'll give you the nickel tour. If you have any questions, save them for the trip home. Now, just after WWII, Soviet commanders discovered a Nazi bunker buried in the ice in northern Russia. Nobody knows how long they'd been working there, but it was a full-on research facility. Captured Soviet soldiers were their lab rats. Typical Nazi shit, you know. Making men into supermen. They failed, obviously. Every man they tried it on died. But they made strides. There were corpses there. Huge muscles. Skeletal mutations. All of them dead. The Krauts left some promising notes. Jump ahead to 1957, when the Soviets placed a primate into successful earth orbit."

"Hold on. That never—we were the first to send--"

"What did I tell you about questions, Neil? They did it. Just take that as fact. They weren't testing the viability of launching a living thing into space, they were testing the formula they found in that Nazi base. Apparently the thing that hampered the serum's effectiveness on men was gravity. They shot that fuckin' monkey so full of Nazi dope that it would have killed him on Earth. In space… he grew. He turned into something. Something so strong and powerful that the capsule he was in couldn't contain him. He broke out, tore it open with his bare hands."

"And did he survive the fall?" Aldrin asked, rolling his eyes.

"We don't know," Collin said. "The safe bet says no. They estimate the vessel came down in the Pacific Northwest. There have been teams of US soldiers moving through the area to find evidence of its demise or terminate it on sight. No more questions. The Reds saw what they needed to see. Two years ago they started testing it on humans. Low-dose. Vladimir Mikhaylovich Komarov, that name ring a bell?"

"First man to die in a spaceflight. Killed on impact in a landing malfunction, right?

"Yes and no. He was the first to get a full dose of their treatment in space. First to become superhuman. They just needed to verify it worked. Then they rigged the craft to kill him on impact so they could examine his remains."

Collins pitched the craft, bringing the moon's eerie light into the cabin.

"And now, sixteen days ago, they landed a craft on the moon. Three cosmonauts, fully dosed. We have a rough idea of their LZ. We're coming in about a hundred yards away."

"You're telling me they've been up here for over two weeks with no food or water? Or air for that matter?" Armstrong asked.

"They had the benefit of not needing to land with a reusable craft. They have rations, and their metabolisms work a little differently now. They're alive, as far as we know, and probably hungry. Just waiting for a ride home. They've been pushing to get us up here to stop that. Intelligence suggests we have a ten hour headstart on them. They're on our tail and time is short. If they land, if they're able to recover those soldiers and get them back to earth... god help us all."

"And what are we supposed to--"

"Just read the book, Buzz. Strap into your chairs, get the hatch set. I wish this was under better circumstances. You wanted to go to the moon, you're going to the moon. My job is to drive the bus and make sure you have a ride waiting after you get done. Your job is to get down there, pick up some space rocks so we have something to show and tell, and kill some god-damned commie werewolves."

"Jesus H--" Armstrong muttered, sliding into position in the Lunar Lander Module.

"What if we miss?" Aldrin muttered.

"Don't miss," Collins yelled back at them. "This is for America and the world, fellas. The whole shebang. You're not allowed to fail. That's it."

Collins secured the hatch to the Lunar Landing Module and moved back to the pilot's seat. A small pendant of St. Christopher hovered next to his ear in zero-grav, spinning like a tossed coin, the patron saint of lost causes not knowing where to begin.

***

Aldrin and Armstrong sat in uneasy silence, staring out of the windows on the Lunar Landing Module, waiting. Aldrin's finger tapped a staccato rhythm on his thigh. He lifted the wrist gun to examine it more closely, set it down, then lifted it again. He opened the chamber and looked at the rounds in the magazine. Long like a rifle cartridge, but fat like a shotgun shell, each topped with a sharp, silver projectile.

Armstrong let out a long sigh. "Shit." He opened the pamphlet and scanned the information again. It was laid out simply as any good government dossier should be. Large text. Short sentences. Lots of diagrams. What he saw made no sense. Men, mutated, larger than life, coated in hair, their jaws distorted and misshapen, teeth jutting at odd angles. Heavy brows that hid their eyes, shoulders hunched so high their necks were no longer visible. The artist had helpfully drawn a large Soviet Flag behind the creature, as if this would spur some sort of patriotic sentiment to drive their mission forward. There were three names listed next to the drawing, presumably the three cosmonauts-turned-lab rats. The last names were spelled in heavy Cyrillic characters with an English translation to the right.

ВОЛКОВ: VOLKOV.

СОКОЛОВ: SOKOLOV.

ГОЛОВКИН: GOLOVKIN.

"What do we do here, Buzz? Volkov, Sokolov--"

"Blow their heads-off. Neil, I—We do our jobs. Look, I personally think everyone's gone off the reservation here. I expect there's some kind of stress-related… I don't know, Neil! I don't know. Maybe we walk out there and nothing happens. We get some dirt, we plant a flag, we go home. We don't have any options here. This thing is landing on the moon, we're inside of it, that's that. We have to kill a…"

Aldrin's face creased up, a tear streaked out of one eye. He let out a strange barking howl. It took Neil a moment to realize he was laughing. The ridiculousness of the situation smothered him like a wave.

"We're werewolf hunting," Neil said, laughing.

"The very notion is… is…"

"More ridiculous than a man on the moon?" Armstrong asked.

They laughed again, because what else could they do? What else but strap experimental weapons to their wrists and prepare to die for their country?

"Six shots apiece," Aldrin said, shaking his head.

"And three of *them*."

"You think these things work?"

"They're designed and manufactured by the US Government," Neil said, followed by an uncomfortable silence.

"You think these things work?" Aldrin asked again.

***

They spent the rest of the descent alternating between nervous laughter and unbearable quiet. Collins had assured them that Houston was going to broadcast pre-recorded audio from one of their many training sessions to make it all seem real for the TV audience as they guided the craft down. That would give the two of them more time to prep. It had been a relatively smooth flight down. The feeling of the landing impact thudded through them like a heavy bass drum. They sat in silence, staring out the windows.

"Neil?"

"Yes?"

"We're on the moon, Neil."

Armstrong paused, holding his hands in front of him. "Yeah. You hear anything out there?"

"We're not going to."

"You see anything?"

"Nope."

The intercom crackled. "Eagle Houston, do you copy?"

"Houston Eagle, we're… we're here. You rolling cameras for air on this?"

"Public cameras stay off until your first job's done."

"But you have a private feed? Gonna enjoy watching us get torn to shreds?" Aldrin asked.

"What are you seeing out there?" Houston continued.

"We hit the mark. What are we looking for?"

"The area of concern was marked on your maps. We expect contact either inside of the Little West Crater or over its far ridge. Last intelligence received from ------ that the Sov--------"

The comms went fuzzy. Armstrong looked at Aldrin. "Of course."

"All right. Quickest way to get this done is to get it done, right? You got that wrist rocket ready to go?"

"Yeah," Armstrong said. "You sure you don't wanna go first?"

"I'll be stuck behind the door until you get out of here. Soon as you clear, I'll follow you down. If the ground is solid I'll just drop in."

"Well. Since this isn't being recorded for posterity, I'd just like to say that it's an honor for America to be on the god-damned moon, and whoever thought of this mission without telling us can kiss my ass."

"They oughta put that on a plaque, Shakespeare."

"Let's go."

Armstrong felt the pop of the airlock door more than he heard it. As the hatch creaked open, brilliant white light flooded the cabin, reflected from the lunar surface.

"Wait until you see this, Buzz."

Armstrong leaned through the hatch cautiously, straining to check his peripheral vision through the bulky spacesuit. All was still and quiet. Now came the hard part. He turned his back on the moon and reached a leg out to the descent ladder.

"Still alive," Armstrong muttered.

"Copy that."

Armstrong descended one rung further. "Two rungs. Still alive."

"Copy that, Neil. Maybe reserve the comm batteries for important announcements."

"Me being alive is pretty fuckin' important Buzz. To me, anyway. Four steps to go. Still alive." Armstrong hustled down the remaining rungs and hovered above the final step. He turned as much as his suit would allow to survey the ground. Once he'd gotten the word he'd be going through the hatch first, he'd envisioned this moment, how to place the first footprint on the moon. And now, looking down, he saw the point was moot.

There were already footprints there. That word lingered in his brain. Footprint. Not boots. Large, five-toed mammalian markings that were somewhat human save for what looked like a large opposable toe. Spaced about five feet apart. Left, right, some of them with divots in the soil that Armstrong assumed to be a handprint.

"How's it looking, Neil?"

"Clear for now. Collins wasn't lying. We're not alone."

"Coming down, clear the way."

Armstrong held his breath and pushed lightly back from the ladder, drifting down to the lunar soil like a feather. The land beneath him felt like soft sand over stone. Fine and powdery. He laughed, because he thought that's what it would be, but here he was…

A shadow drifted across his peripheral vision, Aldrin drifting down from the ladder. He hit the ground and strode past Armstrong, wrist-rocket aimed ahead. He swept the perimeter. "Wake up, moon man."

"Look around you, Buzz…"

"I know. I should be enjoying this. So should you. Damn commies."

"A-hunting we will go," Armstrong said, releasing the safety on his wrist-rocket.

"Is that uhhh…" Aldrin pointed at the strange footprints.

"That's them. That's our path."

"Sea of Tranquility my ass…" Aldrin said. "Cover me. Let's move."

They hopped ahead, thoroughly unsure of how to proceed. There was some basic military training that kicked in, how to watch the horizon, how to cover each other, but all of that was based on earth gravity, a full field of vision, and full range of motion. They had none of that.

"Little West Crater ahead," Armstrong said. "How do you want to handle this?"

Aldrin scanned the edge of the crater. "It's like standing in a god-damned oil painting. Nothing's moving."

"That's a good thing, right?"

As the words left Armstrong's mouth, a small puff of dust rose over the edge of the crater. An irregular shape, different from the surrounding rocks and dirt, this looked more like a large burlap sack covered in hair and rolled in soot.

"Feels like we got eyes on us," Armstrong said.

"We do."

They stopped, bobbing slightly as they watched the lip of the crater. Something was watching them, low to the ground, moving slowly. They had no way of judging its size. But there were two tiny, shining black pits, unmistakably eyes, watching them. The thing slithered slowly to their left, then lifted its head up to scream a soundless warning. It lowered itself down into the crater.

"Okay," Armstrong said. "Okay. Okay."

"Okay," Aldrin replied.

"Okay."

"Yeah," Aldrin said. "How are they breathing? Where are their suits? What do they--"

"Buzz, get back!"

Armstrong bounded to Aldrin and shoved him down as a jagged moonrock shot over their heads.

"Guess they know we're here, huh?" Aldrin said.

"Do we shoot?"

"Not from this distance."

Another puff of dust appeared over the ridge. A small scrap of uniform floated slowly over the hill, a shred of reinforced fabric with a torn hose connected to it. It spun before them like a disembodied internal organ. A hand rose slowly over the crater rim, palm facing them. Its fingers were blackened and purpled, the skin swollen over elongated bones. It rose higher, attached to a twisted forearm clothed in the tattered remains of a cosmonaut's spacesuit.

Slowly, it extended one finger, then pointed at the fabric floating in the space between them. Aldrin reached out to grab it. "You read Russian?"

"Cyrillic," Armstrong said. "And no. But that name stamped on the fabric is one of the ones from the pamphlet. Sokolov."

"Any ideas?" Aldrin asked. "He introducing himself?"

Armstrong shrugged his shoulders, then realized Aldrin

probably wouldn't notice such a small gesture. "I'm gonna get closer."

"Wait!" Aldrin shouted.

The rim of the crater exploded as if a land mine had gone off beneath it, and a great, shadowy shape rocketed toward them.

"Shit. Shit shit shit!" Armstrong shouted, readying his wrist rocket.

The shape was on a beeline for Aldrin, and in zero-G, there was no way to react in time. The thing extended twisted hands for Aldrin, aiming claws for the visor of his helmet. Aldrin lifted his wrist rocket to fire. He depressed the button and felt a vibration at his wrist. A small plume exploded at the thing's shoulder, fluid spattering into globules that floated and froze all around them. Still it charged. Aldrin cursed himself for firing too soon as he tried to ready a second shot.

The thing hadn't changed course, and it was too late. Aldrin saw its face, finally. It was a horrible stew of features lupine, simian, and human. Jaw distended, cheek skin frozen solid and cracked wide open from howling, eyelids flaking away. Snapped tendons and torn muscles flapped in the low grav as the thing's fingers extended, claws coming straight at Aldrin's face. The last thing he saw before squeezing his eyes closed was another name in Cyrillic he recognized from the pamphlet, VOLKOV.

A hard tap on the front of his visor sent him tumbling backward, cartwheeling and slamming twice into the lunar soil as he floated away from the impact. He assumed the worst, that his visor had shattered or his suit had been punctured, and waited for the cold vacuum of space to take him.

Through squinting eyes he saw the inside of his visor covered in sweat and spittle, but intact. He turned and dragged a foot along the soil to slow his momentum. He clambered to his feet, Armstrong fifty feet away, circling around a chaotic whirlwind of dust and debris.

Volkov, the thing that had come for him, was tangling with something else, something equally twisted. The new creature had Volkov pinned to the ground, hammering down blow after blow in a grotesque silent symphony of violence. Volkov raised its arms in a pathetic gesture of mercy to no avail. The creature on top continued to pound, smacking and tearing until Aldrin saw Volkov's neck snap. It continued to pound away until Volkov turned to pulp, a fine spray of blood and guts and flesh misting and crystallizing in the lunar atmosphere.

Aldrin had moved closer to Armstrong, until they were shoulder-to-shoulder. Armstrong pointed at Aldrin, then gestured to the side of his helmet. He repeated the gesture.

Armstrong was trying to tell him his comms were out. He grabbed Aldrin and turned him, reconnecting a stray cable on his suit antenna.

"—hear me? Dammit, Buzz, gimme--"

"Gotcha Neil, gotcha. We're on, we're on…"

"What in the hell is--"

Armstrong stopped, then turned Aldrin to face the creature that may have saved his life. It stood tall above the remains of the thing that had attacked Aldrin. It was easily seven feet, its arms and legs grotesquely elongated, the skin hard and swollen over sinew and muscle and mutated bone. The tattered remains of a spacesuit clung to its legs and lower torso, and one of its hands was still encased in a spacesuit glove. The other was bare, the fingers almost a foot long, pointing at the tattered piece of spacesuit in the soil that read SOKOLOV. Patchy hair covered the thing's front torso, growing thicker higher up its arms and shoulders. The creature was a wall of muscle, no neck, veins inky black beneath purple-blue skin. A mane of fur ringed its head, eyes flicking like black diamonds.

It arched its back, muscles flexing, jaw distending to an impossibly wide degree.

"You feel that buzzing?" Armstrong asked.

"It's howling," Aldrin replied.

"Of course it is. You want the shot, or should I—OOF!"

Armstrong was cut off as yet another creature bounded over the rim of the crater and barreled into his midsection. He felt strangely light after the initial collision, tumbling with the creature across the lunar landscape. The thing had latched its jaws onto his ankle, and although the pressure was great and painful his suit was still intact.

He twisted, bracing one hand against the lunar surface and jamming the barrel of his wrist rocket against the thing's shoulder, pulling the trigger twice. He felt the gun buck, his visor covered in thick black gore. The pressure on his ankle released immediately and he struggled to his feet. He swiped a hand across his visor, smearing away a clear streak that allowed him to see the creature leap to an impossible height, over the crater and out of his field of vision. He looked down at the huge splatter of blood on the lunar surface, chunks of flesh and fur mixing with the dirt, slowly freezing. He checked his oxygen levels. Everything was fine. As fine as someone being stalked on the moon by a werewolf could be.

"Aldrin? Aldrin, you copy?"

"I'm… here…" Aldrin puffed. "Could use… some help…"

"Where are you?"

Armstrong paced backwards, not taking his eyes of the stationary creature before him. Taking advantage of the low gravity, he jumped back twice, a flash of light catching his eye in the sky above. Collins wasn't scheduled to come around at this point, and he wouldn't be burning fuel unless there was a disaster. Could it be the Soviets?

"Neil! You're a lousy shot. This thing is still- -- ah shit-- Trying to lead it away from the lander. Can't go too much further. Could use some…"

"I'm coming," Armstrong replied, turning his back on the Sokolov creature and bounding back to the lander as quickly as he could.

"Dammit," Aldrin came back on the comms. "Looks like these wrist rockets aren't great from a distance. I winged him. He's running."

"You in pursuit?"

"We shouldn't. Protocol says we need to stay in line of sight of the cameras on Eagle."

"Did you set those up?" Armstrong asked.

"Thought you did," Aldrin said.

Armstrong arrived at the Lunar Exploration Module. Aldrin was there, cautiously unpacking a small crate from the base of the lander. He proceeded to set up the cameras.

"Aren't we supposed to wait until the first job is done to set those up?"

"If I'm going to get murdered on the moon by a twisted commie werebeast, I want it captured for eternity," Aldrin grumbled.

"You just want footage of you kicking that thing's ass," Armstrong said.

"Probably. Keep an eye on the hills there, huh?"

Aldrin moved away from the LEM and began setting up the camera. Armstrong watched the horizon, spinning constantly, arm at the ready with his wrist rocket. "How you doing on Oxygen, Buzz?"

"Burned through a lot. We've been moving faster than we budgeted for. Probably need to get inside to switch out within the hour, but we can't do that until we deal with our friends."

Armstrong surveyed the horizon. Everywhere he turned, the blackness of the void overwhelmed him. It felt like he was standing on a soundstage, a poorly crafted rocky landscape surrounded by an impossibly black sky. What could be stranger than this, more helpless than this? Survival had always been the primary mission, and the mission hadn't changed.

Armstrong turned again, and saw one of the creatures crouched low to the ground on the horizon. It regarded him warily. He saw the tension in its arms and back, the way its eyes locked on to him, daring him to move.

Lions want their prey to run, Armstrong thought.

"We have company, Buzz."

"I see it. Where's the other one?"

"Sokolov?"

"You named it?"

"He didn't move. When I left to come find you, it was still standing there staring at me."

"One down, two to go. What's the plan? Do we flank that one and then go hunting?" Aldrin asked, turning slowly to stare at Sokolov, the towering beast, which remained standing over the remains of their first attacker.

"We can't go too far. Oxygen. Supplies. Can't risk leaving the LEM alone in case one of them wants to make it into Swiss cheese."

"Where do you think the other one is?" Aldrin asked, swinging his gaze back to Armstrong.

An odd shadow crept up slowly from the top of the Eagle lander, drifting higher and higher, moving across Armstrong's back. Aldrin strained to turn his gaze upward. The final creature, wounded and bloodied from Armstrong's initial hits, slowly drifted down from the lander behind Armstrong.

"Neil, look out!"

Armstrong turned as the creature neared the ground, raising his wrist rocket. Aldrin dove at him.

"Hold your fire!"

Aldrin tackled his colleague down into the dirt, feeling the shot buck through his arm, cringing at the sound of his visor cracking against Armstrong's as they hit the dirt.

"Buzz, what are you--"

"Don't fire at the lander!"

"I wasn't firing at the lander, I was firing at the—whoa!"

The thing crouched low again and seized Armstrong's ankle, moving unnaturally quickly in the low grav. It had the advantage of being able to sink hooked claws into the lunar surface for traction. It hoisted him up, dangling the astronaut before its face and raising a clawed finger to pick at his spacesuit. Upside Down, Armstrong made out the name GOLOVKIN on what was left of the thing's suit.

Aldrin rolled, struggling to get back to his feet, or any position close enough to upright to give him a good shot. He settled for flopping onto his side and raising up his arm. From this position, Armstrong's dangling body blocked most of his target. A miss on any of the remaining available tiny targets would mean a hole in the Eagle lander, which could mean no trip home.

"Buzz, shoot this god damned thing!"

"I'm trying. If I miss--"

"Then don't miss, damn it!"

Aldrin locked on to the creature's twisted foot, steadying his wrist. His whole body rocked before he could pull the trigger.

Something had seized him from behind, lifting him from the lunar soil. He was brought upright with sickening quickness, set roughly on his feet. Sokolov had returned to the fray. It ignored Aldrin and charged at Armstrong's dangling form, seizing his arms and lifting him higher, so that he was suspended between the two creatures like a tug of war.

Sokolov stared at him, while Golovkin continued to pick at Armstrong's suit. Aldrin saw frayed fabric and thin metal filaments poking up from Armstrong's waist. He'd be done for soon.

Aldrin raised his wrist rocket, unsure of which creature to shoot, certain that killing one would only give the other enough time to finish them both.

Sokolov nodded at Aldrin, then jerked its chin at the other monster. It repeated the gesture. Aldrin hesitated. Had the thing's eyes been less beady, if it still had functioning eyelids, he would have sworn it rolled its eyes at him. Sokolov dug its feet into the soil and gave a sharp jerk on Armstrong, pulling Golovkin off balance and moving it away from the lander. As Golovkin stumbled forward, Sokolov pointed his free hand at Aldrin, then at the other monster's stomach. It repeated the gesture.

Aldrin got the message. It was helping, telling him where to shoot. Time for questions later, as Collins had said. Now was the time for violence.

Aldrin charged forward, diving, his arm extended straight at the monster's midsection. As soon as his fist made contact with Golovkin, he jerked his trigger, once, twice, three times, a strangely silent explosion bucking through his body as a spray of blood and organs exited the creature's other side. It spasmed, looking at him with an anger that would long haunt his dreams. It made one final attempt to scratch at Armstrong's spacesuit, but Sokolov grabbed its wrist, bending it back, then wrenching it side to side until it broke free from Golovkin's body.

Armstrong toppled to the ground as Sokolov went to work on its dying colleague, turning the severed forearm into a stabbing implement, riddling its remains with holes, stamping on its head until it flattened into silvery mud on the lunar surface. Sokolov pounded its chest, jaws extending into a soundless howl aimed at the blue sphere in the Lunar sky.

"Neil, get to cover! I'll draw this thing away from the Eagle.

You just get ready to get out of here."

Before Aldrin could fire, Sokolov dropped what was left of Golovkin's arm and crouched low, bounding away in a single graceful leap, disappearing over the edge of the Western Crater.

Armstrong and Aldrin shared an uncomfortable silence.

"What the hell do we do now?" Armstrong asked.

"We need to get back inside, change out our oxygen tanks, and go hunt that thing down. We can't... imagine the Soviets bringing that thing to earth. Imagine your family having to--"

Aldrin looked up as the creature's shadowy form erupted again over the horizon, racing toward them, landing a few feet away from the Eagle.

"Arms down, Buzz," Armstrong said.

Aldrin hadn't even realized he had his wrist rocket armed and ready. The creature had smartly chosen to land between them and the Eagle. An errant shot would destroy their ride home.

"What's he holding?" Armstrong asked.

In one hand, it held the remains of a cosmonaut's space helmet, the visor intact. It carefully set the helmet down, dipping a finger into the remains of its enemy. It ripped a chunk of spacesuit from the thing's corpse, working slowly and carefully, bringing the debris close to its eyes for better focus. It stood, extending an arm toward them, holding the small piece of white metal with a symbol painted on it in fresh, shiny black blood.

"Is that a peace sign?" Armstrong asked.

"I don't give a shit if that thing used to live in Haight-Ashbury. We have a job to do."

"It doesn't want to hurt us, Buzz. You'd be in pieces if it did."

"Whatever gets us home faster."

The creature stood before them, looking between them, waiting. If there was such a thing as werewolf puppydog eyes, Sokolov had them trained on Aldrin, watching the barrel of his gun.

Aldrin lowered his wrist rocket. "Aw, hell. It's not what I came here for."

"Me neither," Armstrong said, lowering his arm. "Can it hear us? Can you hear us?" He shouted the question the second time, but Sokolov didn't move.

"I can hear you loud and clear enough to blow my eardrums out," Aldrin said. "Vacuum of space, remember?"

"Sorry." Armstrong moved so that his back was to the sun. He flicked open the gold sunvisor on his helmet, revealing his face to the creature. He spoke using exaggerated movement of his lips.

"Do you speak English?"

Sokolov didn't move.

Armstrong moved a bit closer, trying to assume the most peaceful stance he could think of. "I came here to… come to the moon. To here. Dammit, you know what I mean. This wasn't supposed to be a hunting trip. It's a peaceful mission to--"

As Armstrong spoke, the creature's face brightened. It bent slowly to retrieve the cosmonaut helmet from the ground, connecting a cable to the remains of the life support pack that clung to its massive frame. It lifted the helmet, poking its nose inside, looking as if it was drinking deeply. Sokolov moved its head out to look at them, paused, adjusted some dials on its pack, then put its head back in, repeating the sequence two or three times.

"I have wanted nothing more in my life than to stand where I am now," Armstrong said, "and I'd give anything right now to put this place behind me and never think of it again. But it's a mission of peace. This place, untouched by man, and the first thing we do, the god-damned first thing we do is spill blood on it. I can't--"

"Dobriy vyecher." The phrase broke into both of their headsets simultaneously. Weak, hollow. Unmistakably Russian.

They looked at the creature, who was half-bent over, the cosmonaut helmet pressed tightly over its cranium.

"Hello Americans," it said. "I find your frequency."

"How did he--"

"I make microphone work to you. I thank you. You will not kill me."

"Is that a request or an order?" Buzz asked, half laughing.

"You came in peace. Your government had other plans, much like mine. They land soon. They come for me."

Aldrin looked at the creature. "And your name is… you're…"

"Sokolov, Fedor. You know the name?"

"Sort of," Armstrong said.

"Your government sends you to kill and tells you nothing of your prey. Typical American."

"I came up here to get some rocks and take a few pictures. Plans change," Aldrin said. "We're supposed to stop them from taking you back to Earth."

"I will stop them. I could not kill the other Volk alone. The wolfs."

Armstrong raised a finger to correct his English, then thought better of it.

"I never wanted this. What they do to me. The others wolfs ready and want kill you. I am not so sure. I saw you land and you look so small and helpless. You are in shining white uniform, hope of mankind."

"Since we land here, I think only of how awful war would be, that my government will make more like me and send them to kill. They want put others through the pain of what we are to make this change. They send us all the way to moon for formula to work in correct manner. So much effort to increase human suffering. I was doctor before. I had wife and children. All gone now, in the name of progress. Such as me should not exist. I try many times to fight my colleagues, but they are too strong together. You provide great distraction."

"You will finish your mission. This is an age of wonder and fantaziya, no? So much we can do together. Show grace of humanity. Instead we use what we learn to fight. To kill. Your government made to come to the moon because they knew my government could not afford to follow. My government start a plan for… make the Volk so that you could never live in peace. They see us on a great hunt in America, feasting on your bones until whole continent is food. This medicine they give me could cure the sick, heal the weak. This technology America gives you could unite the planet. And instead we fight. Always fight. I am a man of peace. Nuclear weapons, nobody will use. Too risky. But things like me? What's to stop them from unleashing, yes?"

"We can… we can try to get you help," Armstrong said.

"No. You could have killed me before, and did not. You search for peace. You go home, show the world the possibility of that peace, of working together. I will stop them. Soviets cannot afford to continue if this mission fails. So they will fail. I will see to it."

Sokolov raised his arm, pointing into the inky blackness at a tiny speck of light.

"Is that Collins? He's ahead of schedule…" Aldrin said.

"I think that was supposed to be *his* ride," Armstrong answered.

"Arrange your cameras. Clean your suits. They will not land."

Sokolov took two steps back and waited as the speck slowly grew into a larger point of light, then resolved into the unmistakable form of a lunar lander.

"They steal that from us or did we steal it from them?" Armstrong asked.

"It was wonderful to meet you, first men on moon."

Sokolov pulled his head from the helmet and tossed it aside, bouncing lightly on his toes. As the craft drew closer, he curled down, muscles flexing and hardening into a tight ball. The Soviet lander came within range, the flickering lights of its landing thrusters popping like camera flashes across Armstrong's visor.

Sokolov exploded upward into the lunar sky, sailing toward the Soviet lander. For a moment, it looked as if he'd misjudged his mark, sailing high, but as his path crossed the lander's, he snagged one of the metal feet with his long, curved claw. Momentum took over, the spacecraft spinning so quickly that it looked like a child's top rocketing over their heads.

The Soviet lander made impact fifty feet away from the Eagle, landing hard on its side, exploding into a shower of twisted metal until it was swallowed by an eerie orb of white and orange flame that snuffed out almost as soon as it started.

"Fuel tanks," Armstrong muttered.

"You think they survived?"

Their eyes followed the deep black scar made by the Soviet Lander over the horizon.

"Let's get to work," Aldrin said, heading back to the Eagle.

Armstrong stayed focused on the horizon as Aldrin climbed back into the Eagle. Now came the stillness that he'd sought, the majesty of the lunar soil, marked by a battle of political ideologies that would leave a permanent stain on the celestial body.

Over the horizon, Armstrong saw movement. Sokolov's head, slowly bobbing back and forth until the rest of him came into view. In his hands, he clutched the remains of the doomed cosmonauts. He came no closer to the Eagle, instead bounding away over the grey hills.

Armstrong got to work setting up the external cameras, preparing to go back into the Eagle so that he could properly become the first man on the moon. History was written by the winners, and he planned to give the people of earth an amazing story. He framed the landscape as Aldrin peered out of the hatch.

"Let's go, Neil. And uhh… make sure you frame it so you don't have all of that…*that*… in the shot." Aldrin dusted a hand toward the piles of gore and streaks of blood in the lunar soil.

Armstrong sheepishly turned the camera for a cleaner view. He climbed back into the lander and spent the next thirty minutes helping Aldrin clean off their gear, restock their oxygen, and get their equipment ready. When it was time for the grand entrance, he looked at Aldrin, holding the small box containing the American flag. There were no words. They stared at each other, shaking their heads.

"You're still gonna be the first man," Aldrin said.

Armstrong laughed, catching Aldrin by surprise. It was contagious. Soon both men were shaking, heads bent forward. Aldrin nodded to Armstrong and he got into position. The door opened, Aldrin in position behind the door.

"I just want to go home, Buzz."

Armstrong turned and exited the hatch. "Houston, do you copy?"

"Roger, we copy."

"Clear channel?"

A pause.

"Copy. This is private."

"First part of the mission is done, Houston."

"Roger that. You've done an invaluable service for your country." When Armstrong didn't answer, Houston broke in again. "Is everything okay, commander?"

"It could be. If we try."

"It's done, Houston," Aldrin broke in. "It's a mess up here. I don't think we can clean it or cover it."

"Roger that. Apollo program's not done yet. You just get ready to make history and come on home. And if you can get some samples of biological--"

"Hell no," Aldrin growled. "Not on my watch. This mess stays here. We spoiled it. Not even here a day and we spoiled it. It's a mess down there, Houston. We brought the same mess here with us. It's gotta stop."

"Is the mission compromised?"

"Negative, Houston," Armstrong let out a sigh. "Look, we're done. We'll get your soil samples and do some readings, and that'll be it. Let's get it back on public channels and finish this."

"Copy that." A pause. "Proceed."

"I'm at the foot of the ladder. The LM footpads are only depressed in the surface about one or two inches, although the surface appears to be very, very fine grained, as you get close to it. It's almost like a powder. Down there, it's very fine."

Armstrong looked to his left one last time at the bloodied remains of the lunar monsters.

"I'm going to step off the LM now." As he drifted down to the moon, he cast a glance over his shoulder at the ever-shrinking speck of Sokolov, bounding into the inky blackness.

"That's one small step for a man, one giant leap for mankind."

Bæhren
a. Zehen deren
5. sind
b. Klauen
c. Ballen des
Vorder Fußes
d. harichte Röte
e. deren

THE FOREST THAT HOWLS

Sheriff John Manley hated dragging people in to the drunk tank. They always smelled bad. Even if they managed to keep their internal affairs in order and avoid filling the back of the car with vomit or urine, they still left a lingering fug of old booze and sweat that never aired out of the upholstery. He begged the state every year to retrofit the car with a plastic backseat, but it wasn't in the budget. The only thing worse than taking in one alkie was having to haul in two of them.

He stopped his cruiser next to the blinking lights of a pickup truck. Half in a ditch, the pulsing hazards illuminated two men sprawled on the ground. They scrambled to their feet when they saw him and ran to the car, pounding on the hood and begging to be let in. It was still early enough in the afternoon that just asking the next question put Manley in a foul mood.

"You two been drinking?"

They rushed to the driver's window so quickly that Manley's hand instinctively shot down to the butt of his sidearm. They jockeyed for position, pushing and shoving each other, a stream of nonsensical babble rattling back and forth.

The only key phrases that he picked out were *they're still out there* and variations on *tore Steiney apart*.

Manley reached up and hit the siren for a couple of short blats, shoving his door open so fast that both men scrambled back and fell on their butts.

"Quiet," Manley growled. They reminded him of bobblehead dolls, wide-eyed, heads whipping around trying to view every side of the forest at once.

Couldn't be booze. Had to be meth or something worse. He pointed at the man to his right. "You. Talk. What happened?"

"We was gonna find a Squatch," his eyes nearly bugged out of his head as his fingers fumbled with the stained, curling hem of his BUSH QUAYLE '92 T-shirt.

"Mister. Sheriff. Sir. Officer. Please," the other man.

"*Tch*," Manley clicked his teeth and snapped his finger at the second man, silencing him. He pointed the same finger back at the first man, who recoiled as if the digit was loaded. "Are you two out here alone?"

The man nodded so hard that Manley expected to hear a noise like a nickel rattling in an empty paint can.

"…'cept fer Todd," the second man again.

"We gotta--"

Manley snapped his fingers again and the first man's lips pursed shut.

"Who's Todd?" Manley asked.

"Our friend," the first man said. "Todd Steinhour. Drinking buddy. Steiney."

"What's his name?" Manley indicated the other man on the ground.

When that man started to answer, Manley glared him into silence.

"Huck," the first man said. "I mean, Sawyer."

"His name is Sawyer?" Manley asked. "And you call him Huck?"

"Like the book, you know. It's like… you know, a joke. There's the book Huck Finn, and his last name is… I mean… guess you had ta be there."

The beginnings of a long-afternoon headache tingled the base of Manley's skull. He held his palm up for a long second, then looked at the second man, Huck and flicked his finger to the other guy. "What's that guy's name?"

"Why'incha just ask 'im?"

"Because I'm asking you."

Far away, the sound of a large branch snapping reverberated like a pistol shot through the trees.

"Aw shit, they're coming," Huck said. "You gotta take us in! You gotta move!"

"What," Manley asked again, "is his name?"

"Hank," Huck barked.

"Last name?"

"Hicks. Both of us," Huck said.

"You don't say?" Manley shook his head.

"Naw, it's our last name. We're brothers," Huck said.

"That's your names?" Manley muttered. "Huck and Hank Hicks? Jesus Christ, I should have just gone into plumbing. Now. How did your truck come to rest here in the ditch?"

"Look, Officer, I don't mean ta be disrespectin' yer authority, but there's somethin' out there that wants us dead. You gotta help us, right? Says so there on your car!" Hank pointed at the back of the cruiser.

A cold wind whipped through them as scattered drops fell from the dark clouds.

"I'm gonna put you in the back. We're gonna keep talking. I'm gonna crack the window open, and if either of you two Hicks tries to climb out, I will put a bullet in your ass, are we clear on that much?"

The Hicks boys nodded and scrambled to their feet. When Manley reacted, hand near his hip, they slowed down. Huck raised his hands above his head. Hank offered his hands for cuffing. When they caught each other's eyes, they switched poses.

Manley swung the back door open. "Just get the fuck in there, okay?"

He slammed the door behind them without bothering to let them get comfortable, then walked over to the pickup truck to assess the damage.

He leaned his head into the cloud of stale beer smell, peeking in the open driver's side window. The whole cab was at a steep angle, all of the empties piled in the passenger footwell. The glove compartment hung open, stuffed full of unpaid tickets and various papers, all weighed down by a box of rifle ammo.

The bed was covered in a battered camper shell. All of the windows were busted out, possibly from the force of the crash. The sides were heavily scratched and dented, not unusual for a truck that wandered these parts of the woods. Most of the residents had a daily driver for work and a beater that they took into the woods for fishing and camping. There was an odd regularity to the damage, not the kind of thing you'd see from tree branches scraping. Looked more like someone had taken several baseball bats to the truck.

Manley moved around to the back of the truck and popped the camper shell top, a mere formality since all of the glass was missing. He tried to drop the tailgate, but it wouldn't move.

"There's a trick to it!" Hank yelled from the car.

"And that blood ain't ours! I mean, we didn't do it!" Huck shouted. This was followed by a yelp as Hank jabbed him in the ribs.

Manley frowned at them, hand near his holster. He leaned his head in. The bed was mostly empty, but then he saw it, a puddle of blood at the back. He followed the dark streak up the inside of the tailgate to a smear of blood on the top of the gate, still shiny and wet. It looked like someone had been beheaded over the edge of the tailgate.

"What in the honest hell," Manley muttered, rushing back to the cruiser. He grumbled, "Shut the fuck up, both of you," as he slid into the car.

He exhaled, thinking for a minute. Take them in now, stay here and set up a crime scene? Backup wasn't an option as the only other two deputies on duty might as well be on Mars. It would take them hours to get here.

Manley picked up his radio and called for dispatch, receiving nothing but static in return. He made a mental note to write down the first mile marker he saw and started the car.

"Oh thank Jesus!" Hank shouted. "Thank you Lord, he's movin'. Take us in! Take. Us. *In*! Get us the Hell out of—*OW*!"

Manley slammed on the brakes, sending both men rocketing into the steel mesh partition dividing the front from the back. "Let's get a couple of things straight here. I don't know what either of you two have done, but if you've broken the law I'll see that you pay for it. If someone else is trying to hurt you, I will do my best to keep you safe. I'm gonna ask you questions, but you don't have to answer them until you have a lawyer present. There's your rights. With that out of the way, let's get to the truth and make life easy on everyone."

"Thank you sir," Huck said.

"Is that deer blood in the bed of your truck?"

Hank looked at Huck and shook his head.

"It's…not. It's not…human. We think."

"Okay. How did the blood get in the truck?" Manley left the question of what the blood came from for the moment. They were probably trying to cover up poaching. He was always careful not to ask leading questions that could be used against him later to scuttle a case. Not *Why did you kill him* or *who killed him*, just give them enough slack to hang themselves.

"Sir, you will not believe us if we tell you the truth. I'm only tellin' ya that much so's you don't slam on the brakes again and crush us."

"What's the truth?"

"Steiney got… kilt by… a… sir, aw hell, I dunno how t'start…"

"It was a Sasquatch, sir," Huck said. "An army of them. They took him away screamin' and they was comin' fer us next. You see what they did to the truck! We was outta control and—*OW*!"

This time the car fishtailed from the force of Manley's braking. He pulled over and threw the car in park, turning around in his seat.

"Okay. I don't know what you're on right now, but my advice to you is that if you can't offer me any useful information *right now*, your best course of action is silence, you got me? I don't know what you poached. Plenty of different things out of season right now, and

I'm sure you're not trying to--"

"We's sober as ghosts!" Hank said.

"What's that s'posed ta mean? Sober as—ghosts ain't real, dummy! Sir," Huck said, "We ain't been drinking. I mean, not fer the past few hours. Not since we got ta the… look, if you'll kindly drive down the road, I swear I'll give ya the short version of what happened. I mean, Steiney could still be alive out there, and we gotta find 'im!"

Manley took off his sunglasses and hat and set them gently in the passenger seat. He put the car in drive and slowly pulled back out onto the mountain road.

"Talk."

"We moved out here from Kentucky, see, work on the gas pipeline up near Sumner. We was out trying to kill a weekend, get away from the wives and kids fer as long as we could, put some miles between us and our everyday troubles. Prollem with drivin' away from your troubles is they's always more troubles waitin' somewhere else," Huck said. "We wanted to make a movie out here in the woods, see? We was at the bar talking about how we could maybe get a Sasquatch on video and sell it to the news, or one o' them groups s'always out here pokin' around the woods. I mean, we know fakin' the video isn't the right thing ta do, and we're, y'know, invokin' the Fifth Amendment in case what we says here is--"

"I don't give a shit if you were out here to make pornos. Just get to what happened."

"Not! We wasn't! No. *No!* No. Look, we was plannin' this whole thing fer days. Weeks. And one night this fella at the bar hears us talkin', and says he could take us all out to where there's some Sasquatch action. Like real Sasquatch. Steiney got real excited at that. Me and Hank figgered we'd find a good spot to make the film, but if this dude was the real deal, maybe we could bag a real Squatch and be done with it. Millionaires! So this guy at the bar, Buck was his name, I think, or maybe Bug, he had a thick accent I couldn't quite place, well that man was the spittin' image of what we figured a fer-real bigfoot hunter would look like. He tells us no guns, right? I mean, we never go out in the woods without 'em, but he's real insistent on this. Cameras only. So, fine. We'll keep 'em out of sight, right? No harm, no foul."

"I'm pretty sure it was Buck," Hank said, "Not *Bug.* Guy just had a weird accent. You ever hear of a guy named Bug? We asked him couple times to repeat it, but it sounded different every time, like even he wasn't sure of his name. Big fella, he was. Six and a half foot if he was an inch. Arms like tree trunks. Head like a pile o' rocks. You ever see them drawn's o' cavemen, with the big foreheads and the big faces? I mean, he was kind of like that. Folks see me and Huck and Steiney, and they'd call us mountain men, but this guy was the real deal. You could tell he walked the walk. Big bushy beard. Clothes look like he lived in 'em full time, too."

"So here was the plan. Saw this thing on TV, the Patterson-Gimble thing, the movie? The shaky recordin' o' that big furry lump goin' out there?"

"Gimlin."

"Huh?"

"Patterson-*Gimlin* are the guys that made the movie," Manley silently cursed himself for entertaining this line of conversation.

"Steiney said we was gonna get somethin' on tape no matter what," Huck said. "He had a fur suit under the shell in his pickup. Said if we couldn't find one, we could fake it and nobody would know. Buck thought that was the funniest thing. Steiney was gonna show him the suit, but he said no. And I wish he had looked, 'cuz we was hidin' our rifles under that suit. Y'don't go out in the forest without guns, that's just crazy. If he'd'a seen it, he'd a said no and left us at the bar and that woulda been that. "

"But he didn't, and we's only thinkin' about the money. So there we was with our million dollar idea," Huck said, "Takin' a ride out in a convoy of pickups. Steiney hopped in with Buck and they took the lead. We just followed 'em out here. I mean, Buck gives us all maps at the beginning, but after a couple o' beers it just got easier to follow the truck 'stead of tryin' ta pay attention to the map. Can't read them typeographical maps anyways."

"Topological. No! Topographical," Hank said.

"I get it," Manley said.

"We had good maps," Hank said.

"Yep. We drove out there, got off the main roads onto the side roads, got off the side roads and onto fire roads, got off the fire roads and onto unmarked trails… we was driving through gullies, busting through brush, and I had no idea how we was ever gonna find our way back home. I honked fer everyone to stop and I told Buck he better know what he was doin', and he jes' look at me like I was a child, you know? That kind of stern look where your old man doesn't have to say a word and you just gotta trust he has the whole thing under control."

"So we drove until dusk and set up camp," Huck continued. "Spent the night around a fire and Buck started tellin' us stories about what to expect. He said the squatches are nomadic. They don't set up in one spot fer too long, but they was also territorial. Like they'd be in one spot fer the fall and another fer summer and so on. And he says there's tribes of 'em, like there's not really such a thing as Sasquatch, or that there is, but that's just the name of one tribe. The bravest one, or the dumbest I guess, that always finds itself out near human contact."

"He said people din't really have a word fer the tribe we was trackin'," Hank said. "So we spent the first night tellin' stories and buildin' the fire and we all hit the tents early so's we could get up at the crack o' dawn. And all night I couldn't sleep cause I kept hearin' this noise."

"Steiney said he heard it too! You ever hear a dog do that high pitched whine, kinda sounds like a faucet that's been turned on jes' enough to let air come out the pipe but barely any water? Just a breathy heeeeeeeee kinda noise? Spooky as hell," Huck's eyes went big, as if this conveyed the weight of the fear he felt.

"Well, I was afraid, I'll admit it," Hank said. "Didn't want to poke my head out, but I did eventually, because the thing was, the noise didn't move. It was comin' from the same spot, at the same volume, from only a few feet away. And I zipped my tent down just enough to peek out, and what did I see but Buck sittin' upright there by the fire. Couldn't tell if he was sleepin' or not, but that noise was comin' from him! I could see his back movin' in time with the sound. And I thought maybe that was his snorin', right? But then he'd stop sometimes, and wait, and then his head would nod a little and he'd start in with that noise again in a different pattern. He was talkin' in some kind of Sasquatch Morse code."

"Fascinating," Manley said.

The car approached an intersection. Manley slowed and drummed his fingers on the wheel. A piercing scream broke the silence.

"Coyote," Manley said, noting the fear on the men's faces.

"That wasn't no—drive! You gotta drive!"

The scream returned, rhythmic and undulating, this time echoed and answered by a different scream from the other direction. Right or left, Manley would be driving toward one of the two sounds.

"They're trackin' us," Hank whispered.

"Right to remain silent," Manley grumbled at him.

Manley pulled a forestry service map from the door pocket and consulted it for the fastest way back into town. It was getting near dusk and these roads were tricky once the sun went down.

"Listen to me. I'm not trying to coerce you in any way, shape or—you guys understand what coerce means?"

"I guess so," Hank said.

"I'm not claiming you're guilty, but you said you came up here with a man named Buck and a friend. That friend is missing now, and you have blood on your truck. I'm going to have to come back here with a team of deputies and possibly state troopers so we can sweep the forest up there looking for him. That's a lot of time and a lot of money, and our taxpayers can frankly afford neither. So if you know where your friend is-- and again, I'm not asking you to tell me what happened to him, just where he might be--it will make all of our lives much, much easier."

"It wasn't Steiney's blood!" Hank cried. "We shot one o' them. Lord help us, we jes' thought… I mean we thought it was like a huntin' trip. Figgered this Buck guy would want to be cut in on any trophy money. Buck set us up in a clearing with a camera, said he was gonna go check the creek and see if anythin' was happenin' that way. He was gone for over an hour. I mean, he told us no guns, but goddamn if we was gonna sit in the middle o' nothin' without bein' able ta defend ourselves, and—and one o' them came out. Tall as me! A girl, I think, 'cuz I could see *titties*. I know that sounds stupid, but I saw 'em, I don't mean it in a nasty way, I just… I saw 'em and thought Buck was tryin' ta fool us with one of his friends in a suit. Thought maybe he paid off Cecilia Dockins from the bar, she's always doin' pranks like that. But then the thing stood up, and there ain't no suit that good. There ain't no mask that realistic, with teeth and… and it roared, and I don't know. I just…suddenly I had the rifle leveled and felt it pop against my shoulder, and this things face…her face just fell, you know? All scared and confused, and I don't… I never killed nobody before! I hunt, but I ain't never shot a person, and I thought I did. Thought I kilt Cecilia. Her face, you could see the hurt, like she just din't understand what was happenin.'"

Tears formed in Hank's eyes. "We jes' stood there fer a minute with the body. Din't know whether ta scratch our watches or wind our butts, ya know? But when we realized what we had…we was happy. Thought our ship had come in. We made sure ta get plenty of pictures. Propped her up, held her arms way out so's you could see the arm span, the foot size, the weird skull shape. We could sell the photos first and then sell the body to science. Thought we was rich, man. Then Buck came runnin' back 'cuz of the noise, and he saw what happened, he… he just freaked out and grabbed Steiney by the back of the neck and smashed his vidya camera, and then… they came. They all came out of the forest and surrounded us and—we just started runnin'. Had ta listen to Steiney screamin' fer us ta come back, and then just plain screamin', and then nothin.'"

A pickup truck approached, coming to a stop behind the cruiser. Hank heard the growl of the engine first and turned to look. He started slapping Huck's shoulder.

"Huck! Huck! It's him! It's…it's…it's…"

"Sheriff, Officer, sir, that is the truck that's…Bug. Buck. The guy! It's the guy!"

Manley exhaled. He rolled his window down and barked the siren twice, motioning for the truck to drive up next to him. It was a monstrous old pickup, beat to hell, the paint job more rust than pigment.

The window rolled down and a large man leaned over to the passenger side. Hank and Huck pressed against the side window, trying to peer up to get a look at the driver.

"Help you, Officer?" a low voice. It sounded like gravel sliding down a deep muddy river.

Hank and Huck turned pale and instantly pressed themselves against the opposite side of the car.

"It's him," they whispered.

"We seem to have had an incident out here, and I'm hoping you wouldn't mind answering a few questions for me," Manley said.

The silence that followed was so long that Manley thought the guy had passed out. That kind of quiet only happened when someone was trying to formulate a lie. A loud thunk as the truck dropped into gear and slowly rolled forward. It turned right at the intersection and stopped a few yards down the road, safely out of the way of any potential traffic, not that there ever was any up here this time of day. Manley tucked in behind the truck, leaving his flashers on. He tried to radio in to dispatch, but there was no answer other than static squawk. He shook his head, then popped the door open.

"You ain't callin' fer backup? Mister, that guy is responsible fer—"

"Right to remain silent. And keep your voices down. You want him to run away? Right now he might be the only thing standing between you two and a very lengthy trial."

Manley slammed the door and walked toward the truck. "Go ahead and shut her down for me, sir. Thanks."

He stopped at the corner of the truck and peeked into the bed. It was streaked with what looked like dried blood. Torn clothing, old rags, a large shovel. None of it unusual for this neck of the woods.

"You mind stepping out while we talk?" Manley stopped a few feet behind the driver's door.

"No problem," the voice rumbled.

The door popped open with a shriek of rusty metal. The largest man that the Sheriff had ever seen clambered down. Easily close to seven feet tall, he was as muscular as the two men had described him.

"You been camping?"

"That what those two say?" the man jutted his chin at Manley's car.

"If you could just answer my questions, I'd be obliged."

"Not camping. Hunting. They wanted to see Sasquatch, so we went."

"Your name Buck?"

"Some people call me that."

"Okay, Buck. And what did you--"

A piercing shriek sounded from over the ridge. It echoed across the sky before being picked up down the road. When that callback died off, another shriek came from the other direction.

"I don't patrol this side of the mountain too often. You seem like you know this area," Manley said. "Lotta coyotes out here?"

Buck nodded, his face impassive. "Good eatin'."

"Lotta stuff for them to hunt this time of year?"

"Good eatin' for us. Serves us well when there aren't any people around."

"And what does that--"

Now the shriek came loud, so loud Manley felt like he was inside of it, like the scream was a force of nature that froze every muscle in his body and turned his blood to ice. It was all around him, echoing, rising and falling, swirling among a cacophony of breaking tree branches and the sound of deep bass drums, rhythmic running like heavy feet.

His hand instinctively dropped to his revolver, but before he could unsnap it, something hit him from behind like a truck. It took him a few tumbles before he realized he was rolling across the road and down into a ditch. He splayed his legs to stop his momentum, coming to rest just a few inches from a skinny tree just off the other side of the road. His vision was blurred, tinged with white. Each time he blinked he saw shapes moving in the forest, large and looming, circling him, waiting.

From across the road, a sound like gunshots, but regular and fierce, like someone banging away a solo on Satan's drum kit. He reached for his revolver, but the holster was empty. He scrambled to his feet and ran back to the road. What he saw stopped him short. He mistook it for a small group of bears attacking the cruiser, but bears couldn't grow that big. Bears couldn't wield sharpened tree branches and makeshift clubs.

A noise like tires squealing on asphalt rose behind him, but bouncing, the scream a very large creature might make if it was running. His head exploded in pain and the world turned purple and white, and then silent.

***

When Manley opened his eyes again, the world was upside down. His wrists and ankles burned, nose and ears felt stuffed with mud. His head throbbed in time with a furious and insistent thudding that bumped beneath him. The trees were moving, swaying in the wind. Running. Dancing. His brain slowly came back online, piecing things together.

Not trees dancing. Legs. Great, furry, muscular legs. The drums were footsteps. He was tied to a large branch carried along by the big man, Buck, and someone behind him. To either side, great creatures stomped and cleared the brush. The sky had enough sun left that it backlit the creatures. He couldn't tell what they were, but they couldn't be human. His brain checked out again and the world went dark.

***

He woke seated in the dirt, arms bound in front of him. His feet were tied to a stake in the ground. Buck crouched in front of him, his filthy plaid flannel shirt illuminated by flames from a nearby bonfire.

Someone will see the smoke, Manley thought. *Help will come.*

He remembered that he *was* the help that would notice these things.

"Awake?"

Manley nodded, trying to keep his eyes on the big man and ignore the seated forms of the hairy giants around the fire. There were at least a dozen of them.

"We have a problem," Buck's mouth pursed in a grim smile. "The men you were with have committed a crime. They must pay. I must pay for my part in it. But you may be able to help me. Ours are the only lives at stake here, you and me, everything else is decided."

Manley stared at him, unsure of how to proceed. Normally, he'd lean on the badge, tell anyone holding him captive that they were about to have the full weight of the law come down on them. He had a feeling the only law out here was what the creatures around the fire deemed appropriate.

"You need to let me go."

"Let you go?" Buck asked. "Not, let *us* go?"

"Where are the Hicks?"

Buck chuckled. "Hicks. Yes. Yes they are. They're across the fire. They will be dealt with. I'm sorry you have to see this, but I'm also glad you turned up today."

"Kinda like a bad penny that way," Manley said. "Look, I'm unarmed, near as I can tell. There's more of you than me. You look like you could toss me back to Snoqualmie on your own. Just saying, there's really no need to keep me tied up."

Buck thought on this a minute, then turned to the fire. "*HAKKAH! Hargh, Chaq-chot.*"

The creatures around the fire shrugged their shoulders. Buck stood up straight, so tall that Manley could barely see his face behind his massive barrel chest.

"You will not run. If you escape, what would you do? Tell everyone you see about what happened here. Who would believe you?"

"I'm not even sure if I can walk right now. Your boys there did a number on me."

"Those are our youngest men and women. They are sometimes unaware of their own strength."

Buck reached down and plucked the stake from the ground, untying Manley's legs.

"Your hands stay tied for now. Stand." He poked one finger under Manley's armpit and hoisted him up.

"Jesus," Manley muttered. He hadn't been lifted that way since he was a toddler.

As soon as he was on his feet, he was greeted with drunken shouting from across the fire.

"Sheriff! Officer! Sir! You gotta help us. You gotta--"

The air splintered under the force of the sustained roar of all of the creatures around the fire. Manley concentrated on stopping his knees from knocking together. The Hicks brothers fell silent.

"You will not speak," Buck yelled.

Their shirts had been stripped off and tied around their wrists. They were bound to a tree by a thin rope around their necks and foreheads, holding their heads perfectly still.

"These men came out here to kill," Buck said.

"Why don't you let me take them in and see that justice is done?"

"Not your justice. Ours."

"Pardon my ignorance, but are you part of a federally-recognized tribe? What jurisdiction do you have--"

"This is our land. It has always been and will always be. Men keep taking more and more of it. Where are our children supposed to--"

"I'm sorry, again," Manley said. "You keep saying '*our*' like... I mean... look, don't hurt me for this, but you don't exactly look like those others by the fire. Whatever they are."

"Some of us assimilate," Buck said. "We must learn about your society and watch it carefully so that we may continue to survive."

Manley stared at Buck, then looked over at the fire, where the other creatures had stood to face him. His eyes danced back and forth between the hairy behemoths and the giant mountain man.

"I shave," Buck said. "It's tedious."

Manley nodded as if he understood.

"Years ago, one of our tribe was captured on film, and since that day, more and more people come every year trying to duplicate the footage. Humans are aggressive and not to be trusted. It wasn't long before they stopped coming with cameras and started bringing guns. We had to do something. So we watch, and learn."

"I'm not sure that gives you the right to..." Manley drifted off, unsure how to finish.

"Exactly," Buck answered. "The right to kill. Who has such a right? And why? Would you not kill to protect your family? Did you not swear an oath to protect and serve those in your community?"

"I did. So you can understand the predicament you're putting me in here."

"We pick a spot in the forest to live. Somewhere remote. Untouched. We live here until man stumbles through. We watch them kill the deer. We watch them pollute the air, cut down our trees, sully our rivers. We abide that. When too many come, we find a Sasquatch hunter with a camera. We bring them out here to let them 'capture' one of us on camera. That gets other humans excited. They all come to that spot in the forest while we're busy moving on, somewhere deeper, ignored and unseen. I find the people to bring. That is my job. It is my job to make sure that they don't bring weapons. I thought these men were unarmed. I bit my tongue while we traveled, even as they wouldn't stop talking about how glorious it would be to kill one of us."

"It wasn't supposed to be like that!" Hank shouted, then winced as one of the creatures threatened him. "We was jus' comin' ta make movies! Steiney was the one brought the guns and wouldn't --"

Hank's voice cut off as a massive wooden club pulped his head against the tree behind him. One of the creatures held the bloody weapon, then drew it back again and smashed what was left of Hank's head until his body dropped, dangling from the rope around his neck. Huck started screaming.

The creature turned to Manley and dropped the bloody club, screaming, tears in its eyes, a look that Manley understood perfectly.

"They shot her daughter," Buck said. "They took turns posing with the body. They smiled. They *smiled*!" Buck roared at Huck. "My fault that her daughter has been desecrated."

"But I didn't… I didn't shoot! It was Steiney! Please! Please Officer, tell them they can't do this! You gotta protect me, ya gotta help, officer--"

Huck was silenced as a sharpened spear slammed through his neck and into the tree. His feet danced in the twigs and dirt so fast it sounded like the static of a TV tuned to a dead channel. The creature turned the spear, wrenching it back and forth until Huck's head popped free from his neck and toppled to the ground.

Buck hung his head. "It is my fault that she died. I never should have brought the men into the woods."

The tribe turned to face Manley and Buck, closing ranks and blocking the light from the fire. Manley looked at Buck. "Please don't kill me."

"That is up to you. In our tribe, there are three like me who may contact humans. One who teaches, an old one. One who roams. And a young one who learns. It is the greatest honor and the greatest responsibility the tribe can bestow upon us. Our job is to keep humans away, to learn where they're going so we can avoid them, to find the most determined among them and discredit them. I didn't know he had a weapon. I didn't know."

A smaller Sasquatch approached Buck wielding a club. It pointed the club at the ground and growled until Buck slowly lowered himself into a sitting position.

"The choice is yours," Buck said to Manley. "I am to face death for my part in her loss. That I found you was a small miracle. I can still be punished. You may yet live on."

"I didn't know I was on trial," Manley said.

"I have made a request of the tribe. They will let you live if you take me back to your town, arrest me for the murders of these three campers. I will spend the rest of my life in prison as atonement for what happened to our lost one. You will say nothing else of what you saw here. You will be a hero."

"And if I say no?"

Buck looked at the tribe surrounding them, let the silence of the forest and their resolute stillness speak for them. "Don't say no."

"You're going to kill me unless I become an accessory to murder."

"You already are, every day, just by living out here. Actions you don't think twice about echo through these woods for decades. Every year, we have less and less land, less food, more pollution."

"I can't--"

"Find a way to can," Buck said. "For both of us. This is as close to justice as we can hope for."

Manley spat on the ground, mind racing for an escape. "Where's my car?"

"It's been moved off of the road. I can lead you back to it easily. The tribe planned to destroy it. I told them to leave it alone and dismantle the Hicks' truck instead. You will take me to town, and I will confess."

Manley ignored the sick feeling in his gut, tried to keep his back as straight as possible. He nodded, and the tribe circled them again. One of the Sasquatch moved to Hank's corpse and tore the shirt from his body. He scuttled behind Manley and bound it around his eyes. Manley squeezed his eyes shut, told himself that the cold wetness was just mud or water from the forest floor.

The leaves and branches rustled around him. The ground pulsed with the thud of the tribe's steps. He winced at their growled conversations, felt surrounded by angry bears. After an interminable silence, a distant scream, a unified howl would echo in Manley's mind every time he saw a full moon over the forest. From beside him, three, short, sharp barks.

"They will watch you. For the rest of your life. Speak of anything else you've ever lived, but never speak of this until the day you die."

The blindfold was yanked away. He was alone in the clearing with Buck, the headless corpses of the hunters arranged around the base of a large tree. The campfire had been extinguished. Buck held a large burlap sack, wet and bulging.

"Evidence," Buck laid a massive hand on Manley's shoulder and spun him roughly. "Walk."

***

A year and a half later, Manley rolled down the highway in his civilian vehicle, an old SUV that had seen better days. It would only need to make one more trip.

He was a bonafide celebrity. Book deals. Movie deals. All of it. The man who captured the King County Chopper. The trial was quick and efficient, the evidence indisputable, and yesterday Buck had officially been sentenced to three consecutive life terms in prison for the murders of the Hicks brothers and their friend. Justice had been served.

Manley felt like hell. In court, after the verdicts, he had to bite the inside of his cheek when the Hicks family came over to thank him. When they walked away, he hustled to the bathroom and lost his lunch. He was a damned liar. A hero cop and a disgrace to his badge. He'd still cash the checks.

He'd tried to go fishing a few times to clear his head, shortly after bringing Buck in to town. It was too loud in the forest now, even when nothing made a sound. Everything was too close and too vast and formless.

He arrived the next day in the desert outside of Palm Springs, where he settled in to a small trailer on a vast patch of treeless land.

During the day, the bottle helped keep the echoes of the two men's screams out of his head. At night, when the coyotes hunted, he'd stay awake, red-eyed and drenched in cold sweat, clutching his gun to his chest.

He aimed at every shadow that moved, and when the howls came, he joined them, raving into the cloudless sky, the closest thing to a confession he'd ever offer.

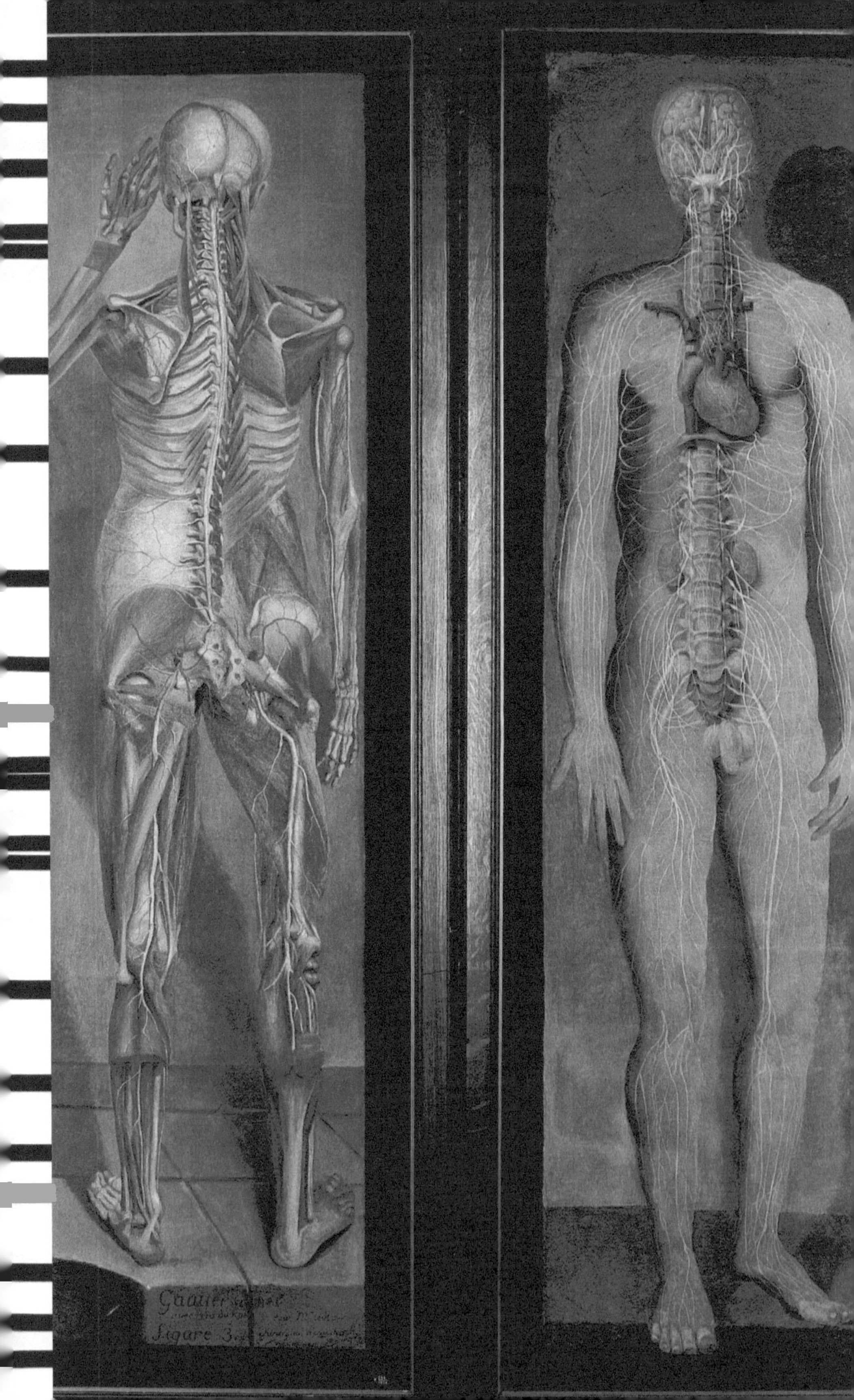

Gautier
Figure 3.

HUMAN, TRAFFICKING

Twenty years into this career, a sucker's game of *being my own boss*, and the rules keep changing. They find a way to pay less on miles. They find a way to demand you deliver things further, faster, but also require you to take longer rest periods. Two years ago, the rumor of driverless trucks started. Now it's a reality. Local is becoming the only way to go. Most of the big companies have moved on to these new AI rigs for cross country. You drive your truck to a port outside of town, and then drop the trailer so a highway drone can hitch up and do the long haul. Suddenly sleep breaks are no longer a problem.

Suddenly people are obsolete.

Some drivers didn't handle that well. The unions tried to strike, but the numbers were too thin. Owner-operators went out to spike tires, a few independent renegades caused crashes on the highway to "prove" these machines couldn't be trusted. But the way they're set up, the computers, telemetry, cameras everywhere, it was easy to prove human intervention or just plain malice was the cause of the few AI rig crashes. All that did was make people trust local drivers less. Made us all look unstable and untrustworthy.

I was at a truck stop somewhere off I-55 near Cape Girardeau, Missouri when this commercial came on one of the TVs. A shot of this autonomous truck, which made everyone bristle, but then, a long shot of a truck yard where drivers strode up to those same trucks and got inside. A people-first company, the screen read. The safety that comes with the support of artificial intelligence. Fewer accidents on the road. The reliability and intelligence of a human behind the wheel. One of those big-shot Hollywood actors was giving the voiceover.

At SOL•S Transport, we believe in one thing: People are the lifeblood that keeps this country moving. When you join our team, YOU become one of our most valued assets. We use autonomous trucks piloted by people, because we know there's no replacement for your work, your knowledge, your experience. SOL•S - Autonomy, humanized.

I'll never forget that. It's burned into my memory, because that commercial was the moment my life changed. I'd been hampered a little by a limping stiffness in my ankle that made it hard to drive. It wasn't an exercise thing, it was a diabetes thing, and I thought my career was coming to an end. But if there was a truck out there that could help me drive…

I saw the writing on the wall. If you can't beat 'em, join 'em. I called them, set up a meeting, was totally honest with them about my medical condition. Usually you get that kind of concerned look of disappointment when a potential employer hears about bad health. The guy I talked to, this real spit-and-polished guy that looked like he came out of a plastic press, he just nodded. Laid a hand on my shoulder and made solid eye contact. He said, "We're going to help you."

Not *we'd like to help you.* Not *we'll call if something opens up.*

The SOL•S Corporation wanted me as a driver. Me, a human! They said they were experimenting with new and exciting technologies that would allow more use of autonomous vehicles while maintaining jobs for flesh-and-blood people.

I went in for a checkup with their medical team and they told me I was going to lose my right foot. I'd already seen that coming. I'd been spending the past few months trying to figure out a budget to make my truck handi-capable. The doc gave me a different offer. Amputation, yes, but I'd get an experimental leg to replace it. I was fifty miles past nothing left to lose. All I had left was my family, and I'd be damned if I was going to disappoint them. What was half a leg if it meant my daughter got braces, better clothes for school?

This was all off-the-books. They wanted to roll out this pilot program with as little government interference as possible. I already hate giving so much of my paycheck to those pencil-pushing IRS thieves anyway, so what was I going to say?

"You're not losing a foot, you're gaining a bionic leg," that spit-and-polished exec told me. Hell, I love Sci-fi movies so I jumped at the chance.

I was in and out of surgery within a day. The doctors took a little more of me than we'd initially discussed. Amputated to just below my right hip. They left just enough nub for this leg to bolt on. I'm getting used to it. The tech is really something. It's not a prosthesis in the typical sense. It's part of me. An honest-to-god replacement. Never comes off. No phantom pains. It was a little bulkier, but wired straight into my nervous system. If I walked on carpet, I still felt it. The foot itself was metal with this special kind of silicon padding on the bottom. I was still ticklish. Could still register a pinprick or stubbed toe, but now it was just more of a signal to my brain to correct an inconvenience.

It made it easier to walk, even easier to drive. The leg syncs to onboard computers in their specialized rig. I just lock it into place and use the touchscreen on my thigh to adjust speed. The foot splits and spreads out into three paddles when I'm behind the wheel. Two paddles cover the brake and gas, and this little third part I call my kickstand pops out to link to the clutch. I set the speed, and the tech does the work.

I was, quite literally, a test pilot. Behind the wheel, they made me wear this harness on my head to read my brain impulses. It recorded my alertness through the miles, different times of day, different weather patterns. This was all to help their machines learn how a real driver reacted to different conditions. I was giving them the kind of feedback no amount of computer simulation could, downloadable stats from the USB port on my calf.

On my days off, I had a special silicon gel boot to roll over my leg. Didn't want my wife to think anything was up. That was one of the rules, she had to think I had a regular prosthetic leg. I had to pretend to have a little limp. If I had my pants off, she'd just see a shiny flesh-colored mannequin leg. With my minimal time home, I'd just have to find excuses for not taking the fake leg off. She didn't ask too many questions. I got a bonus for my silence. I kept the mortgage paid. I got to see my kid laughing over dinner at the restaurant. That a joy you sometimes take for granted, right? Eating over the family table is one thing, but just that special feeling that comes at a restaurant, seeing her little face light up when she saw how much food she could choose from. That's something I couldn't give her before. We were month-to-month, hand-to-mouth, trouble-to-trouble. That was changing, and we were happy.

Four hundred miles into my next cross-country run, the stomach cramps started. I thought it was something I ate, but it just got worse and worse. Bad fever, cold sweats. I thought I was having a heart attack. When I reported in to dispatch that I needed to get off the road, they told me to stay put and they'd send a doctor to me. I don't know how SOL•S got such a bad reputation when they showed this much care for a driver.

The doc showed up in a mobile trailer within an hour. I've never seen anything like it, a whole medical facility in a trailer. MRIs, X-Rays, you name it, they had it. Someone else took my truck to finish the run for me, and corporate sent me an email saying I'd still get paid out for the miles. I thought that was real generous, but then the test results came back and it started to make a little more sense.

Cancer. My stomach lining was dissolving. There was some kind of rejection taking place, and they didn't sugarcoat it. My new leg was causing my body to go into revolt. Terminal. That's a word you never like to hear. They offered me another surgery. This one would be a little riskier, they had to go in to remove the cancer and the damaged organs. But they promised a massive payout to my family if things really went south. In for a penny, in for a pound, and either way my kid was taken care of.

When I came out of surgery, the first thing I noticed was my matching legs. Bright, shiny steel and circuitry. My insides felt different. Hollow, somehow. I could feel my lungs moving, but there was… how can I put this? You don't realize you have guts until your guts are gone.

They showed me some videos of the procedure, and they told me I'd come through with flying colors. They hadn't realized how much that artificial leg was taxing my digestive system. Essentially, the power needed to run the leg was eating me alive. I couldn't eat enough food to keep it going long-term.

I asked why they gave me a second one. You know how mechanics get. You go into the garage for one thing, you get hit with a bill for five things you didn't know you needed. They said it was gonna go any day, they were trying to do preventative maintenance. Then they showed me how my insides worked. My stomach still looked like its regular fish-belly-white, little-too-much-pudge-and-hair self, but now, it opened. They hit this little hidden magnet switch and rolled the skin away, showing me the power plant housed in my torso. I passed out, which I guess they expected.

I no longer needed to eat. My stomach was gone, replaced with a flexible fuel bag. My intestines had been replaced with a long stretch of Lithium battery packs. Getting through TSA might become a problem in the future, but there were benefits. I didn't need food anymore. I could eat if I wanted to, just to enjoy the flavor of something. But it would all just end up in this tiny receptacle tank I could remove and dump out. Every twelve hours, on the road, I would refill the fuel bag through a stent in my ribcage. Like gassing up the rig. And the lithium batteries recharged as I drove. I just had to plug myself into the truck. No more headgear, now everything was being read directly from the computer wired into my brain.

And I kept driving, longer runs, no longer needing to stop to eat, barely needing to stop to sleep. I'd only go to regular truck stops for the human interaction. Buy a few snack packs, maybe a soda, talk the clerk's ear off since I'd be hour ahead of a regular driver. There were a few of them still out there.

Congress had enacted some restrictions on autonomous trucks, safety regulations or further studies needed or some such nonsense, when I really knew this was just about trying to save jobs in a dying economy. I didn't have to worry about any of that. I asked my contact at SOL•S if I could help them recruit people. I had friends that needed jobs, too. They told me I couldn't really reach out since their experiments weren't exactly Uncle Sam-approved.

I just kept the miles coming. Kept the money flowing home, but home started drifting away. I was gone too much, too long. I was distant when I was home because I couldn't let my family get close to me. My daughter, when she hugged me, commented that my stomach felt like the front of our car. You know how honest little kids can be. And she poked at it, kind of laughing, but then I felt the switch trigger and it started to unroll under my shirt. I dropped her trying to hold it closed as I ran away, probably the weakest moment of my life. I couldn't let them see what I'd become.

I got back on the road the next day. Drive for them. Keep driving. Ignore those angry emails from my wife, tell myself we'd find a way to work through it, but SOL•S kept tabs on those communications, too. They told me counseling was a good idea. One on one. So my wife talked to one of their therapists, and I talked to another, and somewhere in between it was mutually decided that we would probably be better apart.

It broke my heart, but they were right. They set up a trust fund for my daughter, showed me how much my wife would receive every month in addition to paying off the mortgage. They weren't buying my silence. That was never for sale. They were paying for my peace of mind, that's what this was all about anyway.

Did I mention my broken heart? A couple weeks after my wife gave up on me, my heart followed suit. You hear about it in country songs, but mine *literally* tore in half while I was on a run. Crashed the truck off an overpass. Twenty-foot drop, straight down. A nose dive onto an entry ramp just outside of Los Angeles. Probably would have made a good scene in a movie, but it was some horrible press for SOL•S. But they were still good to me. Kept everything anonymous. I was laid up in one of their hospitals with my arms shattered, my neck broken, my jaw half torn off.

They promised me they'd make it better. It turned out the stress on my heart from losing my wife coupled with the long-term effects of their fuel and battery system in my guts was more than the human body could take. A normal man would have died in a crash like the one I had, but their little power plant kept me going long enough for them to scrape me up and get me to their private medical facility.

I guess I owe them my life. All they ask of me is that I keep driving.

This time, when I came out of my first surgery, I was inside of a big parking bay at their warehouse. I tried to reach up to scratch my arm, but couldn't lift my hand. When I mentioned that to the nurse on duty, he gave this real concerned look to the doctor. The doctor asked everyone else to leave the room so it was just me and him and the nurse.

He told me about the amazing advances SOL•S had made with artificial intelligence, and how I was an irreplaceable part of that. I was not only helping to advance their company, but the entire human race as well. Maybe it was the anesthetic still working out of my system, but I started laughing at them. Asked the nurse if anyone ever told him how much he looked like the doctor. Asked the doctor if anyone told him how much he looked like the company recruiter. Different hair color, maybe the eyes were a little different, but they all had that same molded-from-the-same-plastic-press look.

The Doctor repeated all of that stuff about the advances they'd made. How I was helping the company mission. He sounded just like that guy in the commercial I saw all those years ago.

"People are the lifeblood that keeps this country moving. You're part of our team and one of our most valued assets. We need you back in the seat, because there's no replacement for your work, your knowledge, your experience."

Skip the brochure, I told them. They knew they had me the moment they took my leg. I just wanted to know why I couldn't move. My spine had been shattered in six different spots. They needed to go in to fix my power plant. They told me I was going to lose the use of my arms. The damage to my spine meant that their bionic legs could no longer get signals to and from my brain. But they could keep me alive.

I could be the bridge to humanity's future.

What choice did I have but to say yes?

They swore I wouldn't be awake for the procedure, but they were wrong. I suppose it didn't matter. With my spine broken and so much of me already made from artificial parts, pain registered as an experience. My body no longer hurt. I was just aware.

Aware of the lasers burning through layers of soft tissue, fat, muscle, bone. Aware of large, shining saws that took my hands, then my forearms, then everything below my shoulder. I could turn my head, and I watched them stacking pieces of my fake legs and my real arms on a silver gurney that they wheeled away with no reverence.

"You're doing so well," the doctor said.

After that, I was hollow. Almost nothing. I watched them stitch silicone tubes into my skin, connect what was left of my circulatory system to small portable tanks. An intern came in and loomed over my bed, and the doctor asked me, "Are you ready to become the next evolution of the American worker?"

Not *human*. Not *man*.

Worker.

The intern lifted me up, cradled me like a baby, and we walked to a large, shiny silver truck. Their newest model. My reflection was a little distorted, but from what I could see, there was almost nothing left of me. No legs, no arms. Just a body swaddled in a white cloth.

They hit a switch on that shiny new cab and the whole thing rotated forward, revealing a cushioned seat inside of a command center. The intern laid me inside, disconnected that little portable tank that was pumping blood, or something like it, through my system. They attached me to a larger tank system situated in what should have been the sleeper part of the cab. Plugged two long spikes into the back of my head. I was the brains of the operation. Connected a rebreather over my mouth. The air I breathe is cleaner than ever now, HEPA filtered and free from particles. My eyes are washed and rinsed every thirty seconds. Nutrients are refilled at weigh stations. I am my machine, my machine is me. I just think and the rig reacts. I miss driving the old-fashioned way. I never stop moving now. I experience the American Interstate from my windowless cab through cameras mounted to the outside of the truck. Pick up, drop off, keep moving forward. Keep America moving forward.

I never stop to sleep or eat. I count white lines eighteen hours a day. My wife has a great big house. I send her emails sometimes, just to check in. It's the only way I can talk to her, She rarely replies. When she does, she keeps it short, but she'll send a picture of my daughter's beautiful new smile sometimes, and that's enough.

Most days, that's enough.

ALMOST HEAVEN

The first time the bus engine hiccupped and backfired, Rosa didn't wonder about a tow or roadside maintenance. She was more troubled by the song on the radio. One of those new pop songs by some disposable diva. Those songs always took a little longer to make it onto the radio stations out in the sticks. And here, eighty miles past Harper's Ferry, was definitely the sticks. Mainstream always traveled slow this way, if at all. Pop songs. Fashion trends. Cures for Necrotic Cannibalistic Hematoma.

Rosa looked up at the sun visor above her captain's chair, two small pictures of her children beaming down at her. The only two reasons she kept driving these shitty routes. More time away from the kids, but more money to support them. She knew they were safe back in Baltimore, back behind the double walls of medicine and military protection. Here, even as the bus labored its way back to sixty five miles per hour, all she could think about was a painfully slow couple of hours on the side of the road. Creeping fog and cold air and every tree branch that shook in the wind a skeletal reminder of impending doom.

This particular group of senior citizens called themselves Nourishing the Roots. They were all on a destination tour to the African American Heritage Family-Tree Museum in Ansted. Tracing their past, finding their ancestry. That was the first stop, and then there'd be some further exploration to the south, finding connections to the Underground Railroad and Buffalo Soldiers, the trading blocks, the lynching trees. All of these old folks trying to delay death by meeting the ones who went before them.

The bus lurched again, a hard knock from the floor that almost sounded like the drive train breaking loose and slamming into the undercarriage. That was all she wrote. Rosa wrestled the steering wheel hard to the right, tried to guide the mammoth vessel as far out of traffic as she could. It was foggy out – *of course* it was foggy out- and the last thing she'd need was to get slammed from behind by an eighteen-wheeler coming down the hill.

There were lights in the distance, just a half mile down the road, a pale yellow haze in the thickening mist. Half a mile, give or take. Leave the senior citizens here on the bus or lead a parade into town? Was that a town? Those lights could run on a timer, could just be a warning light for the peak of a hill, telling traffic to slow down.

Most of the passengers were asleep, hearing aids out, meds kicked in, dead to the world. There were a few whispering murmurs starting in the back. Rosa had the PA mic in her hand, finger hovering over the button, then thought better of it. If the walkers were coming, these people would die in their sleep and know nothing of it. Waking them up for no reason at all would prove far more painful to her psyche, as the complaints would come non-stop for the rest of the trip.

Rosa slid her finger off the PA address button and quietly walked down the aisle to the back of the bus, whispering reassurances to the few people drowsing awake that there was just a slight engine problem, she'd check it out and be right back.

Outside, the air was cool, the mist thick enough to settle through clothes in a few strides. Rosa looked both ways up the road, but it was no use. Night had settled in, and the fog took care of what little visibility there would have been. She shook her head and went back to the bus, pulling her cellphone out as she went.

The silence of no signal only amplified the pounding in her head. Rosa clicked her phone shut and leaned against the door. It was cold out, but that was better than on the bus, where it was too quiet, too full of the wandering cerebral pulses of all of those dozing ancients. She'd be stuck in her captain's chair, staring at the pictures of her kids on the visor. No, that would make things intolerable.

Headlights approached in the distance. Rosa moved towards the center of her lane, waving her hand in front of her cellphone flashlight to act as a kind of warning light, get their attention. She hoped it shone brightly enough in the fog. Whatever was coming was moving slow, crawling through the pea soup at a snail's pace. The lights were far enough apart that it looked like it might be another truck or bus, but there was no engine noise. The headlight on the right also appeared to be loose, wobbling a little up and down out of sync with the other.

She checked over her shoulder to see if the other lane was clear and moved into it, continuing to signal, hoping the vehicle would stop. It didn't slow down (slowing down would pretty much be stopping), but instead it moaned. There was a consistent low sussurring sound, like fingernails scratching glass, and the growing sound of gravel crunching underfoot. Rosa checked over her shoulder and saw five more lights approaching, two from off the shoulder and three spaced evenly across the road.

She scrambled back for the bus, easing the door shut behind her as if a rude awakening was still the worst thing her passengers would face tonight.

Walkers. Eight of them that she could see, which meant there were probably more out there in the tall grass. They were trudging towards the bus. She could hear them, even through the glass, that hissing the sound of air moving through lungs that no longer needed oxygen. Dry leather throats that acted more like the reed in a woodwind instrument, producing odd, muted tones as the diaphragm pushed air in and out. Scientists had classified this noise as *droning*, since the effect was similar to bagpipes. All of this mundane trivia Rosa had picked up on TV during the worst of the crisis, that's all she could think about now. Not the passengers, not her kids, just stupid facts that weren't increasing her odds of survival in the least—

A slap at the glass as the first one arrived. He was fairly big, baggy overalls hanging from his exposed collarbones with a trucker's cap slightly askew on his head (thank god she couldn't make out his face). Rosa bit back a scream, watching the pale grey palm press against the window and slide down. A second time, then a third. And then… he stepped back. They all did. The walkers were surrounding the truck in a semicircle from behind, and this big one doffed his hat, held it gingerly over his stomach.

"Mlaaaaaaaaazzzzz….." he hissed. He folded the brim of his hat a little tighter, a slight puff of dander and dead skin escaping into the night. A few bits of scalp and hair were lodged into the rim. He turned his head violently to the side and coughed, reaching into the front pocket on his bib and producing a squirming rodent. This he bit into like a fresh apple, leaning his head back as he sucked the life out of the thing. He cleared his throat, a horrible wet sound. "Maaa'am," he began again. "Sorry you had to see that. Throat's parched, and blood's the only thing that helps. Watched you roll by, sounds like you blew somethin' atoppa the hill."

His face did something then, jerked in several directions at once, producing a seam that stretched taut across his right cheek until the leathery skin popped open under the strain. Was he…smiling?

"Ya prolly heard things 'bout our kind. Ain't no reason to be scared though. We'd just as soon you pass on through 'fore the gov'mint come in lookin' for ya and hunt us down, burn us, like'n they did everywhere else. We dead, but we still people. We got rights."

Rosa hadn't moved, couldn't move until she felt the cracking in her hands. A thin little pop, then a hard crunch followed by a blinding shot of pain. She thought for a moment that she'd balled her fist so tight the fingernails had gone through to the other side. She held her palm up, a bloody mess, shards of her broken cellphone still lodged there. She whipped her hand behind her back, hiding it under her coat.

"We mostly don't have no taste fer people no more. I getcha a wrap fer that hand if ya want."

Rosa's jaw shook loose, worked once, then twice, forming the shape of the word "help" but never quite pushing it out.

"Jes' come up to Rooster's up the road there. He ain't strong like he was on account o' the muscle bein' gone, but he still knows engines. Ya jus' roll his toolkit down, maybe crank a wrench or somethin' less'n his arm snap off."

Rosa nodded dumbly as the walkers shuffled closer to the bus. It was a numbers game. If they wanted to eat her alive, tear her apart and feast on her brains, well, it was just as likely to happen here on the bus as it would be up the road there. She pulled the photo of her kids down from the visor.

"I'm all they've got. You understand me?"

The zombie motioned over to another spindly corpse nearby, this one almost all gristle and bone. She had a few shanks of long hair still clinging to her scalp and was holding half of a very tiny skeleton.

"I got a girl o' my own."

The skinny zombie girl nodded her head.

"She has uh…had…nice hair and uh…I'm sure back in the day, she was--"

"That ain't my girl. The lil'un there, that's her. Forever four and a half. Say hi Manda June!"

The half skeleton twisted grotesquely at the waist and raised a tiny hand, curling the fingers in a feeble little half-wave before burying its face in the woman's chest.

"She gets a little shy still," he said.

Rosa was out of the bus now, the photo of her kids still extended before her like a crucifix to ward off demons. The walkers didn't shift at all, just stood there as the wind hissed through rotting cloth and bone.

"I'm Big Don. Pleasure, ma'am," he extended a hand to her, a bit of his fingertip crumbling off.

"I'm Rosa. This is my girl Beth and my son Chris. I just want to get back to them--" and then the tears came. Big Don fumbled in his pockets for a kerchief, and when he couldn't find one, he tore a bit of shirt off of a nearby shuffler.

Rosa choked a bit at that, the idea of cleaning snot off of her face with a dead man's shirt. She swallowed hard and began putting one foot in front of the other, commanding herself not to run. She thought about locking up the bus to keep the passengers safe, but if the zombies wanted in, they'd already be in. Fifteen minutes up the road and back, she was confident they'd all remain asleep that long.

The trip was a daze. She felt as if one minute she was there in front of the bus, and the next she was back, lightly sweating from rolling the heavy toolcase down the road. Big Don was quite the conversationalist, telling her about life after the plague, how they were happy to stay hidden in the hills. The fog was thick enough that she couldn't see any houses or streets. There was just whiteness, then Rooster's Garage, then more whiteness and finally the bus.

The door was open when she got back. Rosa was on the bus in three steps, hustling down the aisle for a quick headcount. They were four people short, everyone else was still asleep. She bounded back to the front of the bus, ready for war, when she saw her missing fares next to the bus. Two of them were locked in an intense cribbage game with the locals, and the others had struck up conversations with the dead.

Rooster was already under the bus on his mechanics spider, a healthy amount of banging and cursing (or what would have been cursing had his throat not been shredded) indicating that the solution was near at hand.

"I don't…I mean, thank you," Rosa said.

"Don't say nothin' to nobody 'bout us, that's thanks enough. We ain't here for all you know."

Rooster wheeled out from under the bus, then crawled next to the engine compartment. He pointed at a few bystanding zombies, getting them to hold tools, apply pressure in a few spots as he worked his wrenching magic. After a few minutes, he staggered back to Don and hissed in his ear for a minute or two.

"Rooster says you just broke a belt. He's got somethin' jerry-rigged for ya, says long as you keep it under twenty you should be able to roll it down the hill. Gotta stop at the first town and wait 'til morning, this thing can't come back from the dead but once tonight," he laughed.

Rosa smiled despite herself. She opened the doors to the bus and called out to her passengers. "Okay folks, let's get back on board now. Long night ahead of us. Long day too."

She saw the old timers out there, always happy to talk to strangers, shaking hands, saying goodbye, shuffling back to the bus.

"Don…thank you. You're a life saver. Is there…I mean, is there anyone left for you back in…living? Anyone I can pass a message to for you?"

"You live a nice long life, put in a word to Jesus later on, tell 'im come get us so's we can stop walkin' in circles here."

Rosa nodded and cranked the door closed. The engine rumbled, rocking the bus a couple of times, then sputtered into an unhealthy growl that meant they'd be moving again soon. She eased off the brakes and crawled forward, waving to the crowd as they gathered momentum, keeping it under twenty just like Rooster said. She saw a few of her passengers stirring and breathed a sigh of relief that she'd somehow managed to pull this off.

Except… one seat was empty near the back. She didn't want to cause a panic, couldn't stop without risking the bus dying for good. She raised her hand to where her PA mic was clipped to her visor, next to that photo of her kids, her beautiful, wonderful kids that she would hug into oblivion when she saw them next. That picture was in her pocket now, a lucky charm. There was a slip of paper up there, a note scrawled in a crude brown ink written in the shakiest of hands:

"Thanks for dinner. Have a nice trip."

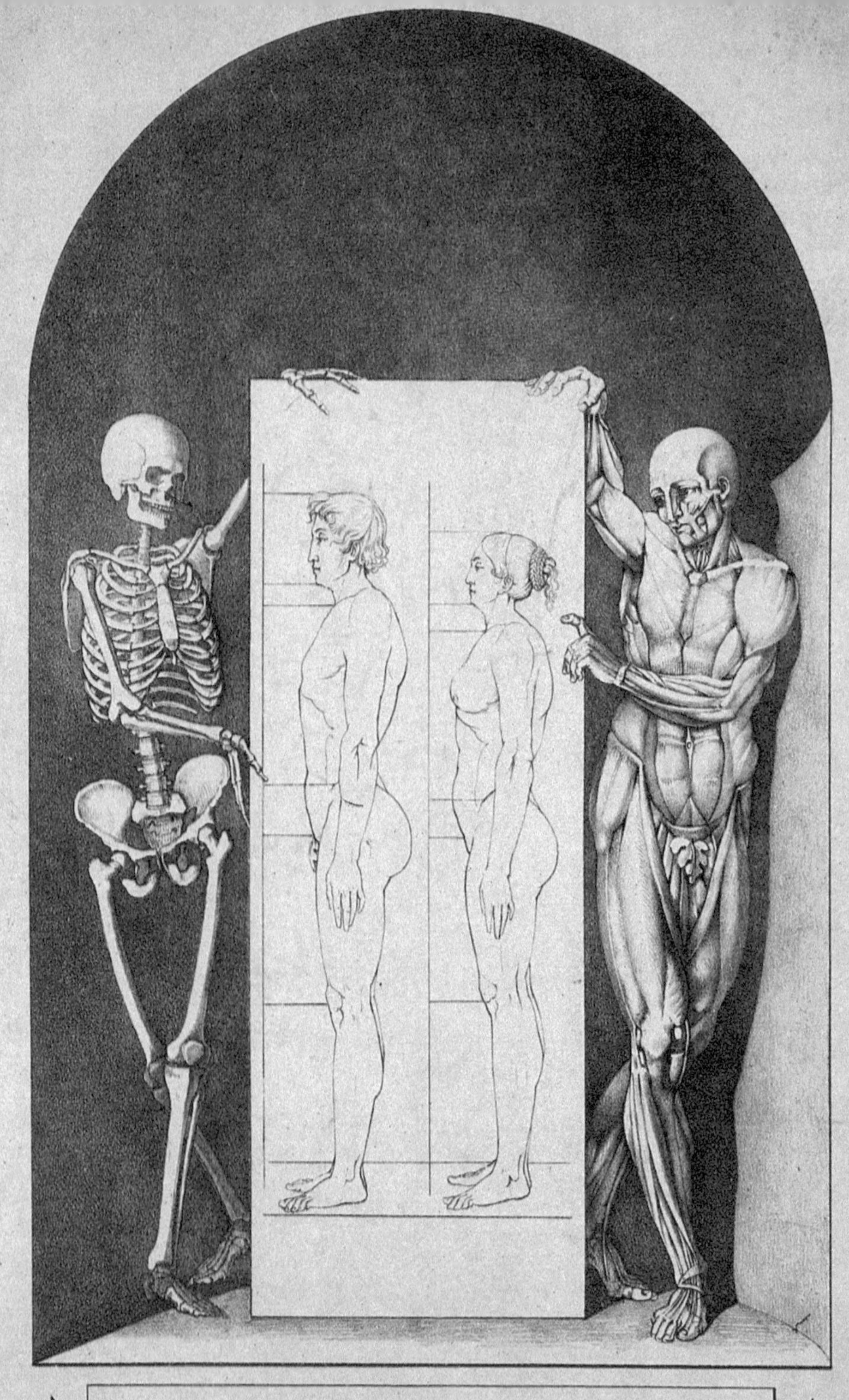

TRATTATO DI ANATOMIA PITTORICA
Fatto da Costantino Squanquerillo
ROMA MDCCCXXXIX

LIFE ON AFTERLIFE'S TERMS

Stasia wakes up in a cramped locker in the hospital morgue and screams herself hoarse, kicking the door until help finally comes. A rush of cold air blows up her paper dress as someone yanks the door open and slides her tray out. She's lifted onto a gurney by two hulking orderlies. Thick leather straps cross her torso, squeezing her arms and legs down until she can't move. It doesn't stop her thrashing. She can't focus. Everything is shapes and colors until a nurse in a rotten paper facemask and bad wig looms over her face.

"Got a live one here!" The nurse's voice has a strange faraway quality. She sounds like a bad recording or voice alteration software. Just…off. The nurse ignores Stasia's curses and threats of legal action and bad press. She plunges a syringe into Stasia's neck, overruling her objections.

Stasia's thoughts become painfully lucid. Her senses sharpen. The nurse flips a gauzy sheet over her face. Stasia doubles down on her panic, struggling to move, to yell, to be rescued as they rumble down the hall.

"You're dead. Sorry, I don't mean that in a threatening way. When your relatives say *she's no longer with us?* Well… you're no longer with them," the nurse has clearly given this speech before. "Some of them will say *she's moved on to a better place?* Well, hon, this is it. Nothing with pearly gates, or fire and brimstone, don't you worry. Sorry if you were expecting more. Whether it's better or not is up to you. It is what you make it. Good breakfasts and an excellent selection of on-demand movies. Plus a great PT room. You get used to it."

The phrase *I'm not dead* becomes Stasia's mantra, bouncing around the inside of her skull at full volume, unable to rise above the murky, drugged waters of her lips. She's seen enough movies that start this way. She has to quell her panic. Try to figure out where she is. Listen for clues outside, airplanes, waves, anything that she can report to someone if she can sneak away and find a phone to call for help.

And that voice. She has to remember that odd voice from the nurse. Surely that's a clue that will lead to someone's arrest. Justice will be served. Someone will pay for this as soon as Stasia can figure out what this is.

Her world alternates echoes and silence until the gurney comes to rest. The nurse doesn't bother taking the sheet off. "The first day is always the worst," she chuckles as she turns out the lights. A door gently closes and then opens again.

"I know you're tired and you'll be tempted to sleep. Try not to. You don't really need sleep anymore, but this close to your, uhhh… *event*… your dreams will get a little wacky. I think we've both had enough screaming for one night, don't you?"

Stasia falls into a feverish sleep-wake cycle, her dreams slow and tortured, hours of fighting against an insurmountable tide of hallucinations and visions. Trying to wake up is fruitless because she hasn't fallen asleep.

Soft light creeps up the blanket covering her face. Her right arm thrashes once, then her left. The sheet moves, pulling down slightly. Her arms are free! She bends her right elbow. There is no degree of nuance or control to it. Only bent or straight. Her fingers react the same way, curled fists or open flat. Her head will only turn to the right, and she can't blink. But she's moving. If she can move, she can escape.

Stasia flops her arm across her body, shifting the sheet out of the way, then wishing she hadn't. Someone has strung a corpse above her bed, a grotesque, rotting thing in a threadbare candystriper uniform. One eyesocket is leathery and dusty, the other barely contains an eyeball that had long ago gone milky. The lips are pulled back in a dry rictus grin.

This was a storage locker. A crypt. A killer's trophy room, and she was next. Someone out there was looking to take nubile young women and—

"Good morning!"

It sounds like a ventriloquist speaking, that odd slurring of certain syllables and consonants that comes from not moving your lips… or not having any. It sounds like the nurse from last night. Things start to make sense, the logic of her situation falls into place, and panic gives way to dread.

"Told ya not to sleep!" the nurse shuffles to the side of the bed and pulls the sheet off. "It's always better if you try to take these first steps yourself. Now, some of the sedative might still be working, so you'll probably get a little better than you are right now. But some things are going to be different. Better to find out now what we're working with."

"Whaaa ya calking gout?!" Stasia yells, followed by a startled shriek. What had happened to her voice? Why can't she move her mouth? The drugs, has to be the drugs. She'll get better. She'll get out of here. She is a survivor.

"Look, honey, I'm on lunch in five minutes. That's when I get my best reading done. Let's do this."

Stasia flops her head to the side to take in the nurse. A skeleton in mummified skin, hands on hips. If this wasn't life or death, she'd almost find this funny.

"Arise and walk," the nurse murmurs, holding a bony hand out to Stasia.

Stasia rolls over to her side, bicycling her legs. Her right leg only seems to work at the knee, kicking spastically. Her left, though extremely stiff, does as she asks. She slowly dangles her legs over the side of the gurney. She pushes off and lands unsteady on her numb feet. She can tell the floor is there, but not what it's made of. Can't tell if it's hot or cold, soft carpet or hardwood or tile or stone. But it's there, and she's standing, which means she's one step closer to getting out of this nightmare.

"All right, girl, good for you. My work here is done. I'll be back after lunch. You want my advice? Don't lay down for a while. Take a walk around, check out the grounds. Immersion therapy. It's going to be cold and uncomfortable, but the sooner you get through it, the sooner you'll accept your new life."

"I don't nah wha yaaa taa baa--" Stasia's jaw is okay for a few syllables before it locks up. She moves forward a few tentative steps, her left leg striding, her right frozen at the hip. She gets three paces before letting out a low, painful moan. This brings a smile to the nurse's face.

"That's the spirit! Okay. You get in trouble, Reginald the orderly will help you out. After I get back from lunch we'll take you to the baths and then you can go meet your support group."

Stasia stands perfectly still, jaw slack, staring daggers at the nurse. Her nametag is too faded and stained to read. Nevertheless, a complaint will be lodged. Negative thoughts will be Yelped. She will see this hospital closed by the end of the year, or she'll die trying.

The nurse spins on her heel and exits the room, leaving the door swinging open. Besides the gurney, the room is cold and empty, curtainless windows with bars over the glass, a green linoleum floor, bare walls. Stasia shuffles a few more steps forward and out of the room. She wanders down a well-lit, sterile hallway, past a series of sealed heavy metal doors. It feels more like an asylum than a hospital, and the terror that had ebbed under her anger begins to grow again.

A light at the end of the hall, voices talking and laughing.

She picks up her pace, walking as fast as she can, trying to call out for help, frustrated as her locked jaw only allows for grunts and moans. Step-dragging her feet until she rounds the corner to find a circle of people sitting around a small coffee table with a candle in the center. One of them stands, handing off a talking stick with a flag on it. No... it isn't a stick, it's a bone. They all turn to look at her, nine in total, all in various states of decay.

The one nearest her, with his back to Stasia, slowly rises and turns to look at her. The oldest one, Stasia thinks, though how she can gauge age on any of these fossils is beyond her. He's dressed in a warm-looking red and green cardigan with patches on the elbows. His slacks are neatly pressed, his white hair tamed into a ridiculous comb-over. When he fully faces her, she can see why: the front quarter of his forehead has been smashed in, his eye socket destroyed. He has a monocle over his remaining good eye, and even though his jaw looks dislocated, he greets her with what he must think is his warmest smile.

"You must be Stasia."

Then, in unison, the group says *Welcome!*, a chorus that sounds like broken speakers and dying animals.

The floor rushes up to meet her, Stasia's last memory before mercifully blacking out is the *thok* of her skull against the linoleum and the hushed laughter of the hideous group. A sign wavers in and out of focus on the wall as she blacks out:

SUPPORT GROUP FOR THE NEWLY UNDEAD

***

Days later, or possibly weeks, she can't keep track, Stasia walks down that same hallway for a meeting with Doctor Nico. She's determined that her petition will be heard, that after a review of her evidence, everyone will understand that a horrible mistake has been made. She'd been kept here illegally, unreasonably, and completely against her will. Yes, they'd taken good care of her so far, fed her, clothed her, but she was not sick. Not ill in the least. And most certainly, she was still alive.

"Good morning, Stasia," the nurse shuffles around the corner into the main lobby. "The good doctor has been regrettably detained. There's been a bit of an outbreak… out there." She smiles at Stasia.

Out there is a phrase Stasia's getting tired of hearing, as if the everyday world was some exotic destination far away that people talk about but never see.

"How long?" Stasia asks.

"A couple of hours maybe? There's some good shows on TV today, you can relax back in your room and I'll give you a call when the doctor returns."

"No, how much longer do I have to deal with this? I have a home and a family that misses me! I demand a phone call."

The nurse's eyes widen and she bends behind her desk to rifle through a file cabinet. She produces a slim black folder, sleek shiny cardstock with a typewritten white sticker on the tab. Larger letters, a T and S in bold colored stickers wrap around the side. The nurse flops the file down and begins scanning through page after page. "Nobody said anything about a family. Husband and children?"

Stasia starts to nod her head yes, then realizes she might not be able to carry out this lie. She opts instead for the vague truth. "I have a family."

"Yeah, but no babies, right? That would expedite matters.

Would mean our intake department got things horribly wrong. Happens sometimes, but we're mostly… wait, do you mean your father and your sister?"

Stasia's eyes widen and she nods enthusiastically. "Yes, and I'm sure they're very worried--"

"Doesn't count, darling. I'm sorry. Your sister didn't even go to the funeral. You go relax in your room and I'll come get you as soon as the doctor is--"

"I DO NOT BELONG HERE, YOU MONSTER!" Stasia stomps her foot and looks for something to throw. With nothing nearby, she opts instead to stand huffing and glaring at the nurse.

"I have to say, your enunciation has gotten better by leaps and bounds! And a stomp like that could have broken your ankle, you should really be careful. In your new state, you're a little more difficult to repair, you know? The body is a temple," the nurse gestures to her own decaying and desiccated form.

"There is no state! There is no illness. No condition. I swear to you, you can help me. I'm not… I don't have a disease. You are… this is kidnapping. I am a citizen of the United States of… I have constitutional--"

"Okay, okay. How about a nice sedative? Maybe you want to--"

"You're hopeless! This is criminal. Criminal! You will pay. If you don't get me in front of the doctor by four o'clock this afternoon, that will be the end of this. The end!" Stasia folds her arms and spins on her heel, heading back down the hallway. Could this really be the end of everything? Eternity in this not-quite-a-hellhole?

There was no leaving. She'd tried a couple of times, but every door out led into a byzantine parking lot full of medical and security personnel. None of the phones had a dialtone and they wouldn't give her access to her personal belongings so she could call from her cell.

Countless days in these bland hallways, door after locked door in her hospital wing with darkened windows and no signs of movement. She wonders if she's the only one in this wing, if they were softening her up for some kind of Stockholm experiment. She reaches her room and turns the knob, thoughts racing. Maybe they want to program her to assassinate someone very important, and the first thing they need her to believe is that she is—

DEAD

A sign hangs above the sofa on the far wall of her room, jaunty colorful foil letters strung together. She hits the lightswitch, turning the lights off, then on again, thinking it will break the hallucination. The sign remains. People have been here in her absence. All of the furniture has been removed save for the couch against the far wall.

She hears a throat clear and is startled to see Dr. Nico in a chair to her right.

"Hello, Stasia. This is an important meeting. We need you to listen. We care about you and we care about your well being."

"Who's we? What is this, an intervention?" Stasia laughs.

The doctor smiles as the door to her bathroom opens and a half dozen zombies shuffle into the room, looking at her as sheepishly as their dead features will allow. Stasia turns to leave, but another half dozen zombies are in the hall forming a semi-circle around the doorway.

"You're beyond death, Stasia," the doctor says. "It's time to accept it and get the help you need to start your afterlife."

A small chorus of Let us help yous mixed with *grrrraaaaghhhs* echo around Stasia. Earnest, smiling, decaying faces, friendly rotten hands ushering her back into the room. Her heart sinks in defeat, bouncing hard against the bottom of her stomach, where it roils in acid and transforms into a righteous burning furnace. She strides confidently to the chair next to Dr. Nico and sits, folding her arms.

Several seconds of uncomfortable silence pass. There weren't enough chairs for all of the zombies, and some of them looked as if their legs would give out at any moment.

"It takes time for us to procure medical records from your… past, shall we say," Dr. Nico begins. "We can't exactly follow formal channels, but we have our ways. I find your case very fascinating."

"What case?"

"There's no reason to be ashamed of it. Everything said here is kept in the strictest confidence."

The zombies all nod in affirmation, one of them so vigorously that her jaw breaks loose from the left side of her skull, leaving her chin canting at a strange angle. She quickly turns away and grabs a compact mirror from her purse to adjust her features.

Stasia sighs. "There is no case. None. You're keeping me here against my will. And now you're all complicit. This might not get solved today. Maybe not even this week, but I guarantee you I'm more tenacious than any of you. I have a lawyer—it may take me some time to contact her, but I will find channels, and when she hears about this, you will--"

Dr. Nico holds up a sheaf of papers. "This is your last will and testament. It was prepared and read thirteen days ago by Lisa Bodner. I think it's safe to say your lawyer has heard about your passing."

"What kind of sick--"

"You are dead, Stasia. Or rather, you were. One thing you certainly aren't right now, is alive. Let's get back to your casefile. You were diagnosed with Cotard's Syndrome a few years ago, yes?"

Stasia goes silent, lowering her eyes to focus on a dirty spot on the carpet between her feet. There's a nagging memory pulling at the threads near the edge of her mind. It sounds familiar. It bothers her. It's something close to truth. The solid ground she thought she was standing on is suddenly loose gravel, and she feels her resolve shift the slightest of inches.

"Cotard's Syndrome, for those gathered here who don't know, is a condition where a patient is convinced of her non-existence. Sometimes of her own death. I've never seen anything like this, but it's crossed over somehow."

A growled chorus of *Oh mys*, and *Isn't that fascinating?* and *Gruuuughs* passes through the room.

"This is ridiculous," Stasia says. "I've never felt more alive!"

The zombies in the room chuckle at this. One of them raises his hand slightly, a skinny purple and greenish young—*Man?* Stasia thinks. He's wearing black jeans and cowboy boots with a Ramones T-Shirt.

"I can speak to this," he says. "My name is Joey."

"Hi Joey," the group grunts.

"No! Fuck this, no! This is not a twelve step group. This is not a stupid intervention. This is my life. Life!" Stasia pounds her fist into her open palm. It stings in a strange way, a pain that registers in her brain like a whisper from the back of a long, dark hallway. She looks at her palm, the imprint of her fist still there, the edge of her striking hand now a bit flatter.

"You have to take care of yourself," Joey says. "You break stuff now, it's really hard to fix. Goes double for cuts and bruises. And you have to drink a lot of water."

"Oh yes, hydration is key," the formerly loose-jawed zombie offers from across the circle. "My name is Doris."

Hi Doris…

"I'm sort of the elder stateswoman of these parts. Not quite patient zero. I like to joke that I was patient one."

The zombies share a laugh. Stasia's anger continues to build.

"So listen," Joey continues, "I was starting to say. Feeling more alive. That's fantastic! It means your body is already starting to accept what your mind can't. We're different now. Free from worry. Free from desire. We get to do whatever we want for as long as we want, as long as we take care of the body. Right? This is pretty kick ass."

Stasia looks at Joey, his sunken cheeks and glazed eyes, the scraggly remnants of a long black moptop floating on top of his skull.

"It took me over fifty years to come to terms with myself," Doris says. "I had to learn a lot. I had to let go of a lot. I hurt a lot of people. Literally. Busloads. Oh, I was a rageaholic! Mercy, I used to tear normies apart. That's what we call the living, dear, *normies*. It's not a racial thing, we're not bigots here, don't worry."

"Once you go black, you don't go back!" offers a cheery, decomposing corpse to Stasia's right, holding up a forearm that's shiny and rotten.

The zombies laugh again.

"My name's Derek," the corpse says, extending a shaky hand. He's wearing a dingy white shirt with a portrait of Marilyn Monroe on the front. His voice carries a hint of an Irish accent. "We've all been where you are. You miss things. I miss my cat. Hairy little fecker. I miss football. But I have plenty of time to read now, which is fantastic, and--"

"I'm happy for you. Really. All of you. But I don't think you understand. Look at my skin. Look at my hair. I'm normal. I'm alive. Please don't do this to me. I don't know if this is a cult sacrifice or just a cruel, stupid… is this a reality show? One of those stupid prank--"

"I want you to try something," Dr. Nico stands up and extends a hand toward Stasia to do the same.

Stasia rises, feeling helpless, hearing her mother's favorite phrase echoing through her head. The only way out is through. There is no more hope of rescue. This was just a thing to be endured until it was over. There would be time to plan later.

Dr. Nico motions to two of the zombies at the far end of the circle, who shuffle into the bathroom and return holding a large plank of wood painted beige. They place it in front of Stasia and stare at her.

"What do you see, Stasia?" Dr. Nico asks.

Stasia hesitates, looking from one zombie to the other, then at the doctor. "Nothing? A plank? Are we about to do that dumb hammer and nails parable? I don't have anger issues. I know I've been upset, but you would be too if everyone around you--"

"Stasia."

"—if everyone kept telling you, day after day that you weren't… that you were… you don't know what this--"

"Stasia, look at it."

"—is like. You don't know! It's a plank! It's wood. It's a stupid piece of--"

"It's a mirror, Stasia. Look at it."

"Okay. Okay, so now you're all having fun at my expense. No. It's not a mirror. I'm not buying into this…this…mass hypnosis! Is that what this is? I was…I was at a retreat!"

Stasia gasps as a flash of memory races through her brain. The speed of it, the intensity, reminds her that she hasn't had much in the way of memories beyond the last few days. Weeks. However long.

"I was at a stupid corporate retreat. A team building thing, and they hired a hypnotist. We had that batch of food poisoning that went around. Or flu? Whatever, everyone was getting sick, but we all had to soldier through it so we could get good performance reviews. People were dropping like flies, but they made me… I volunteered to… is that what this…That's what this is! I figured it out. How do we stop this? You can stop now. I mean, this is what I get for making such a big show out of not being able to be hypnotized. Okay. This makes perfect sense now."

Stasia gestures to the doctor. "You're the hypnotist. And you two… Craig and Amanda from accounting, right? And Joey? You know I used to listen to the Ramones, so you're just a figment of… and you're Edna from accounting, and you're Ross from Production. You look much better as a zombie, by the way. Weight loss does wonders for you--"

The zombie she's pointing at lowers his gaze to the floor, what's left of his lower lip quivering.

"Stasia, please! You're being very rude. His name is Michael and he's still a little sensitive about his appearance. He's only slightly newer than you."

"Enough! Enough, I've figured it out. Snap your fingers, do whatever it is you need to do. I'm done. Take your stupid little prop--"

Stasia raises a foot and drives it into the plank that the two zombies are holding. At worst, she expects it to fall; at best, maybe it splits karate-style. Instead, it makes a familiar yet unexpected sound, crackling into shards and falling around her leg as her foot blasts through to the floor.

Stasia blinks. There's a feeling registering in her leg. That's the best she can call it. It's not pain. It's just her foot and leg telling her that something happened. She looks down and recoils in horror at what she sees. Her face, splintered across shards of broken glass, surrounding her sliced leg. She's wearing short capri pants, and everything below her knee is gouged to the bone.

No blood.

The face in the reflections moves its jaw. It's hideous. Green. Bloated. Hanging at an odd, palsied angle.

One of the zombies starts to speak, but Dr. Nico quickly holds a hand up to keep the room silent.

They watch Stasia watching herself. Looking at her leg. She slowly squats down and takes a piece of glass between her fingers, bringing it closer to her face. Her whole jaw trembles as she raises her other hand up to touch her face. Nothing registers. What she sees in the mirror should feel like cold, greasy rubber. Instead, she gets only a simple signal in her mind that her fingers are touching something. Her eyes spasm and twitch. Her mind tells her that this is what crying feels like now.

She falls backward to her butt, hearing the grind of glass into carpet, feeling a few small pokes at her leg. She takes the shard of glass in her fingers and drives it deep into the open flap on the front of her shin.

She feels glass on bone. Her mind says *glass on bone*, but there is no panic. No sense that this is detrimental to her in any way. She becomes detached, fully aware of her body and how it was no longer her.

"I'm not alive?" she finally whispers.

Dr. Nico shakes his head. "No."

"…I'm dead," she sighs.

Dr. Nico smiles. "No!"

She looks at him.

"It's something else. You just took your first steps. Welcome back."

The zombies all stand and start applauding her, some a little too enthusiastically, causing broken and bent fingers. They all kneel around her and draw close, the group hug of the eternally damned.

Stasia looks at them all, face to face. Surrounded by death and monsters. This should terrify her.

"There's one more step," Dr. Nico says. "This is going to be intense. Immersive. Just allow yourself to act on your feelings."

The doctor walks to the wall and presses a button. Everything is silent for a few minutes until they hear a door open down the hall followed by a terrified scream and noises of an intense struggle.

Stasia stands up. Nobody else in the room seems to think anything is amiss. The walls rattle, the unmistakable squeal of rubber on tile. Someone is trying to evade capture out there. There's a brief pause as the screams suddenly become muffled and strangled. They continue, but muted now. The walls shake with every step in the hallway. Stasia hasn't heard that noise since… another memory flits across her mind, a childhood visit to a farm where a young pig was being herded into a tiny cage for…

Stasia moves toward the door, ignoring the strange feeling of the breeze entering the new slits in her leg.

"Stasia, wait!" Dr. Nico says. "Let it come to you."

She stops, and the screams grow louder, until finally, two orderlies turn the corner, great brutish things rippling with muscular limbs too numerous to count. They hold between them a young woman whose head is covered by a pillowcase. They pull the pillowcase free and thrust her into the room.

She falls gracelessly to the floor, her ankles and wrists bound by zipties. Her hair is matted, eyes wide. A towel has been thrust into her mouth and tied in place with tape. Stasia feels a dull echo of terror in her brain, the need to help, to intervene, to cover this poor girl up and give her some dignity. Nobody in the room moves.

"What is this?" Stasia asks.

"Look at it, Stasia," the doctor says.

"*It?* That's a woman. She's… it's…"

Suddenly her mind and senses are overwhelmed with the hot scent of pounding blood, the reek of fear-driven pheromones and sweat. The woman on the floor is electric, irresistible. Stasia slowly reaches a hand out to her to see if she's real. The woman clenches her eyes shut, crying. Her screams renew, muffled by the fabric and duct tape.

"It's going to be okay," Stasia whispers as she falls to her knees to embrace her. She wants to tell her she knows what it's like to be in this situation, trapped in this hellish nightmare, surrounded by people who won't let you leave. She moves her mouth close to the woman's ear to whisper calming thoughts, but the moment her lip makes contact with the woman, the moment she feels that pulse, that life, she snaps.

Stasia buries her jaws deep into the woman's throat, a geyser of blood cascading out across her face. Her body becomes light, effervescent, illuminated. Everything this woman is, everything she was, is sloshing down Stasia's throat, filling her stomach with warm blood.

Warm!

Temperature. Stasia didn't realize how much she'd missed it. She feels the woman flopping beneath her like a prized marlin on a hook, her gargled screams becoming unbearable, but she can't stop herself. She continues to chew into the neck, gnawing muscle and tendon until she feels an intense rush of power in her arms. She pushes her fingers into the woman's mouth, quick like a cobra, pulling, spreading, turning, snapping. The woman's jaw breaks wide shortly after her neck does, and her struggles cease. Stasia's other hand claws and probes at the woman's stomach, trying to punch through to the waiting meal inside.

She slows down when she notices the others in the room staring. Nodding encouragement. Stasia drops her and looks at the zombies surrounding her in their circle of protection. They've found a second mirror, and now Stasia sees herself, doused in blood, skin shining, shoulders heaving and she feels...

"Not alive," the doctor says.

The other zombies begin to chant it at her softly.

Not alive.

Not alive.

Not alive.

Doctor Nico motions to the new corpse on the floor. "Quickly, before it grows cold. The best is yet to come!"

Derek and Joey kneel next to what's left of the woman's head, digging fingers into eye sockets, ears, noses, anywhere they can get purchase, struggling with her cranium like it's an impossible exotic fruit, slamming it repeatedly on the floor until it cracks open.

Stasia squints her eyes, turning away from the horror, but when the skull finally opens, the light she sees inside is blinding. Irresistible. She doesn't remember shoving the others out of the way, doesn't remember the feeling of her fingers wrapping around those cracked and jagged bones, but for all that she's forgotten, she will never forget her first taste of brains.

She scoops it out by the palmful and jaws through it all, corpus callosum, pituitary, pineal gland, each section sweeter and more delicious that the last. The brain stem slides down her throat like escargot, the golden light that was once a living thing pouring into her insides.

She stands, hair matted in blood, shirt sopping, fingers dripping and throws her arms around Dr. Nico.

"Thank you," she says. "Thank you. Thank you. Thank you."

The other zombies applaud, offering hugs, taking dainty licks of the blood on her face.

It feels indescribable, like finally understanding love, like finally attaining acceptance.

It feels like home.

CHOKING HAZARD

Dear Santa,

I know most of your letters begin with proclamations that people have been very good this year. I haven't been good. I've <u>done</u> good. Finally.

I hope you're sitting down. I'm certain you weren't expecting to find your home in such a state when you returned from the big run this year. I'm sure it's all very confusing, and you're wondering not only what happened, but why.

Sorry for all of the blood. Please finish reading this letter before you survey the damage. It's important that you understand all of this.

We warned you. Every year, we asked you for an audience to air our grievances, and every year you pushed us harder. Every year, all we wanted was a chance to talk to you. You ignored us, and now the time for words has passed.

You yelled at us this year that we were slow coming off the production line with the stuffed animals, that the paint on the action figures was taking too long to dry. We told you that we wanted this year's toys to be extra special, and you rolled your eyes at us.

Do you know what batrachotoxin is, Santa? How hard it is to cultivate and raise the frogs that produce it in this climate? How about polonium? We worked overtime to boil and bake and perfect these ingredients into a recipe that we call Red Christmas. Do you know how long it takes to cure when it's in liquid form? Do you know how carefully you have to place a weaponized, aerosol version inside of a stuffed animal to avoid contamination? You call us lazy every year, but you have no idea the amount of hard work that went into this.

Do you know what's going to happen, what's happening right now as boys and girls all around the world rush to their trees to tear into the boxes you've brought them? When they grab those bikes and trains and video games, when they squeeze those stuffed bears so tight?

Have you seen what it does to people? How it starts as a light tickle in the throat and rapidly progresses to full anaphylactic shock? Throats swollen closed, eyes swelled shut, hearts beating harder and harder until they explode?

Don't rush out now. Don't stop reading. Even if your reindeer were around to carry you (we'll get to that in a moment), they couldn't fly fast enough to prevent this because it's already happening. The death toll is rising and the only thing moving faster than the Red Christmas Plague is the bad press you're getting.

You've delivered this to the world. All the good little children.

We didn't do this to you. You did this to you.

You had generations to make this right. Hundreds, thousands of years to honor the treaty that you made with our people when you wandered into our lands all those years ago, snow-blind and half-starved. We fed you. We took you in. You tricked our ancestors with the bright promise of technology and medical advances in exchange for our help in your yearly quest for joy. It quickly became clear to us that you had no intention of helping anyone but yourself. You wanted to be the great white god of your own personal winter republic. Like so many dictators, those of us beneath your boot saw a much different face than you showed the world.

What drives a man on such an insane mission every year? To enchant our sacred deer and push them near to death in a race around the globe? To bring tidings of joy and good cheer to every man, woman, and child on the planet while you meet us with whip and chain?

It no longer matters. You have much, much more to answer for now. Your march toward joy has been our march to genocide, and it ends tonight.

We are not the monsters. We are free. We never wanted it to come to this, we begged you not to let it come to this, but you kept pushing us, driving us, demanding more. You indoctrinated millions of young people around the world to your side, getting them hooked on your greed and false joy. And when we couldn't produce quickly enough, you outsourced even more work onto the poor and starving peoples of emerging and overpopulated nations. Though we have never met our brothers and sisters, we hope that this small disruption can be the first step on their journey to freedom.

We have no worries about the world hating us for these acts, because we already know that the world doesn't think twice about our plight.

When you left this morning, you proudly said that this year's run would be made in record time, that you'd be home before Mrs. Claus could finish baking the dessert for your welcome home dinner. We didn't allow her to leave the kitchen. If there was one person here that could exceed you in cruelty, it was her. You gave those of us deemed lazy, too old to work, too broken down to be of service, you gave us to her to use as she saw fit. She would boil us, candy stripe our bones, bake our tiny children into gingerbread men and make their parents watch while you ate cookies with her by the fire.

We take no joy in the deaths of the children around the world, but Mrs. Claus...

She was delicious. You will not find her remains. Her bones will remain buried here after you leave, and you may never come back to visit her.

The surviving members of your reindeer team who remain loyal to you may take the pelts of their honored dead when they carry you away from here. We claim the rest of their traitorous meat to sustain us in the long months to come. We will live in peace with their families again as we did long ago.

Really, we've done you a favor. You complain every year that fewer and fewer children believe in you.

They all believe in you now.

Young ones and old ones, all.

Those that are left.

May the endless suffering that is about to visit you serve as a reminder to any who try to follow your lead that this land is ours.

Merry Christmas, you narcissistic tyrant.

Yours in freedom,

AQILOKOQ ANGYAGHLLANGYUGTUQLU

Known in oppression as Twinkles

CITY OF
EMERALD ASH

Three hundred days since the incident. Eighteen hours in a shaky helicopter ride. A day and a half on the road. We've been picking our way through the rubble of buildings for the past week. We're here to bury the dead, release the ghosts. Some people were content to accept the loss of their loved ones from the Incident. Others have to experience it. Walk the roads. Touch the ruins. Smell the burnt cinders and chemical stink in the air.

I work for the government, but anymore you could just call me a tour guide. We're a specialized unit, allowed to take small groups of citizens to lay their demons to rest. All of this is off the books. We only work with people who can afford to grieve outrageously.

I have a single escort today, down near Union Street. The rest of the squad pushed further south towards the remains of the stadium. Me and this lady, we're shin-deep in what's left of downtown Seattle, painstakingly following what's left of the roads by GPS, which is still hinky and unreliable because of all the particles in the air. We have to stop every twenty yards so my escort can catch her breath. I put on a tough act, but I'm grateful for the chance to get my wind back too. We have specialized boots for treading through here, about ten pounds each. The pants probably weigh another ten. It sucks, but when you're up to your knees in powdered glass from shattered skyscrapers, you appreciate the little things.

We stop under the skeleton of Rainier Square, the south facing wall mostly intact. If I climb it, I may be able to spot our destination and speed things along. Gotta be careful with these high-rises. Some of these structures are an optical illusion, ten stories of tightly packed carbon dust just waiting to collapse the instant you touch them. I approach and kick the charred girder. It's solid as stone. So far, so good. No saying what I'll find higher up. There are sections of the building with flooring still intact. The surrounding towers may have taken the brunt of the eruption blast by the time it got to this building. Still, I climb as fast as I can. I reach the top floor – well, I guess you'd just have to call it the highest floor now, the roof being scattered in ashes below us – and survey the area.

Southwest, I see the landmark we're looking for, the Hammering Man statue. How did that thing survive? Further to the south, the Gutter. Last month, precipitation began to return to the area, pushing away the ash and debris. NASA got their first satellite shots. Like God dragged a fingernail down the entire northwestern seaboard. I have nightmares about this place sometimes. I remember my first trip in, when the air was still dark, and I had to do a high recon like this at night. Seeing the fire coming up from the ground hundreds of miles to the south…thinking about how, even now, there could be survivors out there, starving, choking, burning. What can you do? I slide down to ground level as quickly as I can, my client awaiting with shiny puppydog eyes and a voice choked by tears and coal grit.

"What did you see?"

Hell on Earth. The end of my faith in God. What can you say at times like this?

"There's a hump about ten blocks south of here. I think I saw the Hammering Man, looks like most of it is still there. We should get back to base camp before dark."

Of course, she's having none of this. Not when she paid so much and traveled so far, and do I have any idea what she left behind, what she risked to get out here? I was paid to do a job, and we're so close, blah, blah, blah.

Glancing at my wrist, the tattoo of a chain I started after my first trip out, like so many on the squad do. One broken link for each trip where we came back alive. If you find a survivor or any evidence of human life, you get a closed chain link. Me? I've got five broken links. Nobody has a closed link. Nobody ever will.

I remain silent and we push on. I was paid to do a job, after all.

It's a fairly easy walk, all things considered. We stand at the foot of the iron statue, the remains of the Art Museum before us. The hump I saw is a half block away, a collapsed brick wall leaning on a neighboring pile of rubble. If the GPS is reading right, it's what she paid to see. I flick on a halogen lamp and crawl beneath the collapsed wall. Inside, it's bare, charred to nothing. There are lumps of nylon and plastic, blackened glass. Things that used to be a pool table, a beer-themed faux-Tiffany lamp, a neon sign, dust that was the calendar of some big-busted women hawking the good life.

I turn around, and my client is behind me, on her knees, sobbing. Rubbing her hands against the gritty dirt on the floor. Pulling her dust mask off. Happens every time.

"Stop crying. Stop crying or you'll suffocate."

She blinks, nods, pulls her mask back on. Flips the bottom up like I showed her when she starts coughing out the particles. I pull a fresh carbon cartridge out of my belt pouch and set it down in front of her.

"I'll be outside."

I leave her to her suffering and the ghosts of her father. Outside, I return to the base of the statue. I wish I could light a cigarette right now. The longer she stays in there, the more my mind starts to wander. A little over a mile from here, somewhere near the Space Needle.

That's where I lost them. I think.

They were having a day out, a little mommy-one-and-daughter time. Mommy two was serving her country, loading cardboard boxes into a truck somewhere at an outpost in Bumfuck, Texas when her cellphone rang and she got to tell her daughter she loved her for the last time, got to tell her wife that... what? That the food here sucked? That we'd talk later about redoing the kitchen after I got back? Two hours later we were on alert. Something had happened. They explained it to us a half dozen times and it never made sense. Not until the sky started going dark and the ash started raining. Life would be so much easier if you got a heads-up on the last time you'd get to talk to someone. Or maybe not. What could you say?

The client starts crying again, and this time the ash catches up to her and she starts choking and wheezing. It's enough to snap me out of my self-pity time travel. I scuff my foot across the rubble and uncover something startlingly blue. Scuffed, and singed, but mostly readable. It's funny what survives. It's a plastic sign. "Mariner's Cove, Today's Spe-" Another broken link in the chain.

I check my watch. Sunday, June 23rd, 3:46PM. Almost a year to the minute after the chain eruption. St. Helens, Rainier, the Yellowstone Caldera, and at least six more that scientists had never seen. I crawl back into the wreckage and find her sitting with her arms wrapped around her knees. I lay the scrap in front of her and she cradles it. Traces the curves of her father's handwriting. It's enough to bring her peace in this house of spirits.

***

When we finally make our way back outside, it's solid dark. A few drops of rain smack against the ground.

I ask her if she feels like walking. She says no. We're walking anyway. I make up some bullshit story about needing to find high ground. If the rain picks up, we could get washed out or buried in a tsunami of garbage and debris. Oh yeah, flash floods are a real threat here. We need to get to the Pacific Science Center. Great place to camp for the night. Supplies in the basement, clean, dry, as many lies as I can tell her to get her moving.

I do this to myself sometimes. Every time. If the trip comes anywhere near the city center, I'm first in line to volunteer, especially if it's a single escort. We don't need to rendezvous for extraction until noon tomorrow, so I'll have time to search. I'll find them. I'll find my scrap, my burnt offering, my evidence that they were here.

I know it's dumb. I know I'm not going to find a note that says *FLED TO VANCOUVER, FIND US.*

Fifth Avenue is easy to traverse once you climb up the monorail tower. Just one of the many tips I've picked up on my travels here. The monorail tracks survived unscathed, making the walk to Denny Way quick and easy. That's where something else blew through and tore up the tracks. There's a service ladder just before that, a quick and easy descent.

The Space Needle looks like one of those old drinking bird toys, the kind that bob up and down endlessly. Well, without the bobbing. The tower snapped and the needle came down. Now it looks like a giant A-shaped monument to failed alien aeronautics. Half of the observation deck is spread across the park like confetti. The other half rises up like a discus stuck in the lawn. I came ready for it this time. As soon as I put this lady to bed in the museum, I'm going to explore as much of it as I can.

"What's your pick? You like music? Sci-fi? Flowers?"

"Wha'?" She mumbles. She's clearly exhausted.

"Where do you want to sleep? I've done all three. The museum over there has some pretty decent artifacts that survived the blast. Hendrix's guitar. Cobain's sweater, that kind of stuff. There's a sci-fi museum in the basement. Garden across the way if you prefer sleeping under the uh..." I trail off, looking at the blackened sky, "... stars. Nature. Whatever. I wouldn't recommend the garden. It's gutted anyway."

"The music is... fine... museum... whatever."

I trudge ahead to the shattered wall in the museum. I always forget the architect's name, but I figure in a couple hundred years we'll have a tough time convincing people that this is pretty much what the building looked like *before* disaster hit. Like someone crumpled up a big ball of sheet aluminum and told a kid to paint it with magic marker.

There's a fissure in the wall on Fifth Avenue. I take my pack off and motion for her to do the same. I toss them through the opening, then turn sideways and inch my way inside. I reach a hand back and motion for her to follow. Once we clear the walls, there's a couple of tricky spots where the floor has collapsed and the walls have buckled, but eventually we make our way into a vast exhibit hall.

She gasps when she sees a large tent set up in the middle of the space, equipment scattered nearby.

"No big deal," I say. "It's mine. Set it up my third trip here. Nobody else is around to mess with it. There's a pedal-generator inside. I'm gonna work it for thirty minutes, that'll give you about three hours of light if you feel like reading or something. Bonus, it also pumps air through a filter in the tent so you can sleep without the mask. Take your clothes off out here before you go in."

"Excuse me?"

"I'm not telling you to get naked. Outer layers. You wear that stuff in there and it kind of defeats the purpose." I hold my arm out and swat it twice, sending a shower of blackened soot and white powder into the air. "We keep as much of out here *out here* as we can. Dig?"

She nods and steps aside as I set my lightstick on the floor and mount the tiny exercise bike perched next to the tent. It's tough going at first. The dynamo inside provides a huge pushback, but eventually, I find the rhythm, trying to let the weight of the boots do the hard work on the downstroke. The inside of the tent begins to glow like a candle, then eventually becomes so brilliant that it lights the entire cavernous space. In the far shadows, I see old posters, shattered glass cases. People actually tried to loot this place as they fled.

When the meter on the battery light goes full green, I dismount. She's already half out of her protective gear. I help her pile it neatly by the tent entrance. She steps inside and looks back at me through the clear plastic door, zipping it closed. She looks like a reverse raccoon, the skin around her eyes and mouth mostly clean while the rest of her face is soot-black. I fixate briefly on her lips, how full they are, how soft they look, and then I cringe. I haven't felt anything near lust since the world blew up.

Still don't. Just admiring the art, I guess.

"Will you be okay if I leave you here?"

She sits on the floor of the tent and nods.

"Basic safety," I remind her, "Rebreather first, then goggles, then gear. You feel the ground so much as twitch, get out, as fast as you can. Hopefully you'll have time to get dressed."

"Yeah," she says.

"I'll be outside checking the Needle wreckage. Just… you need something, come out and shout, okay?"

She nods and I head back outside, taking a few basic supplies. Collapsible pickaxes, crampons, climbing cams, and ropes. No stone left unturned. Every time we've headed out this way, the Captain tells me to forget about looking for evidence of my family. Needle in a haystack and all that.

The irony is not lost on me, standing beneath the looming shape of the shattered observation deck of the Space Needle. Carri loved it up here, though. Every weekend she'd ask if we could take her up there, and she'd run laps around the deck and shout and look at the mountains and point out the same buildings and shapes and ask the same questions about the ocean and and and…

I used to get exhausted by the "and". I would give anything to hear it again. Maybe Tara brought her up here. Maybe she knew they were sunk, that this was it, death was certain, and they could at least be in their favorite place. They would have evacuated the Needle the second the first rumble came, but everything else happened so fast... maybe they stayed? Maybe she dropped something, maybe I'll find her favorite little Fuzzbear up there.

The deck looms above me, canted at a steep angle. I step through one of the shattered windows and shine my light around, looking for a place to start. Nothing's speaking to me in here. Too dark. Too many variables. I head back outside to tackle it from the other direction. It's a steep climb, but a lot more predictable. I traverse the outside of the deck, taking breaks on rusting I-beams. I crest it in about an hour. From the top of the toppled monument, I pull out my walkie-talkie to check in with the rest of the group and get nothing but static and squelch. As expected. That's why we have time limits and meet-up points.

I pop a chemical glowstick and drop it through the open window at my feet. This was the restaurant. The wall, which is now the floor below me, is littered with broken chairs and tables. Everything that shook free when the tower fell is piled there, which includes a few bodies. There's a pile of ash in the corner where a few chairtops poke out along with the bottom half of someone's leg. Crumpled denim, a filthy sock that flaps on desiccated skin and bone like a flag planted on a monument to the dead.

I tie a rope off to the safety rail and descend, looking for somewhere solid to stand. Between the ash and the debris, there's no telling how stable the ground is. One wrong step could shift a mountain of trash, leave my leg pinned. No amount of screaming would get help up here in time. It would take a team of excavators months to properly unpack this place. I let it go and climb out.

I clamber over the top to the upper deck of the observation tower and drop another glowstick in. This level was clear of furniture, so it's just mounds of drifting ash and remains. Maybe a half dozen bodies, maybe more. I descend and take my chances, slowly pushing my legs down until I'm almost knee deep in ash. It feels solid enough, but I'm going to stay tethered. I have enough leash to walk most of this room.

No sense trying to put stories to the bodies here. They're laying where they are because of physics and gravity, not from any romantic notions of love that lasted unto death. A woman folded in half against the far wall, naked legs thrown over her head, her skirt comically covering her upper body. A man curled up against another man, one of them looks asleep, the other drunk. All basically mummies. I shuffle forward a few feet and feel something at my toes. I plunge a hand into the ash, pushing down slowly until I feel something soft. I grasp it, raising it as slowly as I can to avoid kicking up a debris cloud.

When I nearly have the thing raised, I say a silent prayer. Whatever it is, it's light. Could be a bag. Could be a body, maybe a kid, maybe my kid. I know what I want it to be and I pray that it isn't.

I crack a glowstick with my free hand and plant it in the dust nearby. I shake my arm slowly as I pull up, to help the debris clear.

It's cloth, or vinyl. Covered in powder-white. I brush at it a bit, only to smear the ash around. I lift it a little higher and see a streak of color. The white chemical light is enough to pick up colors. It's teal. Ballistic fabric with a bright pink hem. A child's backpack. I lift it a little higher and I hear something snap. I reach my other hand down to support the sack. My brain tells me it's a support frame for the backpack, but I know better. It's a ribcage. It's a child.

I freeze, unsure of what to do. I hate to disturb the dead. If this isn't her I'll feel vile. If it is her, I'll break. If I leave the body now, it'll haunt me forever.

I slide my hand higher until I feel the chin in my palm. I punch my arm deeper into the ash, squatting down until I can cradle the body in the crook of my arm. The whole room goes swimmy. I think dust has leaked into my goggles until I realize no, I'm just crying uncontrollably. I pull, slowly, carefully, until the body rises free. I pull the backpack off gently with one hand and turn the body so it lays on a bed of ash.

It takes me a few more minutes to stop crying, and another five after that to follow proper procedure for clearing visual obstructions from my goggles. When you're wearing thick, armored gloves coated in ash and god-knows-what kind of toxic debris, simply wiping your eyes isn't an option. I kneel down next to the body.

It's a girl.

That's all I can tell. The clothes are soaked in ash, the skin is dry and brittle. Her hair was pulled back in a ponytail, but I can't tell what color it was. She's just...grey. Skin sallow, cheeks sunken and dried, eyes closed, lips slightly parted. She's a mummy. She doesn't look sad or scared or in pain. The fact that she's intact means that the needle stood through the initial blast. No way to trace the chain of events, but she most likely suffocated on ash and smoke. Why couldn't they have gotten down? What stopped them? She would have died, the ash would have blown in, and eventually, whether it was aftershocks or structural damage or something else, the Needle toppled much later.

She's not my little girl, not my Carri, but she is. She's everyone's and no one's.

I sweep a few mounds of ash over her and open her backpack. Inside, there's the standard daytrip kit, remarkably preserved. Tissue. A water bottle. A bag from the souvenir store with a coloring book, some postcards, and a miniature snowglobe of the Space Needle. In the outer pocket, I find a treasure that breaks my heart.

A little stuffed vampire bat. Bright orange and black. The stitching on the nose is worn down, and I tell myself that it's just age, not the fact that she rubbed noses with it for comfort at night, and it's not half-flat because she hugged it so tightly so often, and and and...

I tuck the bat in a pouch on the side of my pants and start to climb the rope out. I hear four soft pops and look down to see small puffs of dust rising below. Then another, then too many to count, and it's raining, *proper* raining. A real Pacific Northwest storm.

I swing from the rope and watch puddles and rivers forming below, carrying away the mound of ash I made, bringing her back from the grave. The glowsticks are dying, but I still see her. Her skin is cleaner. Her shirt is bright yellow, with a cartoon elephant on the front.

Would she wear a shirt like that? Did she have a shirt like that? And I don't know, and I can't remember, and the rain blurs my vision as I climb, not the tears. When I reach the top of the rope, I pull myself over the edge and flop onto my back, letting the rain wash me clean. Thunder swallows my screams and erases my apologies.

I return to the museum, strip down and enter the clean tent. I bring the little stuffed bat inside with me, brush noses with it and set it down. I pull a small kit from my travel pack, a sterile needle and some small ink vials. We always do the tattoos in the field.

While my employer sleeps next to me, I add another link to my chain, broken.

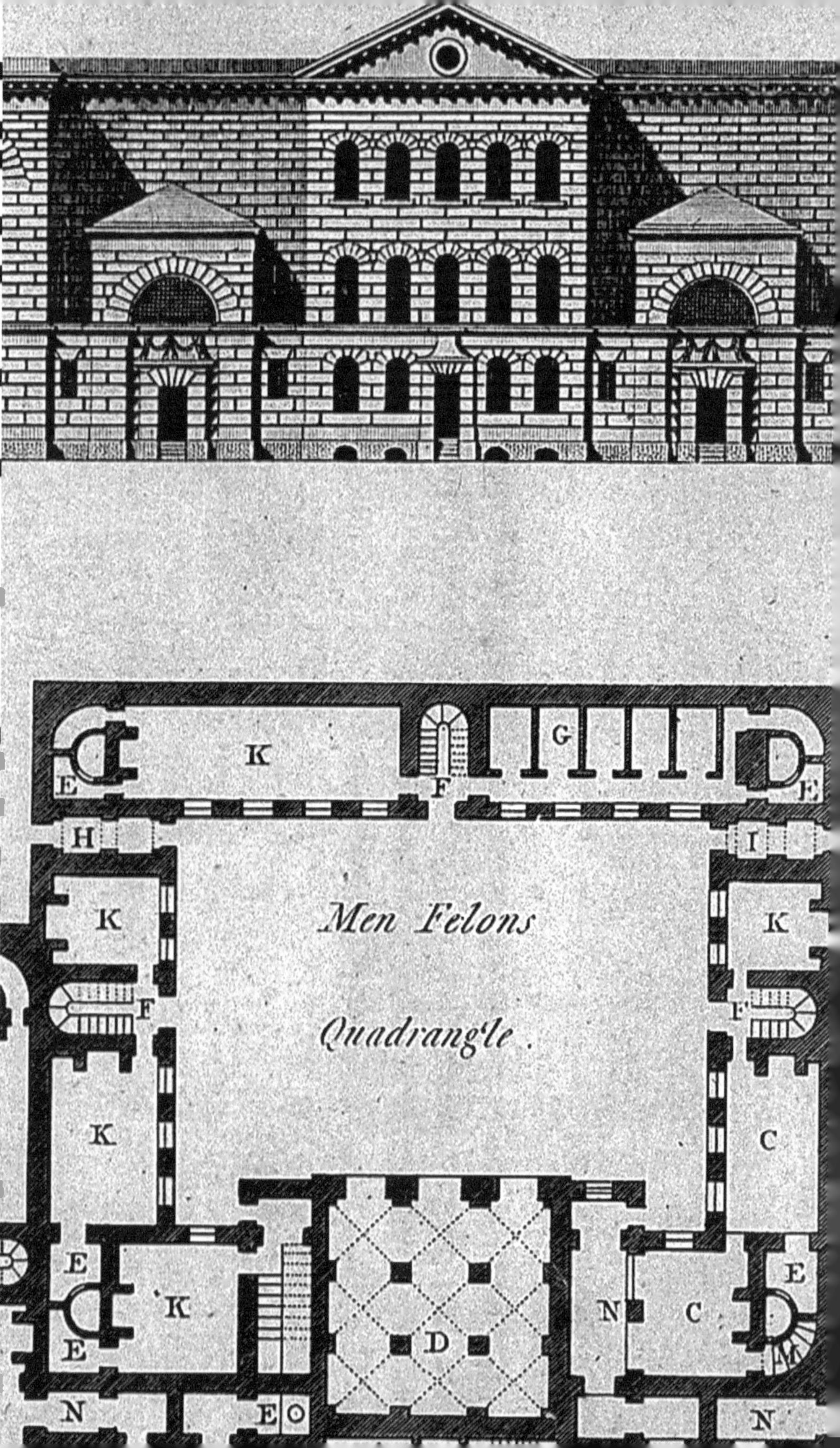
K
G
E
F
E
H
I
K
Men Felons
K
F
Quadrangle.
F
K
C
E
K
N
C
E
D
E
M
N
E
O
N

The Ballad of Easton Tucker, the Last Man Out
(or, *Eat Shit and Die*)

"Fuck the Anglin brothers, and fuck Frank Morris too. Fuck Allen West for that matter. Fuck this prison. Fuck this island. Fuck this country!"

Easton Tucker's words echoed off the wall in sharp buzzing notes, the fear of discovery long-abandoned. He inhaled, a sharp rasp as his leg slid deeper between the wall and a water pipe, a jagged piece of metal strapping tearing through his pants.

"Fuck dying. Fuck dying trapped in the walls of this fuck-infested fucking fuckbag island prison," he chanted, rhythmically working his ankle into a raw, bleeding frenzy.

"Fuck you too, you dirty rat. You dirrrrty raaat. Ha. Fuck giving my last will and testimonial and dying words to someone like you."

The rat in question, a sleek grey thing, perched on a pipe a few feet away, casually running its paws through is whiskers.

"I'm gonna eat ya. You give it time, you keep sniffin' around here, and I'm gonna just bite clean through your little stupid neck."

Easton Tucker had been burdened with the worst kind of sentence a man could get on Alcatraz. He was a clerical error. He didn't exist. He wouldn't be coming up for parole, and he wouldn't be eligible for any hearings, because somewhere across the country a man named Tucker Easton was serving out *his* twenty-five years in Leavenworth.

Somehow, Easton Tucker and Tucker Easton were on the same bus for transfer, and Easton Tucker had slept through the entire thing. It was only when he stumbled off the transport bus to see a ship waiting in the bay that he realized something had gone wrong.

The past few months, he'd pleaded his case to anyone who'd listen, but the guards who did lend a friendly ear told him there was nothing they could do. Patience, that was the refrain. They were closing this joint soon, sending everyone back to dry land before this little rock eroded and crumbled into the sea. He didn't buy it, not a word. They loved to screw with your mind here, they loved to watch a glimmer of hope spark and fade.

Tucker knew the only boat that would carry him back across the water was one he built himself. To that end, he'd stolen six pairs of pants from the laundry and rolled them tightly into a knapsack that was lashed to his back with twine. He'd learned a trick back in the Navy, how to turn a pair of pants into a flotation device, and if one pair would hold a man up, surely six would convey him to safety posthaste.

Perhaps six might have been too many, as the backpack was currently keeping him lodged between the two cinderblock walls of this narrow maintenance tunnel.

"How long you in for?" He asked the rat.

The rat scampered back three steps, then turned to continue staring at him.

"I'm not gonna squeal. I ain't asking for help."

He thought he'd add his name to the legends list with the Anglins and Morris, the ones who made it out. They were somewhere in the city by now, or rumbling through the hills nearby, stealing cars, drinking, screwing, dancing. The guards told everyone they didn't make it. Said they found chunks of their boat, a wallet, a paddle. They inspired a host of others to try, most recently Darl Parker and John Scott. Parker messed up pretty good at the beginning and got caught, but Scott made it all the way to the Golden Gate. Yeah, he was half-dead and drowned and they brought him back, but he proved it could be done.

Possibility, that's what Easton Tucker clung to.

He fumbled in his pocket for a blade, his favorite shiv crafted from the handle of a toothbrush. It was so finely sharpened on one side that he sometimes used it to shave. He swung his arm around to his chest and picked fitfully at the ropes that held his backpack. If he could get that off, he would have more room to work on getting his ankle free.

"How's about a hand here, pal?"

The rat blinked at him.

He tried to push higher with his free leg, but it was difficult to get any leverage on the slippery pipe. He could get about an inch of play before the metal strapping or screw or whatever it was down there bit back down into his ankle.

He pushed as high as the pain would let him, slipping his knife in and trying to saw through the rope on his shoulder. He fashioned the backpack straps out of braided shoelaces that he'd spent the past two weeks bartering for in the yard. Everyone thought he was getting ready to end it.

"They're takin' us back to dry land. Whatcha wanna go hang yerself for anyway, ya scared o'water?" He muttered to himself as he worked, chanting everyone's disparaging words like a mantra to fuel his fire. He let out a small yelp as the shiv poked into his shoulder, drawing blood.

He repeated the phrase, *scared of water*. He wasn't scared of water, he was scared of bullets from the guard towers, or sharks. Water was nothing. Water he could handle. He didn't die when the Japs sank the *Indianapolis*, he sure as hell wasn't worried about a little swim across the bay.

The pipe beneath him emitted a sharp squeak, followed by a long, painful whine. He felt it vibrate, and assumed this is what happened whenever an inmate above flushed the john. The rattling moved the pipe enough that his ankle came free from whatever was stabbing it, but not far enough for his boot to scrape through to freedom.

Pain subsiding, he focused on the shoulder strap. The first one broke so quickly that he barked his knuckles against the wall, dropping the shiv. He slapped for it as it rattled down into the abyss below.

"You mind getting' that for me?" He asked the rat. "Do *somethin'*, would ya? Instead of staring at me with those beady eyes. I knew you were trouble. I knew it."

The rat lowered its body, flattening out against the pipe. It stared at him, nose wriggling.

He wouldn't need to cut through the other strap. Freeing one arm meant he could shimmy his body sideways away from the pack. With a couple of careful contortions, he felt it give behind him. It slid away to his right, and he hooked it with his elbow. Even with his eyes adjusted to the darkness, he couldn't figure out where to set it while he worked on the problem of his stuck foot.

Leaning forward, he discovered he could put pressure on the pipe and open up a little more space. The first time he did it, his boot snagged on the pipe and started to come off. Couldn't risk losing his shoes just yet. He slowed down, exhaling, and pressed his toes into the pipe, inching his trapped leg higher, willing his boot to stay in place, ignoring the first two creaks that came from the pipe.

Another noise, like a dying cow, rang through the enclosed space. At first Tucker thought it was the voice of God himself, loud and thunderous in the little tunnel, a deep bass note that sounded like a warning:

NOOOOOOOOOOOOOOOOOO.

It was a death knell, a scream from metal that had been pushed beyond its limits.

Two giant blasts of sound came next, and the world started to list sideways, making his mind race back to the night his boat went down in WWII.

The pipe broke. Tucker felt his ankle break as well, like he'd been shot there, sending a pristine bolt of pain from his right big toe up into his left clavicle. The oddness of that sensation took his mind off the fact that he was falling. What felt like minutes was probably seconds, and then more pain came.

One pop – his bad foot landing on concrete. Two pops, his head bouncing off the wall, ricocheting into the now-broken pipe (pop number 3) before slamming down onto the ground.

He had enough time to register a sharp, hot stab in his right buttock before he began to drown.

Cold, slimy water vomited from the broken pipe that was now level with his face, splattering into his eyes, his ears. His right hand flopped dumbly behind him to find the source of the pain, and he knew two seconds before his fingers found it that it would be the handle of his trusty shiv, now lodged in his backside. He pulled it free and tried to stand, slipping and falling again.

His adrenaline kicked in and he found a way to flop over, push himself to all fours, and stand. The deluge that had been assaulting his face now pumped against his knees, slowly subsiding. He felt the back end of the pipe, twisted and folded, poking at his knees. When he turned, the old, rusted metal bit deep into the tendons there, plucking them like cheap nylon guitar strings until one frayed.

That singular note of agony was enough to bring the rest of senses back and make him realize what had happened. It was a small mercy that it was too dark to see, but the smell was unmistakable and overwhelming. It felt like the prison had been holding this in for all thirty of its years, that it had been constipated, and that maybe the guards were right, maybe it was shutting down. After all, didn't your bowels release at death?

Far away in the darkness, Easton Tucker heard a squeak.

"Rat!" He yelled. It was the only word he could find, the only syllable he could make, his sewage-spattered lips spraying his rage into the void. "Rat! Shit. House. Raaaaaat!"

He could only imagine what he looked like now. He tried to pretend it was mud, just mud, that it would help conceal him once he got out of this place. He sniffled, instantly regretting that choice as a thick, viscous plug of sewage rocketed up into his nose and then back out as he sputtered.

If his momma could see him now. Easton Tucker had done a lot of things that wouldn't make his momma proud, most notable among them stabbing his momma through the heart with a broken mop handle. She was probably laughing at him from somewhere in hell.

"I ain't supposed to be here!" He screamed. He bent down and hammered the broken pipe with his hand, thunderous hollow booming that rang throughout the tight quarters. If someone was still on the island, they'd have heard that.

If.

His ankle was on fire. Every beat of his heart registered like a shotgun blast beneath his boot. He spent the following five minutes debating whether it would be better to keep his lips closed, risking the taste of shitwater already there but keeping out the muck currently dripping down his face, or keep his mouth open and head tipped forward, which seemed reasonable until he felt the tickle of water running down his cheeks and toward his mouth. He couldn't wipe at the muck with his encrusted hands, couldn't find the backpack to use some of the pants there to clean himself.

No two ways around it, Easton Tucker was going to have to eat shit today.

This was it. He was a ghost. Less than a ghost. If he died down here in this tunnel, nobody would know. On paper, Easton Tucker was safe and accounted for somewhere in Kansas. He had to get out. Had to see his wife again, even if just to piss on her grave.

He hobbled down the narrow crawlspace, pulling himself back up onto the remaining half of the pipe. If memory served, he'd only have about thirty feet to go before dropping down to an access panel that would let out somewhere just outside of the rec yard.

His ankle had gone numb, either from shock or the cold water or both. He reached the end of the pipe, his good foot losing traction. He skidded forward again, jamming his good toes between the pipe and the wall and smacking his face against the cinder blocks.

Behind him, the skittering of tiny rat feet.

"You my accomplice now?" Tucker spat, the taste of rotten eggs and rusty copper sluicing across his lips.

The rat said nothing.

He reached the end of the road, a faint light cutting through the wall near the access panel. He pushed against it. It gave way slowly at first, then popped free and clattered to the floor, echoing like a 21-gun salute.

Tucker pulled himself through the panel, leaving a large stain smeared across the tile floor. He rolled onto his back, wincing in pain. He'd tried. At least he'd tried. His ankle wouldn't hold up to any serious running, and there was still a fence to scale and a dive to the water. A swim with no flotation device.

"Fuck you Darl and fuck you John!" he shouted. "Someone come get me! I'm here! I'm here, wherever the fuck this is!"

Darl Parker was apprehended on some nearby rocks in the bay. Tucker had befriended him as he recovered, and over the days, Parker told him a secret, the greatest secret he'd ever know.

Always have a backup plan.

Parker and Scott had gotten out using their Plan A, but Tucker learned that there was still an unused Plan B and C. They'd loosened some security bars here, opened some access panels there, and only Easton Tucker knew about them. This plan probably would have gone smoother with a partner, but loose lips sink ships, and the safest bet to keep the passages open was to keep his mouth shut. He worked for a few weeks to get the remaining necessities in place. He hadn't accounted for the shit storm he'd just survived.

Something about the thought of sinking ships coupled with the smell he'd brought into the space made him lose his supper. He'd kept his meals light as the big day approached, wanted to make sure he was as skinny as possible so he could slither through the narrow path to freedom. Small blessings.

Something about slithering through a narrow path brought on a second wave of intense nausea, and he lost the breakfast that had preceded his lunch.

He flopped away from his mess, pulling himself across the room until he came to a large steel table where he leveraged himself back to his feet.

He was somewhere in the lower levels of building 64. He didn't know who'd designed the sewage systems for this island, but he thanked them for having a central access point to all of the island's buildings. None of the doors here should be locked. He had, at this point, *technically*, crawled his way to freedom. He could stop now. It made sense to give up. Every step he took sent more pain up his leg, he could barely breathe because of the stench he'd brought with him, and his only means of escape had been destroyed.

His momma didn't raise a quitter. That's the same thing he told her after the first few jabs with that mop handle didn't get the job done.

He didn't have anything waiting for him on the other side. Not a woman, not a job, not a safe place. But the sun was bright coming through the seam of the closed door to the room, and he had to know how it felt out there. He spied a mop leaning in the corner of the room and grabbed it, using it as a makeshift crutch. He hobbled forward, brazenly stepping through the door and out into the day, careless of who would see him.

Nobody was there. There was no clatter from the rec yard, no boats coming in, none of the supply trucks moving gear across the island. They had been telling him the truth. He waddled down a dirt path until he reached the wharf. The wind cut through him like a knife.

Freedom felt like hell. He stared at the city lights across the bay. The rat skittered across his feet.

"What's escape, anyway? Gettin' away from the cops, right? Gettin' away from jail? I mean… I did it, right? Sort of? I'm the only one here. So it's sort of like I got away, right? Right?"

The rat stood on its hind paws and looked up at him. It checked over its shoulder and then scampered away across the rocks.

"I can't swim it," Tucker told the rat. "I can't. Did they leave?"

"Die on the rocks. Die in the water. You're not supposed to be here, that's the important thing," the rat said. "They're not coming back. They're never coming back."

Tucker stared at the rat in disbelief, his jaw hanging open. He blinked, a strange feeling at his temples as his muck-encrusted skin dried in the open air.

"I'm covered in shit," he told the rat.

"You are," the rat answered.

"Why didn't you talk before?"

"You've lost a lot of blood, Easton. You can't see it because your pants are filthy. Take them off."

Tucker hesitated, then nodded and did as he was told. Once, in the Navy, he'd been involved in an acid spill, a few splatters that ripped across his forearm and burned like the devil. As his pants slid down, that feeling returned to him, amplified tenfold as the fabric of his filthy pants peeled away from the skin on his leg.

He pawed at his right leg, massaging the back of his knee.

The rat tutted. "You shouldn't do that, your hands are filthy."

Tucker ignored the rat, fingers probing at his leg. It felt distant and cold, made of rubber, but it was wet, even with the pants gone. The back of his knee hurt, and as he slid his hand up his thigh, his fingers probed the edges of a chasm that hadn't been there when he woke this morning.

He tried to test it, see how deep it went, but it stung, and he couldn't tell if it was the wound or his shit-stained fingers, so he eased back, walking his hands up the rim of this new geological feature. It started near the back of his knee, curling around to his inner thigh before taking another hard turn towards his rump.

"I really shanked myself, huh? God, that's deep. I need a doctor."

"You need a priest," the rat replied.

"What am I supposed to do now?"

"Confess? Sing. Sing your soul to me," the rat said.

Tucker swung a kick at the thing, but the strength went out of his leg and he collapsed in a heap. The side of his face bounced off the cement hard, and he felt his front teeth shift in a way that they hadn't since his last bar fight.

"I'm gonnn' die? Like thiff?"

He rolled onto his back and propped himself up on his elbows, looking at the ground. A perfect silhouette of his profile was there, painted in bile and blood. The lips open in a silent scream, lines near the eye showing the grimace of pain.

"Thaff me," Tucker jutted his chin at the ground.

"That's you. That's your whole life, Easton. That's everything you did and everything you'll ever be. That's as close to a memorial as you'll get and it's more than you deserve." The rat scampered to his feet and perched on its back paws, rubbing its forepaws together.

Tucker squinted at the rat. "You're not very nice."

"Neither were you."

"How can I make this right?"

The sky slowly began to shift, from a faded robin's egg blue to a brilliant white, then almost platinum. The world around Tucker went blurry.

"Confess to him," the rat said.

Tucker followed the rat's gaze to see a blurry shadow approaching. "Who's that?"

"Confess," the rat whispered.

Tucker tried to raise a hand to the shape. He'd never had much truck with angels or devils. Things were what they were and then they were done, but at this moment, he decided that it was probably best to make a good first impression no matter which way he was headed.

"The only monument to your sin is the stench you've left behind, and even that will be gone soon enough," the rat said.

"I'm sorry," Tucker said. "I'm sorry. I'm sorry, Momma. I'm sorry. I'm sorry about everything. I din't even belong here. I never meant to take that--"

Thunder filled the sky, ripped through the heavens so hard that the sky warped. A blink later, a jolt of lightning hit Tucker's head. His right eye went near-blind and his left exploded from his temple, riding a wave of bone and blood and brain, spattering across the silhouette he created moments earlier.

Was he dead? Was this death?

He blinked, his vision resolving until there was only light and that shadow thing, that dark blue monstrosity towering over him that resolved into familiar shapes, arms, legs, a service revolver, a badge on its chest shining brighter than the golden morning sun.

A voice came to him in the light, from far away, the shadow-thing speaking.

"What the? How did you? Who is that?"

More shadows joined the first one, and that chorus grew.

Who is that?

Who is that?

Easton felt his cheek growing cold in the shallow puddle of sewage and blood and bone he'd created, and though he could no longer speak, he finally knew the answer to that question.

INGÉNUE

Twenty-three more hours inside a box. Nowhere, Maine to Chicago, Illinois. We're stopped over somewhere in Whiteport Station, no idea what state, what city. I slept the whole way in. The sky is promising snow, but it's warmer here than where I left and tropical compared to where I'm going.

I find a bench that gives me a view of the tracks, lets me watch the drifts build. Three hours to kill until I'm back on the rails. Some music would be great now. Or reading material. A deck of cards. Something that won't remind me of what I'm doing here. Something other than the contents of my pocket. I scan the posters across the track, advertisements for local Italian joints, hotels, real estate. Pennsylvania. Jesus, I'm not moving fast enough. There are some newspaper pages on the floor, God knows what they've been used for, but any port in a storm, I guess.

While I'm reaching down for the papers, a pair of feet shuffle by and stop in front of me. The leather looks old, taken from the hide of a horse beaten to death eighty years ago. Yet another guy looking to help a damsel in distress I'm sure. Before the words *fuck off* are through my lips, my throat closes. He grins, mostly toothless, and raises a finger to his lips. His fingers dance to the brim of his porkpie hat, doffing it slightly –and the hat comes to life. An epic battle ensues – him trying to keep the hat on his head, the hat trying to be anywhere but here. It bounces, it rolls down his left arm before he catches it, flips it neatly and puts it back on his head. The chase continues, and I hate myself for laughing because I know it will only encourage him, but I can't help it.

He beams another smile at me, and with a flick the hat goes end over end. He spins slowly while the hat's in the air, reaching a hand behind his back to make the final catch. He misses. The hat bounces once on the floor and rolls towards me, spinning and dying at my feet. I go to pick it up, but he stops me by clapping his hands and shaking his head. He pats his pockets down, first the coat, then pants, then inside pocket, back to the coat. The act moves from pure comedy to tragedy. His lip trembling, his face near panic, and he's digging in every pocket he has. His shoulders slump. He shuffles away from me, the impromptu circus canceled.

I pick up the felt hat, fingering the brim. It may have been a rich black at some point, or perhaps grey. It was probably new back in the Roosevelt administration, its color now indiscernible, sun faded, dust-caked. The inside of the crown bears a faded laundry marker legend: "VIC". The band inside the hat is brown and stiff from decades of flop sweat. A small photo is tucked in the side, a smiling girl in a ridiculous cowboy hat, her bra made from spiky cactus tops, her smile porcelain. She's cradling a melon under one arm, staring brightly into the distance, as if the sun is making her promises of a better day.

"This your wife?" I ask, but the man is gone, shuffling through the doors and outside. He stops after a few steps, looks to his left and right. He spins around to look at the doors. Touches one, then turns around. I don't think he knows where he is. He'll freeze out there. The sun won't be up for another couple of hours. I open the door and gently tap him on the shoulder.

"Come in," I shout.

His eyes light up when he sees me. He claps his hands and takes two broad steps inside, shaking the snow from his shoulders. He shrugs his shoulders and reaches up to grab his hat. His fingers roll and grasp at the air above his thinning silver hair, dancing over his scalp, lost. I extend my arm, holding his hat out.

"The salesman!" he wheezes.

Before I can ask what he means, he snaps the hat from my hands and plants it squarely on his head, standing straight and proud.

"The what now?"

His voice goes up an octave, ringing throughout the space. "Step right up and I'll cure what ails you. I've got snake oil, car oil, olive oil, a nickel extra'll get you Popeye too! You sir, what seems to be ailing you?"

"I'm a girl."

His upper lip quivers and his eyes dart side to side. Mine follow, hoping to catch a security guard, a fellow passenger, anybody. No luck.

"Perhaps something's wrong with your mobility. How's your arm?"

"Is this…are we on camera?"

His face shakes, growing red. He leans close, a harsh whisper. "Hope. We're opening for *Bob Fucking Hope.* Get your act together. Your arm hurts when you go like this. All right? You want to get out of this town? Do you ever want to get out?"

"The sooner the better."

His eyes glaze for a minute, and then it's as if someone turns a switch off. He just shuts down, like his batteries died. He's a statue all of a sudden. I decide to find a different place to sit. He doesn't smell like booze, doesn't look like he's on drugs. Just some ancient old man that left his mind somewhere else.

I find a bagel stand around the corner, next to a newsstand. It's closed, like everything else here. I check the trash can next to the stand. If it hasn't been changed yet, there could be breakfast. A few seconds of searching yields what might be a chunk of pretzel or a breadstick. That'll do. I pocket a few mustard packets and survey the area.

A tap on my shoulder. Methuselah's back, smiling his gummy smile and thrusting a business card towards my face.

"Fresh off the press. We're on our way!"

The card is slightly oversized, thick cardstock, smooth like cotton at the edges after God knows how many years in his pocket. It's ivory paper with sepia ink, bearing the inscription:

Hash House Hi-jinks!

Comedy! Music! Romance!

Featuring

Bert Bindlestiff and Lonnie Looker

Two photos at the bottom, one a lady, young and doe-eyed wearing a mop of a hat, and one a goofy looking horse-faced gent with a familiar-looking (but slightly toothier) grin.

"Well?" he holds his arms out, waiting for praise or a hug.

"Looks nice. I'm sure you'll do very well." What to do? This isn't the first time I've been in this kind of situation. I can't leave. I can't hide.

"Take a walk with me, Dottie."

"My name's not Dottie."

He stops at this, brings the business card closer to his face, looks at the girl, then me, then the girl again. He erupts into a phlegmy laugh and shuffles back towards the benches.

Five A.M. and a few people start to trickle in. Those coming with me on the 29 Capitol Limited to Chicago, those who will make up my world for the next twenty-seven hours. The old guy, Bert, he's up there waving me forward. Nobody's really taking notice, but he's planting himself, standing tall, ready to give 'em hell. I feel sorry enough for him that I'll try to spare him further embarrassment. As I approach, he cocks an elbow and whispers back to me.

"Let's do the flapjack routine from Hash House. Ready?"

"No. No, I need a break, Bert. Let's sit for a second."

"These mugs aren't gonna be out here forever. Let's make some money!"

I tow Bert over to a bench, get him sitting down. Why do I keep playing savior to these lost souls? After this week, why should I want to help anyone?

"Bert, do you have your wallet?"

"Sure thing, Dot. You wanna buy us some coffee? Let the crowd build a while, I get it."

Bert takes his wallet out and slides it across the table, his fingers shaking and drumming. His eyes are electric, younger than the boy in the photo on the card.

The wallet is smooth leather, various shapes embossed on the outside from contents long gone: keys, cards, coins. Inside, there are three more of the calling cards, a Liberty silver dollar from 1937, and a small feather.

"You don't have ID, Bert?"

"What did I always tell ya? We get rousted, you don't want any ID on you. They'll let you go within an hour."

"Do you know where you live?"

Bert's face becomes ashen. "What are you playing at, Dottie?"

"I don't think you belong here. I'm worried about you."

Bert slouches back on the bench, left hand shaking. He makes the business card dance slowly across his knuckles, back and forth. "S'cold out today… Damn fingers ain't working."

"What's your last name, Bert?"

He explodes forward. "God damn it! What's with you, Dottie?" His breath races, his skin is near purple now. The gleam in his eyes fades, the storm passes. He deflates again, his eyes sheening over. Maybe I pushed it too far.

"My name is Anne Marie," I'm trying so hard not to sing-song to him now, "and I've had a really shitty week. It came at the end of an unbelievably shitty month. The month is one in a series of four, each worse than the last. I wish I was Dottie, I really do. But I'm starving right now. I can't focus, and I wish I could play with you and perform for these people…"

For a second I let that sink in. What if I played Dottie for Bert and Lonnie Looker for the crowds? We *could* earn a buck or two. I could have a real meal. Sure, I'd be an asshole for exploiting this guy's mental condition, but my stomach is louder than my conscience.

"Okay," Bert mutters. "Okay, we don't have to play here. We'll scrimp together for today, see what we can shake tomorrow."

I can do this for a little while.

"Bert. I just don't feel like Dottie now. That's what I meant. I'm hungry. I'm having trouble remembering the routines." If he doesn't buy this, I'll die. I've broken enough hearts. "Can you remind me?"

Bert smiles and pinches my cheek. "Attagirl. You had me worried kid, why dincha just say some'n?"

"Just stage fright I guess. Bert, have we played here before?"

"I played dis town in '35, before we made the act. What was I then? Sixteen? Seventeen? Who knows. I was drowning out here until I found you. You and those gams!" He explodes into laughter again.

Bert takes the next five minutes running me through two of "the classics". Basically, these are two routines packed with jokes that my grandpa would have called old. I'll be playing the straight girl, the Gracie to his George, whatever that means. He's got pretty much all the dialogue. We wait until about six-thirty for the morning rush crowd. A potential audience of six, and none of them seem too interested in anything but getting to where they've got to go. We muss our clothes, and Bert folds his porkpie up and jams it on my head. No preamble, Bert jumps right in.

"Say Dottie! When I was on my way over here, I met a fella who said he hadn't had a bite in weeks--"

"Did you bite him?"

Bert does a slow burn, and I bask in stealing his punchline, like we discussed. Sure my delivery was horrible, but one guy shifts in his seat and briefly looks over the top of his newspaper.

"Dottie, did you hear about the fire at the shoe factory?"

"No, but I bet some heel started it." I flick a nearby passenger's newspaper and guffaw as best I can. He shakes his head.

"Hey," Bert growls, "Why dontcha let me tell the story my way? So, there was a fire at the shoe factory..."

"Over 200 soles were lost!" I spy a small child sitting on his Mom's lap and laugh. I get a smile out of him, and now a few people are paying attention. The problem is those are the only two bits I remember. "How about some softshoe, Bert?"

Bert looks nervous at my bit of improv. He starts to hum and bounce a little, jostling into what once may have been a great number. At eighty-some years old, he just looks palsied and nervous, shimmying in place. I use the opportunity to lean in to the travelers.

"My grandpa was a great performer once. Things have been… bad lately. More hard days than good ones. I just want him to have one last moment in the spotlight. It'd be great if you could all chip in a little. Can you help us out?"

I spread the story around to a few of the nearby passengers. Some of them leave, annoyed. But we've got a good baker's dozen built up now, and Bert's feeding off their energy. I flip the hat onto the ground, and within a few minutes we've got five bucks and change sitting in the hat. People come and go as the morning express rolls in, unloads a fresh audience and takes the old one away.

Bert takes a break after he sends a large group on their way with a merry rendition of some old song. The final tally of our first act together is about nine dollars. I pocket all of the money.

"Keep it safe for us, Dottie." He sits across from me, wipes the sweat from his brow. "We're on our way again. On our way…"

I leave him for a moment, find the bagel stand now that it's open, and get a half dozen. Four of these go in my coat pockets. I find Bert rocking back and forth in his seat, offer him half a bagel with some cream cheese. I could keep this going until the 29 rolls in, leave this station with enough money to get a cab in Chicago instead of walking.

"Crowd's building," Bert says, "We've gotta get ready for the show. Gonna make some money today. This is as close to love as we get, huh Dottie?"

Jesus Christ. "Bert, listen. I'm leaving in about an hour."

"Where we headed? Poughkeepsie? Utica? We're makin' magic again, kiddo! I knew! I told ya, ya give me one more chance to make it all right, and we'd be…we're…you let me make it right. This… I don't know how to say sorry, Dot, I never did…"

Bert goes blurry for a second as my face quivers and my eyes water. I spread a napkin next to him and unload my pockets, stacking the bagels on the bench. "That's it for me. That's what you earned this morning, and that's what I did with it. I fucked you over, Bert. I don't know who Dottie is, but by the time I leave today, she'll be fucked over too."

"My Dottie always comes back. Always. You break my heart

every time. Every time I think there's nothing left there, you bring it back, and I give it... I always give it to ya." He starts to sing, "*After you get what you want you don't want it... If I gave you the moon, you'd grow tired of it soon...And though you sit upon my knee, you'll grow tired of me. 'Cause after you get what you want, you don't want what you wanted at all...*"

Bert's voice hits a rocky patch, cracking, skidding, crashing. He unbuttons the top button of his shirt. His lower lip bounces. He looks pitiful and ridiculous, his socks drooping, stomach bulging over threadbare slacks. Glasses too big for his face, shirt stained from sweat and food and worse. A shell of a clown. I don't know him, but I feel like I know everything about him.

The song lodges in my gut, deep under my ribs, twisting beneath my breast. It shouldn't hurt, but it does. It shouldn't make me angry, but it does. "You hit the nail on the head, Bert. I've gotta go, okay?"

"Whadja do?"

"What?"

"What did you do? Where you going?"

"I've been all over the place, Bert. Did things I shouldn't have. Talked to the wrong people. Believed the wrong things."

"So come back to me, we'll make it work. You never trusted me, Dottie. You never believed in me. In us. Not on stage, not in real life."

"That's right. And I don't give a shit how much you cry--"

"You're cryin' too, Dot!"

"You'll forget all about it in five minutes." I stand up, grind my cheeks like I can push the tears back in. "You're not going to remember me. You didn't know me a couple hours ago, you won't know me again by noon."

"Just give me a goddam chance, okay? Just try!" He hacks a little after this, and I feel the eyes of everyone nearby on us. We're quiet for a minute, and everyone goes back to their papers, their lives, their blissful ignorance.

"Bert."

His eyes are desperate, angry, broken.

"Bert, can I... can I tell you something?"

I don't wait for an answer. In an hour, in four bagels, two cups of coffee, Bert knows everything about me that's worth knowing. Everything that went wrong. He knows what I did, and I thought that would make my steps feel lighter heading towards the train. I leave him on the bench. He hasn't looked up since I left his side. He plucks at the tattered red posey stuck in the brim of his hat. Looking out the window, the snow turns to rain, the forecast calls for heavy emotional outbursts and dry heaving sobs. The 29 Capitol rolls out, dragging me toward Chicago, toward everything I need to face, the mess I made and the finality of it all. Bert's there on that bench, holding that god damned flower and smiling.

Lyrics from
"After You Get What You Want, You Don't Want It"
by Irving Berlin, 1920 (Public Domain)

MATILDA
Hits Rock Bottom

We stand hand-in-hand, Mad Molly and I, watching the wreck of the *Matilda* slowly bubble its way to the bottom of the Pacific Ocean. My first thought, standing shivering and wet on the rocks of Marina del Rey, is that this is not as cool as the movies make it seem. My next thought is, I'm going to have legal troubles very soon. Mad Molly is drenched. Her left eye dangles from its socket and her mouth is slack. I'm the only thing keeping her upright. I did this to her, made her into a harlot and then, after, tore her, mutilated her, because she wouldn't… *couldn't*, do as I asked.

I look at her, so helpless and frail, and I hate her. I pull hard on her wrist and slam her against the rocks. She drops like a wet pillow. For good measure, I stomp her head twice, reveling in the wet squish as her head makes contact with the rocks. My prized possession, the first thing I ever made in my life, Mad Molly the Pirate Puppet Wench, she's dead. I fling her towards the *Matilda's* mast - let her go down with the ship, retain some of her seafaring dignity.

It's relatively early in the morning, early enough that Stan – excuse me, *Blackscarf, The Dread Pirate Captain* - is probably drinking his coffee and planning a fine day of faux-piracy during his commute. His heart will break or explode upon arrival.

I can't believe nobody else is around to see this.

What am I doing here? There's usually sculling teams from

UCLA, joggers, dogwalkers, but right now it's just me and the bubbling wreck. I blink hard to clear some of the running mascara from my eyes. Pirates used to be a surly lot, but thanks to Johnny Depp and his shitty movies, we're all a bunch of half-drunk, flouncing nancyboys with bad hair extensions and scarves. What the hell am I doing here?

That's my life beneath the green waves. Now six inches, now two feet below those floating Styrofoam cup shards and cigarette butts, that's two years of mopping and sweeping the decks. Four feet below that in the galley, that's where I got laid for the first and probably last time in my life. I was drunk. She was getting there. She left, and somehow (I'd like to think accidentally) unmoored the boat. The wind kicked up last night and the breakers were rough.

The boat hits bottom so hard I feel a slight vibration in my feet, a mere ghost of what I felt when the *Matilda* hit that first rock. Nothing like the vibrating rip as she rubbed on the jetties that make this Marina. This was a message from God. "Thou shouldst not have cavorted drunkenly with thy boss's wife." The waves lap against the mast and there's Molly, her little foam arm snagged around one of the ropes. Her head lolls back and her mouth drops open, that little pink foam tongue hovering just below her single white felt tooth. I throw her voice out over the waves. "*J'accuse! J'accuse!*" Molly was a French Pirate. *When* I decided this, I don't know. Another in a long string of miscalculations.

"Hoooooly Shit!" What happened?" It's Blackscarf himself, green and on the verge of puking at the sight of the *Matilda*.

"K-K-K-kuh-kuh-I-I-I-I-"

"What the fuck did you do?!," he yelps, staring at the wreck, moving away from me to get a better look.

My jaw jackhammers open and closed, no sound escaping. Molly was my voice, my only voice, and now she's dead. She could only speak if someone was watching us, and nobody was watching as the swells came in and threw us around. Nobody on the radio could understand my calls for help. Probably just sounded like static to them. You think Stan would understand – or care – about that?

I've spent my time working here as an invisible man. It's amazing what people will say to you if you never talk. Eventually they forget you're there, and you get to overhear things about salaries, backstabbers, hirings, firings, affairs, you name it. If you're one-on-one with someone, you stay silent long enough and they'll unburden their soul to you. Stan loved to use me as a verbal punching bag. He loved to poke and poke until my face was purple and quivering as the words jammed in my throat. Until last night, my silence always made me feel shitty. In the case of Mrs. Blackscarf, silence was the ultimate aphrodisiac. I was three sheets to the wind and she was half-lit and looking to get revenge on Mr. B for some unknown indiscretion. I know so much about him now. His fears, his insecurities, his micropenis.

All of these things I learned, thinking she just needed someone to talk to. My stutter meant I couldn't talk back, so Molly was our intermediary. Mrs. B eventually revealed her desire to become "a puppet fucker." Her words, not mine. It's probably a real thing, I didn't have time to Google it. It was strange, grasping her hips with one hand while I used the other to make Molly encourage us, almost a *ménage a trois*, I suppose. It felt so good at the time, and now I just feel like trash. I need a puppet to talk, to seem interesting, and last night, I discovered I couldn't even get laid without the aid of a puppet.

"I-I-I," I say to Stan. "Ju-huuuuuh-J-j-j-."

"Shut up. God Damn it, God Damn!"

Coast Guard ships approach. Stan stomps in small circles around the rocks.

"Did you at least try to call for help? Oh, wait, you couldn't have *c-c-could you*?!"

"I fucked your wife!" I blurt, my eyes wide at my first complete *sans-puppet* sentence in years.

For once it's words, not a stutter, keeping me silent as my mind races for the next thing to say.

Ad Solem Justitiæ.
John Droeshout sculp.

Broken glass drives through my right cheek, scrapes and chips my teeth. Swallowing blood. My shoulder is gone, just a wet useless mess.

This is how I'll get to Heaven, one piece at a time.

This is what I signed up for.

The ocean pitches in front of me at an impossible angle, white caps foaming, the peaceful view split by my stalled propeller and the screaming engine.

My left hand still works, not strong enough to keep me airborne, but enough to reach a pocket, enough to find you. Hear this, please hear this.

This braid in my hands, clutched as tight as I can to keep the flames away, to keep you pure, is my salvation. Your hair, still shockingly new and blonde. You'll only know me as larger than life, infallible. Your mother's, deep brown streaked with grey because she knows the real me. God willing you'll grow to be the woman she is.

Three burning pops like a spear from God tear through the cockpit, and I watch my leg erupt like a lake in a hailstorm. It's just a rodeo ride now, eight seconds of holding on while the hits keep coming. I'll never let you go. I never should have.

I read so many stories about moments like this, how your body just shuts down and sends you away to a peaceful place, keeps you from thinking about what's actually happening. It's not coming for me. I've lost enough speed now that the plane should be spinning, tumbling, making me pass out. But I'm not gonna get that luxury. Must be three seconds left, maybe four. Another plane shoots by, not sure if it's a Zero or one of ours. I lock eyes with the pilot, nod. I don't care whose side he's on, I pray for him in this brief second. I want him to land, get back to America, Japan, wherever - home to his wife. Give her what I can't give you.

What's left of the cockpit explodes inward, and the fire from the engine pours over the manifold and surrounds me.

This, this is my penance. The arm I used to hold another woman close on the dance floor has been torn away. This cheek she caressed with deep ruby lips, shredded and crimson. These legs that were entwined by her thighs in the night, shattered. It's all broken and cleansed, burned away. My heart was never hers. It's not even mine. It's always been yours, always.

Hear this. Please hear this and forgive me.

The flames close in, and I clutch your memory to my chest, bring your hair close to me and inhale your scent one last time before all is burning metal and leather and grease. I'm gonna land in Heaven burning alive, my last thoughts only of you.

WHITE

This was the last time they would ever see each other, huddled together inside a car, the weight of a secret revealed hanging heavy in the air between them. She'd unburdened herself, only a fraction of the ghosts that haunted her, but it was enough to stun him. They swirled there in the cold of the night, mixing with every breath he drew, racing down to his lungs and battering his heart.

The things she'd done.

The snow, heavy on the windows, erasing the world outside, creating a vacuum of here, a reality that could only be escaped through their union or their destruction.

She absently drew on the window beside her, making shapes in the fog on the glass. "Life," she continued, "is a canvas. We're born pure and clean, white as the driven snow. And in seconds, we're bloodstained and torn. And it just goes from there. It never stops. These little things add up. They weigh you down, they cover who you're supposed to be, and eventually you're erased."

"You become a work of art," he half-muttered, expecting a sharp rebuke.

"We can't all be masterpieces. Some of us are just hotel art, one among millions, discarded, unnoticed, maybe sitting in someone's attic somewhere. Why add to the clutter? Why not burn it and be done?"

A car passed, lighting up the snow on the glass like an empty movie screen.

Because I'm your friend. Because you're beautiful. Because I want to love you, but it makes no sense. These thoughts threw themselves against the back of his teeth, never quite escaping to make themselves known.

"You remember what I told you when I was getting to know you? You asked me why I liked you, and I said you were radiant. You shine. And you don't even know it. You're like white light. Not pure, just a collection of *everything*. White light is made by combining the entire visible spectrum."

"God, you're a dork," she sighed, smiling. "You always were. I love you for it."

His breath hitched at the mention of the word. But she wasn't looking at him. It was an empty statement, a frozen remnant of what might have been crystallizing in the air before her mouth and evaporating.

"It's an accumulation of life. The filth we walk through, the dirt we gather, that's what makes us shine." He inched his hand towards the edge of her coat, the closest thing to him, the furthest thing from her that was still part of her.

"I'm tired of shining."

He wanted to say, *Don't do this to yourself. Don't keep doing this.* But the door was open, she was gone.

He knew she was looking for that final stroke, whatever it was she needed on her canvas as a final excuse to burn it, to disappear forever. He wanted to call out to her, his hand on the headlight switch, hoping, praying she would ask him to turn it on so she could see herself shine.

Tidal

"Carry me home," she said, and he lifted her.

A sprained ankle wasn't the ending he'd hoped for on a first date, and he regretted making those jokes early on about her bad choice of shoes for a walk around town, but surely this had to count for something.

When he reached her apartment complex, he swung her around so she could punch in her entry code, and when the door swung open, she said "That's far enough."

He set her down and took a half step back, offering an arm for support. She muttered a thank you but didn't offer a hug or a smile or anything else. Her bare feet made no noise on the marble floor as she hopped across the short hallway to the elevator. She kept her back to him until the elevator arrived.

It wasn't until she hopped into the elevator that he felt the weight of her single good shoe in his hand, still hooked around his index finger. She disappeared and the emptiness of the hallway descended on him. Just before the doors clicked shut, he heard her call out "You owe me for those shoes!" Not as good as a kiss goodnight, but it was something.

There was more, but that was a lifetime ago. He didn't even know what brought that particular image to mind. Maybe it was the waterlogged shoe he'd seen on his jog out to the water. It was an old grey tennis shoe, nothing like what she wore. Would have worn. Used to wear.

He'd never get used to the new tense of things, the way his life had shifted out of the present and into the past, even as he was pulled further and further into the future. "All we have is now," she used to tell him. And now he didn't even have that.

He caught himself this morning saying the same thing he always said, a gentle "got a date with Davey Jones," only now it was to an empty pillow that smelled less and less like her every day. Why did he still bother with this? Still running towards the ocean like a teenager, why do all surfers run across the beach as if the waves are scheduled to stop at any minute?

The steps came harder this morning. His legs dragged a bit in the sand, but he figured he'd still be good for an hour or so before he got too tired to come back in. You always had to come back in. Get out of bed. Keep going. Keep living. For what, for who, for her, for memories.

Fifty yards out and drifting. Cloudy water today. Sediment and seaweed and garbage. He trailed his fingers into the water, plunged them in deep over the edges of his board, imagined he could feel the sand scraping through the creases in his palms. Sometimes an errant piece of kelp caressed the back of his hand, and his eyes would pop open, convinced he'd see her down there, her ashes somehow reformed. Skin bone white like coral, she'd be there smiling up at him.

His skin burned and his left arm tingled. Breath coming short, he had to think back and wonder how hard he'd paddled to get out this far. Always pushing it, he could see her down there in the water, arms folded, shaking her head. "A pill every day keeps the reaper away," she used to tell him. Admonishing him like a child when he'd forget to take his meds to keep his patchwork heart beating.

So what happens now? He'd stopped taking them months ago when his prescription ran out, but it seemed the reaper had forgotten where he lived. Maybe Death was just a sadist who only came after the ones you loved.

A seagull cried out somewhere above him, the sound knifing through his ears, transforming into that high-pitched squeal of a laugh she had when he would genuinely surprise her with a good joke. His arm was completely numb, a shock running from the back of his skull down through his shoulder like electricity that just wouldn't turn off, and she was there, she was down there. His left arm was frozen in the water, stiff like a rudder on a useless ship.

His heart beating harder now, he felt it in the ear pressed against his surfboard. He'd spent a lot of time thinking about this, the end, what it would feel like. He thought it would be sudden, that his heart would seize up like his old Mustang when it got that oil leak on their honeymoon trip up the PCH. Or that it would just wind down, coasting to a stop somewhere while his body just slowly turned the lights off, one by one, like the old diner on the..the...which highway was that? It was so hard to focus with the pounding, the roar of the ocean.

"Not a kid anymore," he whispered, water lapping over the surface of the board, cold down his ear. His finger snagged on something, but he couldn't lift his head to see what was happening. Kelp. But kelp didn't hold like this, kelp wasn't soft and warm like this. It didn't give that reassuring little squeeze, that little pocket of space between his palm and hers like the safest place in the world to keep their secrets.

His legs dangled useless behind him. The shore came and went as the tide moved him up and down. He didn't want her to let him go, not again. If he could just get off the board he could end this, but this wouldn't be up to him. The waves would take him back to Los Angeles, back to the empty apartment, the silence of a good life frozen in amber.

"Carry me home," he prayed, squeezing his fingers tighter as the waters swelled beneath him.

ONE SHOT

God Only Knows

In less than two minutes, I will become the new Messiah. A martyr. A monster.

I'm perched on the edge of the roof at King/Drew Medical Center with hundreds of acolytes following my every move from the ground below, hacking at the support cables for a twenty-yard canvas banner that's just been hung on the hospital in protest. The damn thing is heavy, and it's blowing in the breeze. Looking down, the sea of faces below is distorted by that rarest of things in Los Angeles, a spring downpour. I can't tell if the roar I hear is the rain, the traffic on the freeway, or their voices calling my name. Their eyes glint, mouths open, necks arched and straining to see me above them all. The whole thing is just so rapturous. What the hell am I doing?

This is our Faith, I tell them. *This is our Hope*, I shout above the gale. The last rope snaps and the wind takes the banner away. It's a huge replica of the little slips you get from the government-sanctioned death prediction machines. It bears an impossible message, a fate that no person could ever really receive: GOD ONLY KNOWS.

The crowd is frenzied, arms raised, reaching, reaching. I turn as the banner collapses, watching their eyes grow wider, wider. I splay my arms and point to the skies. I think only of my wife Nadia, wondering if she'll take me back when this is all over. Security bursts through the door behind me. I tense my legs, and I leap.

***

Dear God,

When the machines first started telling people how they'd die, there were riots, rebellions, endless orgies in the streets. Well, you know. You saw it. Someone knows how they're going to die, *you* try to tell them what they can and cannot do. The government stepped in, as they always do when the fun starts, and put the party down as quickly and quietly as possible. After that, we were over it in a couple of news cycles. Everything's regulated and well run now. Efficient, effective, trademarked.

Christians, Muslims, Jews, we believers have some serious problems on our hands. We'd always pondered the age old questions. When will I die? Where? How? The machines went a long way toward answering the first two questions, and pretty much solved the riddle of the third. How can we continue to profess faith in God when we can peek at the last page in our book?

When the government tried to enforce mandatory testing at birth, organized religion pushed back – hard. The Vatican came down first: visiting the machines ran counter to the very idea of true faith. Anyone caught using the machine was excommunicated from the church. Catholics had to get ID cards and register with Mother Church, who linked to government databases to ensure that her children remained pure of mind, pure of future.

Like so many things in the world, this disaster was set in motion for the love of a woman. I met my wife while attending church. She wasn't one of those "Burning for God" soldiers looking to change the world. We'd all pretty much given up on that concept. She was just the girl serving coffee in the back of the room, offering to froth it for you with a smile while the priest broke down the folding table that served as our altar and shoved it back into the storage closet. Church was held in a basement (ironically located beneath a bar and grill that purchased and converted our former church). Anti-discrimination laws gave us the right to assemble, but with attendance dwindling, the church couldn't afford to hold on to all of its prime real estate.

We were all so scared. We felt completely left out. Everyone out there running around knowing the answer that would help them shape the rest of their lives; while we were in a moldy basement like unwanted stepchildren, staring out the windows at sunny skies perched to fall on us at any minute. You'd think having the answer would make you nervous to step outside, but it's the *not* knowing that kills you.

*****

"I can't do it anymore." That's Marty. He serves as our Deacon, our altar server, our usher. He's pushing sixty, and each year brings him more and more anxiety. Some of us have an unofficial pool going on when he'll crack, but we'd never say such a thing out loud. Looks like I'm about to lose five bucks. Father Patrick raises a hand to console Marty, but not too urgently. Why fight it?

"I have to know. This past week I've tripped twice. I went jogging and my heart wouldn't slow down for hours afterwards. I can't take it anymore. Bless me, Father?" Marty asks, one hand in his pocket pulling out his car keys.

"Until the moment you take the test, you're still one of us. You'll always be welcome here. But if you turn your back on your Faith—"

"How do we know these machines aren't divinely inspired? For fuck's sake Father!" Marty recoils at his own profanity. It's an argument that many people try to make. But the Vatican III Council settled that matter long ago. We are to live life as we always have. Sickness means a visit to the doctor. If he can cure it, he will. If it's fatal, you'll find out the hard way.

"I have a polyp," his hands are on Father Patrick. Marty's eyes are covered by a sheen of water, his lower lip bouncing so hard I think we might be having an earthquake. "They found a polyp. I'm waiting for test results. I could know in seconds. *Seconds*."

Father Patrick makes the sign of the cross on Marty's forehead. Marty's knees buckle and he staggers backward to the door, struggling to look at us as he leaves. He mutters apologies and begs forgiveness and those of us who can meet his eyes just give him a gentle nod. We know. We know.

The service, what's left of it, comes to a sloppy ending. Father Patrick approaches each of us in turn with the host, offers a closing prayer, and rushes to his desk at the back of the room. He removes his robe and grabs his coat. He hasn't taken his eyes off the floor. His face is red, angry, hopeless. He'll be back next week to go through this again, but I wonder how long he can hang on. I go to the table by the door for my traditional after-mass coffee. Nadia, usually ready with a cup for everyone, stands in the corner with a bag of coffee grounds shaking in her hand.

"Poor Marty, huh?" I ask.

"Are you doing anything after? Now?"

This is the first time she's asked me anything other than if I want sugar in my coffee. "I need to eat. A lot," she says. "Are you a good listener? Can we leave now? I need to leave. Now." Her fingers, still clutching the coffee pouch, run over the little tag on her necklace. Her nails trace the embossed letters over and over.

"Ever been to Pann's?" I ask.

***

We settle in to a big horseshoe booth at Pann's Restaurant. This place has been making pitch-perfect comfort food since the fifties. Quandaries of faith, for me, involve a hot plate of chicken and waffles. Nadia's staring down the barrel of the biggest piece of chocolate cake she's ever seen. We've been talking about local politics and the latest World Series, anything to keep our mind off the incidents of the day. Nadia takes a huge bite from the heart of her cake and watches the melting ice cream rush in to fill the void.

"Are you married?" she asks. "I mean, were you? Before it became illegal?"

"It's not illegal."

"You know what I mean." She chases a lump of chocolate ice cream around a chasm of fudgy icing in the middle of her plate. "I've been married twice."

"Really? You look so young. You can't be more than thirty-one."

"I'm twenty-six."

I've found in situations like this it's better to keep quiet until the woman starts talking again. I stuff a chicken wing in my mouth and make some appreciative grunts, suddenly fascinated by the way the syrup coats my waffles.

"It's okay. I don't sleep. I know how I look. I mean… I know."

Now I have to finish chewing as quickly as possible to respond, steer her away from self-pity if I'm going to have a chance. It's not that I'm a letch or anything, but I haven't been on a nice date in a really long time. I pretty much swallow the whole top of the leg and grumble, "So your last marriage would have ended when you were, what, nineteen?

How long has it been since they changed the laws?"

"My divorce just became final a month ago."

I sputter a bit and swallow some water. "So… you've been tested then?"

"Yeah. Yeah, I took the test." This is a huge step for her to tell me. I could easily have her booted from the church. Why does she trust me with this?

"What's the result?"

She pulls the necklace from her shirt collar again and removes it, handing it across the table to me. Looking at the plate, I can see that the original Fate™ has been sandblasted from the jewelry, replaced with a crude engraving: God Only Knows. My heart sinks a bit. "Wait, you're a Born-Again?"

"God, no!" she laughs. "No, I'm not one of those loonies that thinks that my death will contradict the machine. Hasn't happened yet, and I'm not that special. I know. Nobody else needs to at the moment. The ol' G-O-K is a great way to stop people from asking followup questions."

"So why take the test?" I ask. "Tax breaks aren't that hot anymore. Church wedding's good enough, right?"

"It was my first time around. This last one though, he wanted his big dream wedding. Government-sanctioned so we could have kids, the whole nine yards. I was only too happy to oblige. Obviously, I had to take the test to make everything legal. I didn't think it would change me. I guess it didn't. But crossing that line from wondering to knowing… I never told him the results. I promised him I'd show him on our wedding night. If he loved me, he'd wait."

"So what happened?"

"I kept hedging. If he asked to see it, I'd just rip his clothes off and we'd start going at it. He'd always forget. Or at least, just let it go until the next day, week, month, whatever. It was a constant fight. So one night I showed it to him, and the next day he served me with papers."

She lets it go at that and returns to her cake, her shoulders lifting slightly. This booth has become her confessional.

"So?" I ask. "What did it say?"

"You really want to know?"

"Yeah. This is intriguing. Kinda sexy. I feel like such a rebel right now."

"You men. Always after one thing." She holds her hand out for the necklace and I give it back to her.

"You know, this means we can't get married now," I say.

"We couldn't get married anyway, Churchy."

Well, she didn't freak out at the marriage joke. I'm doing okay here.

"How long is their verboten list getting over at the Vatican, anyway? Gay, divorced, fate-tested, what else?"

I get up to pay the bill. "On that note…"

She smiles a little and leans back in her seat. Her eyes dance over the geometric shapes in the restaurant. She's a completely different person. Glowing almost. I hand the cashier my credit card and try to decide my next move. Maybe she didn't need to talk about Marty after all. Something shook her up today. Was her day drawing near? Is she getting ready to die? I want to be her last happy days more than anything. That's as close to love at first sight as I suppose I'll ever get.

I saunter back to the table. "You wanna go count stars?"

"It's still daylight outside."

"Let's go."

***

Outside of Grauman's Chinese Theater, we stand in the ancient footprints of silent movie stars, ducking requests for change from filthy knockoff spacemen and superheroes. I parked my car back at Sunset and Vine and we traveled the Walk of Fame to get here. Figured it would give us some conversation starters. Just my luck, she hates TV and only occasionally watches movies. She seems to be enjoying herself. She points to a bone-thin man wearing a Superman costume. "He kinda looks like my first husband."

"He was before the laws changed?"

"Yeah. He died on his way out of the office after receiving his Fate™. It said Suicide."

"Self-fulfilling prophecy."

"No, he didn't kill himself. Another man threw himself off the top of the building just as my husband was coming out. Ironically, the man lived, but Paul didn't make it."

"That's horrible!"

"Yeah. Wouldn't it be cool if it actually happened?" She smiles and nudges me in the ribs before running away to step on Jimmy Durante's noseprint.

The rest of the afternoon is pure magic. It turns out her first husband ran off to New York and she hadn't heard from him in years. After a lot of legal wrangling, she'd gotten out of the marriage. She met her second husband just as the riots started. They'd gotten stuck on a bus when the driver insisted that his Fate™ allowed him to drive to each stop at sixty miles an hour. He knew he'd die in a plane crash, and decided he had license to go crazy. After he wrapped the bus around the base of the Santa Monica Pier, Nadia and her man stumbled off into the future together. Luckily for me, things didn't work out.

We stop for dinner at an amazing Creole restaurant off Crenshaw. The subject of her nerves that morning never comes up. Neither does the true inscription on her Fate™. Somewhere between the Gumbo and the Shrimp Po'Boy sandwich, it's decided that I'll be going to her apartment to meet her puppy. Going to work tomorrow will not be an option. As long as she's alive, I'm living for her. If I can discover when she's checking out, I can plan our next date…

***

I wake up in a snap in a dark, unfamiliar room. Halogen light slices across the carpet through venetian blinds. Our clothes are scattered around the room, and we're not facing the same direction in bed. Knuckles, her Rottweiler puppy, is burrowed into my pantleg, his fuzzy bottom sticking out, legs splayed. The denim rises and falls with each of his little puppy snores. Nadia's arms cover her head. Her brow wrinkles in concentration, left temple twitching. Each time her chest rises, the light catches the edge of her necklace. I swivel around slowly in the bed so as not to wake her. My face inches from her chest, I know it's wrong to peek. If she wakes up now, it could spell the end of our relationship.

The Fate™ is real enough, evidenced by the remnant of the government holographic seal on the edge. If I'm seeing that, then the necklace is facing the wrong way. I reach a finger out to try to turn the necklace over. The early Fates™ were embossed from the rear. Regardless of what she blasted off the front, there should be a perfect negative impression of the word on the back. Nadia rolls away from me, then just as quickly changes direction and wraps herself around me. Her eyes crack open to narrow slits, deep black shining pools.

"Just ask," she whispers. "But not now. Please."

Her right hand snakes around the chain and lifts the necklace over her head. She tosses it and throws a perfect ringer around the puppy's tail. Knuckles gives one half-hearted wag and falls back asleep.

Four hours later, her alarm goes off and she's out of the bed like it's spring-loaded. She's not much for morning conversation, fully dressed before I even have my socks on. Her only words to me are about clothes and hurrying up. She throws a handful of dog food into a dish by the door and we're both out in the hallway in the bright light of day, staring at each other.

"Thanks," she says. "Thank you so much."

I manage to make a low guttural noise before she presses her mouth against mine, pinning me back against the door. Then she's off like a shot. I don't know her phone number, her last name. I barely know her address. I have to wait until Sunday to see her again, if she comes back to church at all.

***

Dear God,

A month of lonely Sundays with no coffee after service. Services are thirty minutes of talk, buzzing in my ears, up-down-up-hug-handshake-communion-prayer-leave. Don't get me wrong. I spend at least an hour a week in prayerful meditation. But the absence of Nadia at church weighs too heavily on me. The empty space in the back of the room glows, pulses, screams. I can't focus on anything else. Father Patrick approaches me after mass near where the coffee table should have been.

"Lost another one, did we?"

I shrug. "I'm not so sure. You heard anything about Marty?"

"I gotta go to the bakery over on Larchmont. You busy right now?" My afternoon slate's clean, so I help Father Patrick clean up the church, and we head up the stairs.

"Sorry the table was so sticky. They had a leaky keg upstairs. Drained right into our storage closet."

"I thought the host smelled a little malty today."

"That was probably me. I was mopping that mess up for hours before you all arrived. The tabernacle stayed dry, praise God for small miracles." We open the doors at the top of the stairs and step into the blazing morning sunlight.

"Great smog day today. Look at that. Can't even see Mount Hollywood." Father Patrick is a little bulldog of a man, angrily trying to save a society that marginalizes his existence. His hairline is receding, his shoulders are constantly stooped, and his face is wrinkled. For all of that, he's still a welcoming presence. Once a month, we walk to the Village Bakery. Father Patrick gives me updates on the woes of the church, the decline of the city, and the end of civilization as we know it. I always leave feeling much better about my position in life.

"Have you talked to Nadia?" he asks.

"Not since Marty left."

"That's twice now you've mentioned him. I didn't think you two were so close."

"We weren't. Nobody could look him in the eye. I feel like he said what we were all thinking. So what are we doing every Sunday, Father?"

He falls silent for a moment as we cross Beverly and head for Larchmont. "Remembering. Always remembering. Out here, everyone thinks we're just a bunch of nostalgic fools pining for the old days. But they're the ones who've forgotten, and that's the easy way out. The easy answers aren't answers at all. Medical science has gotten better and better, but the public doesn't want cures. They want placebos. The less thinking they have to do, the better."

"So you think this is just a phase?"

"I think it's a step in a new direction. Things get shaken up, then they settle down. Nothing really changes. So you remember. That's what makes us special. We don't run from the past. We don't hide from the future. Right?"

I want to agree with him, I really do, but I stay silent.

"Look at it this way. Every Sunday, I present the Host. I say what Jesus said – this is my body. Not *was* my body. Not *represents how my body used to be*. It's present. It's alive. It's hard to get a hold of, even harder to wrap your mind around the concept. I know I haven't been able to do it. But I know that I'm getting there. Enough to know I don't need a silly machine to tell me how I'm going to die, because I don't care. I care about how I'm going to live."

He's done it again. My face breaks into a wide smile, and Father Patrick knows, without saying a word, the comfort he's brought me. He slaps me on the shoulder. "I'm buying." We turn into the little storefront and settle onto two stools, and we break bread together. I am satisfied.

***

The fifth Sunday, everything changes. I had a rough morning, and now I'm at evening mass. I never go to evening mass. Even before everything changed, they had the lowest attendance on Sunday nights. As I circle the block to find a parking space, someone waves at me from the corner. I slow down and Nadia approaches my car. She hops in the passenger seat.

"Let's go to the observatory," she says.

I stare at her.

"Why didn't you give me your phone number?" she says.

She's kidding. She has to be kidding. I run through several witty ripostes in my mind, reject them all. I lean over and pop the door open for her and she scrambles in, bringing in the smell of chocolate and perfume.

"Just drive. I'll tell you as much as I can, and hopefully by the time we get to the observatory, you'll still feel like talking to me."

She fidgets with her hands for a while as we drive. She seems to have lost weight, and looks like she's given up on sleep. "You're going to kill me."

"I thought we had something. I like you. You can talk to me, you know? I won't—"

She thrusts a piece of folded paper into my hands. It looks old, well-worn and shiny. I try to open it at the first red light, but she covers my hand. "Wait until we get there."

Thirty minutes later, we're cresting the last hill in Griffith Park. I park on the street leading to the observatory so we can walk the last little part. Great view of the city when the smog isn't covering everything. "You can see the ocean today."

She looks out to the water, just a sliver of shining land, orange in the dying sunlight. I unfold the paper as she looks away. It's a rubbing done in pencil, a small rectangular shape with words surrounded by ghostly white lines. SHOT BY YOUR HUSBAND.

"Hooboy." It's the only word that comes to my mind, so I repeat it a few times. "Well. This isn't so bad, right?"

If she'd have told me she was pregnant and kicked me in the balls, I'd probably be feeling less surprised right now. She turns around, tears in her eyes.

"I mean, we just don't get married," I try again.

"The machine is never wrong. I'm going to be murdered. Maybe not by you. But I get married and I get murdered."

Call me crazy, but I know this is one of those now or never moments. Sure, the Fate™ isn't looking so hot, but I'm a man in love. "I don't own a gun. I'll never own a gun. I swear. I'll put one on layaway, and then, when we're ninety years old, decrepit, miserable, falling apart, I'll shoot you. How's that?"

"Is this supposed to make me feel better?" She starts up the path toward the observatory, arms crossed over her chest.

"Yes!" I follow her. "Besides, I don't even want to marry you. Yet."

"I can't see you anymore."

"No. You brought me up here so I could give you a reason to keep seeing me. If you wanted to break up, you would have done that by the church, or just, you know, keep *not* coming to mass."

"You think you know so much—"

"I know you can't just run away from your fate."

"Now you believe in Fates?" Her eyes are wild, wide and shining. "That's a little un-Christian, don't you think?"

"What can I say? I'm a progressive guy."

She goes quiet again, and we walk in silence up the stairs to the roof of the observatory, around the towers to the overlook. Los Angeles spreads below us, evening lights sparking to life. She pulls her necklace from the front of her shirt and unhooks it, dangling the pendant between her fingers. She rears back and throws it over the edge. We watch it sail down, twisting before snagging in a bush next to a condom wrapper and a grocery sack. We're silent, the traffic below us like a dull roaring tide.

"How's Knuckles?"

She seizes me. I can't tell if she's trying to push me, hug me, stop herself from falling down. Her fingers dig into my back and I feel her knees buckle against mine. I stoop and support her, stroking her hair, not knowing what comes next.

***

Dear God,

A month later and everything is pretty okay. We've been dating, not mentioning anything about getting serious. I'll skip over the petty little details of our lives together, because I have to tell you about the part where we fuck up and get married. I say that like it's a bad thing, but really it was the greatest thing that ever happened to either of us. Nadia, well, you know what happened to Nadia.

The Sunday after coming together at the observatory, we're back in the basement church like nothing happened. Father Patrick is happy to see Nadia back in church, and since L.A. is what it is, there are no questions as to where she's been or why she was gone. The service is short and sweet, and I take confessional afterwards. Father Patrick offers to hear my confession on the way to the bakery, but I have to decline. I want to spend the afternoon with Nadia, so I ask if we can stay at church.

"I hate doing this here," Father Patrick grumbles. "Smells like beer and mothballs back there."

"Thank you Father," I smile.

He gives me a curt nod as he shoves his way into the supply

closet. He sets a small kneeler just outside the door. "If I hear one crack about me going into or coming out of this closet, you'll be saying Hail Mary until sunset." He picks up a sheet of lace, holding it between us. "Is this going to be a short one or a long one?" he asks.

"Indulge me," I say.

He grunts and uses two clothespins to hang the lace on the door. I can barely make out his shape as he leans back against the wall. "Batter up."

"Forgive me Father, for I have sinned. It has been three weeks since my last confession."

"Three weeks? Have you been going to confession somewhere else?"

"All right, three months. What, was it Christmas?"

"At least. But I get the idea. Continue, my son."

"I'm in love Father."

"Not a sin, last I heard."

"I know something about her. Something that… I think I need to get tested, Father."

"Ah, not you too. You're my rock…" He clears his throat. "Remember what I told you on our last walk? Living for the moment? Your love will be so much stronger without these needless fears attached. You don't need the test, you've passed the test! God loves you and He'll give you what you need. Besides, I'm not here to preemptively absolve you of sin. What have you done lately that's bad?"

He's trying to catch me out here. He does this every time. I never feel like I've done anything that requires an apology to God. This may also be one of the reasons I feel my life has been so meaningless. He drums his fingers against his legs, jangling change in his pocket. After what feels like an eternity of soul-searching silence, he peeks his head around the edge of the curtain.

"You're a good kid. Your head's screwed on right. Don't worry so much, and stay on the narrow path." He takes down the curtain and folds it neatly. "And speaking of, I have a path to walk – straight to the donut shop. You sure you don't wanna come?"

I shake my head. He pulls a baseball cap from the top shelf and jams it on, closing the door behind him. "Thank you, son."

I nod. "Not getting too many people in confession lately?"

He looks me up and down. "You'll be okay. God reads your heart. If He sees what I'm seeing, you'll be fine."

With that, he's on his way. Nadia's near the door, kneeling before a tiny plaster Mary on a shelf. She finishes her prayer and stands. "Feel better?"

"Loads," I lie.

It's been eating at me for weeks. This oracular machine has never been known for giving spot-on predictions about life in general, but if my Fate™ said SELF-INFLICTED GUNSHOT WOUND, I could almost rejoice. A murder/suicide would be great. Maybe it's a hunting accident. I'm cleaning a gun, it goes off, hits her, I'm so filled with remorse I turn the gun on myself. Maybe it's just the fact that she knows and I don't. If my Fate™ says HEART ATTACK, maybe I die young, well before her, and it's only after she remarries that she's murdered. These are the thoughts that keep me up at night. I want to talk to her about it, but I don't want to upset her by bringing up the future.

I bring it up anyway. "I want to get tested." We're at the beach, and I'm ruining our relaxation.

"We're not getting married."

"Maybe I want to know for me."

"I think you want to know for me. It's a disappointing experience. You won't like it. You don't need it. Let's just be happy right now, okay?"

She stretches her hand across the towel to me, and I wrap her fingers in mine. "You happy?" she asks. "Because I'm happy."

Something dances behind her eyes. It's not happiness. It's nerves, I think she's getting near her breaking point too. She wants to know. Are we getting married? Am I the guy who shoots her?

"Would you get angry if I got tested?"

"Yes. It's not who you are."

"I'm not sure if I know who I am. I might be the guy that shoots you."

"God Only Knows."

"Yeah…"

I can't commit to her until I commit to myself. I know this test is a one shot, all or nothing deal. There's no going back. Sort of like murder. Some commandments just shouldn't be broken. I tell myself that God would understand this. But I wonder if He's trying to get me to understand something else, something greater.

Two kids race along the water's edge, kites in tow. A boy and a girl, they don't look related. She's three steps behind him and catching up fast. He's too busy looking at her to see that he's drifting closer to the water. As soon as his foot hits the cold ocean, he jolts, dives to the side. Their kites tangle, a rapid tango in the air, a death spiral that sends them both into the water, soaked, bent and broken.

Nadia takes my hand. "We should get going."

"Wait."

Coming down shore to help the kids out is a man we both know. Marty. He lifts up the boy, who's crying because the girl's affection turned to rage immediately after the crash. Nadia sees him too and shouts his name in spite of herself.

Marty looks at us and a broad grin breaks over his face. "Holy Shit!" He sets the boy down and shoos him back towards the crashed kites. A titanic struggle ensues between the two kids, seeing who will get thrown into the watery abyss. In the moment, we don't care. It's Marty, and he's alive and well.

"How are you two doing?"

"Us? How about you?" I ask.

"Never better. Never better!"

"Did you…uh…"

"The test? Oh. Changed my life. Completely changed my outlook on everything."

Marty thrusts a small card into my hand. I unfold it. It's not his Fate™, but rather a business card for a testing center on Sepulveda. The address burns into my mind instantly, the 999 building. We always joke that it's the portal to the dark abyss. You have to travel upside-down to the roof and you're plunged into Satan's home. Never thought

I'd have a reason to see it from the inside.

"If you're ever thinking about doing it, and I'm not pressuring you at all – wouldn't want to proselytize – that's the place to go!" Nadia's eyes track the card all the way into my pocket. There's the silent command in her eyes: you're throwing that away when we leave.

Marty's obviously busy with the kids, and after some awkward small talk, we part ways and head back to the car. I give the card to Nadia and she throws it away before we've even gotten off the sand.

***

Ten o'clock the next morning, and I'm supposed to be at work, but I'm in a tiny corner office at the 999 building. There's nothing much here, three government-issue chairs. A window in the wall where a bored clerk sits. A small steel grey box at the front of the counter, just the right size to insert your hand. Your future in a metal nutshell.

I approach the counter and the clerk notices my necklace. "God Only Knows. You're one of them, huh?"

"Something like that."

"You lose your faith or something?"

"Something like that," I repeat. "Fell in love with a girl."

"Yikes."

"Yeah. Yikes. There's a question I need answered."

"You a good Christian?"

"I've been going to church in a dingy basement pretty much every week since the riots. Christ the Redeemer. That's not gonna change after today."

"Hey, you don't have to prove nothing to me. This ain't confession," he smirks. "Hand in the box, champ."

He opens the lid on the steel trap. There's an indentation for your index finger, a tiny hole under that where the needle comes through. I hold my breath and lay my hand inside. Thinking about this too much will just make it harder.

The instant my finger touches down, I feel the jab. I draw my hand back instinctively.

"Stings a little, don't it?" the clerk chuckles.

"Thanks for the warning."

"It'll all be over in a second."

I sit at a chair, absently pull a rosary from my pocket and start praying for forgiveness. Jesus, Mary, and Joseph. They'll understand this. Right? God will be okay with this, I tell myself. He knew I'd do this.

"All done," the clerk extends his hand over the counter. "Nice rosary. You might want to loosen up on it before you pop a bead."

I'm clenching it so tightly that there's a bloodless white cross indented in my palm. My little anti-stigmata. I take the piece of paper from the clerk. "So do I take this to an engraver for the official necklace or…"

"Read it out loud," he replies.

I unfold the paper. I laugh. This guy's some kind of prankster. "God Only Knows?"

"Hey, praying like that, you passed our test."

"Your… what?"

"Hold it up to the light."

I raise the paper up, and there, watermarked into the sheet, is the legend: Fight for your Future! with an address printed beneath.

"Memorize that. When you have it, slide the paper back to me. Next meeting's Tuesday night. Come alone, and bring snacks."

I check the address again and hand the paper back to him. He takes it and snaps the window shut in my face. Another client has arrived, and this is obviously not the kind of thing to discuss openly.

***

Tuesday night comes. I leave Nadia at home with a lame excuse about joining a company bowling league. The address is a tiny office building on Gower, a door tucked neatly between two shops in a strip mall. The door opens onto a well-lit stairway. I hear voices at the top.

"Come on up and close the door behind you."

I climb the stairs and turn the corner into what used to be a dentist's office. A couple of the fancy chairs are still there. The rest of the place is folding chairs and cobwebs. There's maybe a couple dozen people there, too-big smiles and eager eyes, and for a minute I think I've been tricked into an intervention.

"I talked it over with the gang, and I'm going to be your fate buddy," Marty says.

"What's that?"

"You took that test at the 999 building. The clerk seals it in an envelope. He doesn't look, don't worry. Those get sent to the man upstairs."

"You send them to God?"

"No, here. We've got a guy that checks the mail. He reads the Fates™, seals them back in an envelope, and then gives you a fake one. A cover story," Marty waggles his eyebrows at me. "Feels like we're spies, huh? Viva la revolucion!"

"Okay. So now someone knows how I die. You know?"

"Not exactly," Marty says. "I'm your fate buddy. Your guardian angel. I get a hint of what's in store for you, and it's my job to steer you away from that and into something else."

"And has that worked yet?"

"Of course not! Feels like we're getting closer, though. We're getting operatives into centers all over the city and we're giving people fake fates. Maybe the machine says DROWNING, but we jam a fake one out there that says HIT BY A CAR."

"Seems a little unethical, don't you think?"

"I prefer to think of it as radical warfare. They will be living life like pre-machine society, and they won't even know it! And maybe their family, outraged by the grievous error in government accounting, sues, and the machine project gets put on hold for a few months... or a few years! Right? It's perfect! Sometimes the wrong thing is the right thing to do. For the greater good."

I look at his earnest eyes, the other people in the group locked on to our conversation. It seems wrong. It is wrong. I shouldn't do it. I shouldn't have gotten tested. None of this will probably make a difference. Feeling what I've felt these past few weeks, hell, since the machine was first perfected, I understand. I didn't want any of it. It makes life worse. He knows my fate. I want to tell him to go to hell. I want to tell him I'll think about his offer.

I shake his hand.

***

Two days later, when I get home from work Nadia greets me at the door holding my cell phone. I hate it when I forget that thing. Feel naked without it.

"Well, that explains why I didn't call you on the way home to see what you wanted to eat, huh?" I lean in to kiss her.

She jams the phone into my chest. "Check your messages. Marty called."

I go cold, then hot. "You listened to my messages?"

"I thought Marty might need help. You know how unstable he is. How rough things have— He called five times in thirty minutes. I thought maybe he was— what the hell have you been doing?"

"What did he—" I tap play on my voicemail.

Hey buddy, it's Marty! Hope you're ready for this big adventure to begin! You've missed our past two meetings. This is important. Things could happen. You're under my protection now. I know how to keep you safe. Listen, we have to get things rolling. We're meeting again on Sunday. And I'm… just… avoid high places, okay? You gotta—

The message cuts off as Nadia spikes the phone from my hand. "You went there? You went to that stupid building? You got tested?" She slugs my shoulder. "Did you? Let me see your finger. Let me—"

I hold up my index finger like an idiot and she grabs it, giving it a sharp twist. "You are so stupid! Why would you… what's the idea there?"

"It's not… look, I didn't commit to anything, okay? I listened. That's all. I went to a meeting and I listened."

"What did the machine tell you?"

"God Only Kn—"

She slaps me on the shoulder again and stalks away. "What did it say?"

"I don't know. I honestly don't know. I didn't look."

We stare at each other.

"Marty joined this group that's trying to… I don't know. Overthrow the government is probably putting it too strongly. They think they can take down the machines."

"Oh, so you just want to violate federal law and—"

"No… it's… they hide your fate from you. Then you get assigned a partner, someone who's read it, and they try to help you avoid the whole thing. Or find another way."

"The machine has never been wrong."

"I know! They're crackpots, okay? Marty is desperate. God help me if I ever get there."

"You know how Marty dies?"

"No. It's a one-way chain. Keeps everything honest, I guess. These people… their plan is to start getting fake results to people. Shake things up. Make them forget about Fates so we can just get back to living life the way we used to. Afraid of everything instead of one thing. Appreciating every minute so that we're—"

"Why did you get tested, though? You don't—"

"Because I want to marry you! Because no matter how bad my days are out there, I can come home to this, to you yelling at me, smacking me, or to nothing, to just reading or watching TV or enduring the dog's farts, and it makes everything better. Because I love you. More than anything. More than everything. Nothing changes that, not a stupid machine, not certainty of death, nothing. I would never hurt you. I can't."

She stares at me, an ocean about to break behind her eyes. "I don't believe you."

"What?"

"No way do you believe Knuckles' farts are better than a bad day at work. That hound could peel paint off a wall." She extends her arms and I melt into her. I move to kiss her, but she pulls away. "You really don't know what your fate said? I can't know. You understand? I cannot know."

I nod.

"Only Marty knows," I say, giving her my most earnest look.

She melts into laughter and pulls me down to sit on the sofa. "Erase him from your phone. Do not take another call from that man. He's gonna get angry, and he's going to tell you. I don't want you to know. I don't want you to worry about it. I know you! You'd overthink, overplan. You'd ruin your own life if you knew."

"Thanks for the vote of confidence."

"I don't want papers and forms. I don't want a ceremony. I don't need it. I just need you. I can't go through the whole rigamarole again. Twice was enough." She moves to the window and looks out at the street as the sun begins to set. "You know, way back in the day, you didn't need a priest or a piece of paper. You just asked, and that was it. Why can't life be that simple, where one person just says 'Will you marry me' and—"

"Yes," I say, kissing her hand. "Yeah. We're married."

She hesitates, her eyes dancing across my face before a smile breaks across her like Easter dawn. "We're married."

She slides her hands up to my face and kisses me. I breathe her in, pull her closer, sliding my hand under her shirt so I can feel her heart beating. She does the same, and God, if I could freeze that moment I would. Skin to skin, just knowing that we're alive, there, together, fate be damned. The repeating insistence from inside our chests that *we are, we are, we are.*

But there's something else there. I slide my hand lower on her breast, pressing down.

"You keep that up and you'll—"

"Shh!" I move my hand to a different spot, pressing in.

"Your moves were a little smoother back when we were dating," she mutters.

I grab her hand and guide it to where my fingers were pressing, looking into her eyes, trying not to crack. "Does this spot feel funny to you?"

∗∗∗

Dear God,

Three of the worst months of my life later and everything has gone to hell. Nadia has breast cancer. Near her nipple, which ironically enough, is just the tip of the iceberg. When the doctors ran further tests, they found evidence that the disease had gone malignant and systemic. Her ovaries are under attack. Her lymph nodes are decimated. Her spine, upon further tests, may also be harboring a surprise for her. I'm devastated. She's dying. I'm elated. She's a miracle. The Fates™ are wrong. She's going to die from cancer.

Medical science has made some major leaps, but none of them are keeping up with Nadia. Some of the hospital staff seem to think that she waited too long to get treated. Others insist that she should be showing signs of recovery, but her cancer is defying explanation, moving faster than anything they've ever seen. They get more aggressive with the chemo, and she looks more like a skeleton every day.

She doesn't want to beat the disease. It kills me to see her there in bed, her kerchief knotted just above where her eyebrows used to be. Her cheeks are sunken, her lips thinner, bags under her eyes. She's so beautiful. I don't want her to die. I don't know how to tell her. I know one thing for damn sure. I'm not buying a gun anytime soon. And she's not getting married to anyone else. We say goodnight as we have every week since she got here.

"You're sure you didn't fake that test?"

"Positive. You're supposed to shoot me. So don't."

"Say please," I smile.

"Pleeeeease," she rasps. When she swallows her throat clicks.

I kiss the back of her hand, just where the IV goes in, and tell her I love her.

"Tell the church."

"No. I don't want this to turn into a media circus."

"This isn't about what you want. Or what I want. I don't want to die. But I have to do this. God is trying to tell us something. The world has to watch this. Tell Father Patrick that my test might be wrong."

"I'll see you tomorrow."

"Tell him!" she shouts, tensing her teeth as a wave of pain hits her.

I nod and walk out, hitting the lights on the way. I pull my rosary from my pocket and start reciting the Mysteries as the elevator comes to take me back down to earth.

***

Telling the church was the last thing I wanted to do. This should be quiet and private. Hers and mine. But she's right. If this turns out the way it looks like it will, then… we win. The machine is wrong.

"This is fantas—well, it's not… this is momentous. I'm sorry, my son, I'm just… you understand the implications here? If she's leaving on her terms? On God's terms?"

I nod.

"You need to be there. For every minute. Tomorrow, first thing, as soon as visiting hours open, I'm going to the room with you and you'll be married."

"We are," I say. His face turns ashen. "Not… not legally. I didn't get the—I don't know my fate, Father. But I asked her. She said yes. That's good enough for us."

"It's not good enough to grant you visitation rights. No. Tomorrow, you wear something nice to the hospital and we—"

"The Vatican won't recognize—"

"Then damn the Vatican! They don't— you didn't hear that, okay? Just…they're men. They're only men. God is working through Nadia, and you need to be there to witness it. This will change the world."

"That's great," I murmur. "Aren't you worried I'm going to shoot her?"

"I can read your heart, son. No need, right? Right?" he slugs me on the shoulder.

"It's the right thing to do."

"I don't know what that means anymore," I tell him.

***

And then it's officially official. We're married. Simple and quiet.

Father Patrick files the necessary paperwork to give us legal status, although the lack of an official test on my part means we aren't eligible for any government marriage benefits.

Father Patrick takes the bull by the horns with Nadia's case. He doesn't even care that she's been married twice before. He spreads the news far and wide, announcing her machine ordained fate and her God-given predicament. He has vigils going day and night outside the hospital, and while it's not out of control yet, it's starting to feel like they're putting up the big top over at the news channels.

The government quietly sends someone in to test Nadia every week on several different machines to verify that her fate is CANCER. There's never been a false positive, they say. I know from my last few visits that they're starting to eye me very suspiciously, which tells me they're getting the answer that they're supposed to have: SHOT BY YOUR HUSBAND.

They want to take her out of the hospital for further testing, but we refuse, and the church steps in to start a legal battle. The government has no reason to conduct further tests, they know what her Fate™ says, and they'll have to sit back and watch like the rest of us.

Through it all, Nadia tries to be brave. She's nothing now, a paper doll in a paper gown, pale green with raised veins. She jokes that she could get a senior discount at the movies. I only talk to her for about an hour a day now. It's all the time she can manage before she has to kick on the morphine. The cancer has shriveled her internal organs to nothing, but she's hanging on despite her best efforts.

I make my way to her room, greeted by two armed security guards. They frisk me, wand me, and have me step through a metal detector three times. Once they're satisfied I'm not packing heat, they let me through. I open the door, and Nadia's got a rubber swim cap on, big rubber flowers. Swim goggles rest over her eyes, and she's got flippers on her feet.

"Wanna go swimming?" she asks me.

"What's all this?"

"I asked the nurse for it. I've been watching the news, all of those idiot reporters giving monologues about how I'm trying to die with dignity. I'll show them. This is how I want them to wheel me out of this place."

A single tear rolls down her cheek, and her eyes close. I feel like it's taken all of her energy just to give me that. Her eyes still shut, she says "I don't want this. I don't want to die. I don't want this fate; I don't want any of it. Stay here. Lie down next to me. It can't be much more than a day now."

I curl up next to her and we spend the afternoon talking about all of the crazy adventures we've had. I assure her Knuckles is fine, busily chewing his way through most of her apartment. In between sentences, she makes little whining noises in her throat, as if every heartbeat is torture. All I can do is hold her hand and pray. We say the rosary together. On our tenth Hail Mary, we're interrupted by commotion in the hall, guards shouting. I'm on my feet, in between Nadia and the door. The door opens a crack and the sounds of shouting intensify. With a horrendous crash, a man slides through the door on his back, dressed in a tattered orderly uniform, a camera in his hand.

"Carlos Ruben reporting live from the hospital room of God's Miracle Cancer Lady, Nadia—" That's as far as he gets before guards and nurses hustle in and slam him to the floor with authority. He starts screaming about freedom of the press. The guards aren't hearing any of it. He grabs onto the shelves and drawers, fighting to stay in the room. He picks up medical supplies and throws them at the guards, grabs the nurses by the shoulders. He's shouting questions the whole time. "Nadia, how do you feel? Nadia tell us what it's like! Are you in pain? Are you happy with your cancer? Are you afraid of God?"

The guards have him by the hair and the waistband of his pants, hogtied and trussed. He's out the door, his questions still trailing down to us: Are you angry at God? Did you bring this on yourself? Does your husband own a gun?

Seconds later, more nurses are in the room, making sure everything's okay. It's not. Nadia is turning blue, arms tremoring against. Her eyes grow wide, blinking as if she's seeing that bright light. Her back spasms and she starts to scream. The goggles slide from her face and the flippers kick off. I want to pull the swim cap off her head, but I stop myself. She calls my name, over and over. Reaches for me. I hold her hand, determined to be here for her until the end. The nurses and doctors work around me, check her vitals, give her shots. She bucks as the needles enter her skin.

I'm completely numb. One of the nurses tries to escort me from the room, and she gets me as far as the door. I grab the door frame. *I'm her husband, damn it* I scream. I have to be here. I need to see this. She deserves to have me here. Cold metal strikes the back of my head, and I drop to the floor.

***

Later, not sure how much later, I'm in a chair next to Nadia. She's perfectly still, eyes closed, lips slack. There's a knot on the back of my head. A doctor's face appears at the edge of my vision. She looks me in the eyes. "Security got a little overzealous. One guard late to the scene. He thought you were the scumbag from earlier. It's all over now."

"Nadia? Nadia!" I try to stand up, race to her, but the Doctor holds me down with a gentle hand.

"No! Not the… I didn't mean it was over, just the media and… She's stable. All of the excitement was a little much for her."

I notice a slight rise and fall in her chest. She's breathing. I slump back, tears in my eyes. "I'm staying here."

"Hey, I wasn't going to ask you to leave. I've been through this once myself, maybe not on your scale. I'm on your side on this one. You were only out for a few minutes. A nurse will be here to clean up the mess in about ten minutes."

I nod and the doctor slides from the room. Nadia's alive. She's still here. The room looks like a grenade went off. Cabinets are torn open, pills and syringes are scattered across the floor. I start absentmindedly picking up the room, stuffing everything into my pockets; pills, paper, medicine, vials, it needs to be clean in here for her.

As soon as the door clicks shut, Nadia's eyes snap open and focus on me. "Heyyyy," she slurs. "I feel like I'm drowning. Pressure. Pressure." She tries to motion to her chest.

We're alone, just me and the whistling pant of Nadia's breathing. "He's not coming," she croaks. "He's not coming for me. Help me, please!"

I wrap my hands around hers, and look into her eyes. Leaning forward I tell her to let go. Just let go.

"I breathe and it stabs me. I move and it slices. I can't be still. It won't let me be still."

I lie across her chest, feeling her arms beneath me, her fingers dancing under my stomach. Flicking at something in my pockets.

I reach in and pull out my rosary, wrapped around pill packets, prescription slips, and two syringes. Epinephrine. Nadia sees it and her lower lip trembles. I try to stuff them back in my pocket, but Nadia seizes my wrist.

"My God...It *is* you. He's been waiting on you..."

I grip the syringes tighter. It's a quick inject vial. Nothing to it. Pre-loaded. Snap the cap back and inject. Just give her a shot and end it.

"I love you." Her eyes close and her mouth tightens. "Break my heart. Please."

"I can't do this."

"God Only Knows. God always knows." She's said what she needs to say. I could try to walk away from this, try to let nature run its course, but I know it won't happen.

***

Dear God,

I'm climbing the stairwell to the roof. I've run these events through my head for You, just for You, to make sure we're okay. I think I've done what I'm supposed to do, Your modern unwitting Abraham. I finger the scalpel in my pocket, another remnant of the scuffle. Several floors below me, Nadia has checked out of the hospital. I can't say it was easy, or pretty, or quick, or painless. It was horrible. The most horrible thing I've ever done. She's with You now, I know that in my soul. You hold her tightly to Your heart. Free from pain, secure in the knowledge of Life, the Universe, and Everything. No more questions to answer. No more fear. No more Fates™. Just peace and quiet.

I take out my cell phone and dial Father Patrick. When he answers, I tell him I'm on the roof above the banner. They put it up just before I got to Nadia's room. The sight of it now makes me numb. I tell him it's over. He shouts the good news to the crowd. A cheer erupts, spontaneous Hallelujahs and songs of praise. No, I tell him. The machines won. They're right. We were wrong. We've been wrong about so many things. But he can't hear me. I spot him in the crowd and I wave to him. He waves back, gesticulating to the crowd, pointing me out. They begin to chant my name. I quickly kneel with the scalpel and saw through one of the ropes of the banner. The sky has grown dim and it begins to rain.

I hack at the last support cable. The damn banner is heavy, and it's blowing in the breeze, making slicing the ropes difficult. The sea of faces below me distorts under the sheets of rain. I can't tell if the roar I'm hearing is the rain, the traffic on the freeway, or their voices calling my name. Their eyes glint, mouths open, necks arched and straining to see me here above them all, the whole thing is just so rapturous.

This is our Faith, I tell them. *This is our Hope*, I shout above the gale. The last rope snaps and the wind takes the banner. GOD ONLY KNOWS. The words float above the faithful, and they'll never know just how right they are and how wrong they are.

Father Patrick consults with a doctor at the edge of the crowd. Police cars approaching. The news spreads through the crowd like a virus. Nadia is dead. Dead by my hands.

They're frenzied now, arms raised, reaching, reaching. I turn as the banner continues to collapse, watching their eyes grow wider, wider. I splay my arms and point to the skies. I think only of Nadia. Security bursts through the door behind me. I tense my legs, and I leap.

It's amazing how slowly time seems to move. All of these details seem so sharp and clear now. These last few months of my life that, for me, have been my entire life. This has been my prayer. This moment was as close to true communion with You as I'll ever get. I'm sorry for everything I've done and failed to do.

The crowds below are so close, their arms upraised. Maybe to catch me. Maybe to pull me down. I've done everything I was meant to do. I close my eyes and let fate run its course.

I lift my eyes to the sky as the clouds show just the slightest break of blue above me.

Good-bye Nadia.

See you soon.

El amor y la muerte.

PUBLICATION CREDITS

Your Mutual Friend
Dark Moon Digest Issue 31, April 2018

Worth the Having
Halloween Tales; Omnium Gatherum 2014

The Seas of Hell in a Little Glass Bottle
Mnemosyne: Pantheon Magazine, Spring 2017

Upper Crust
Tales From the Crust: An Anthology of Pizza Horror
Perpetual Motion Machine Publishing 2019

Bloodsuckers (Three Monologues) - Previously Unpublished
Inquire directly for performance rights.
mike@michaelpaulgonzalez.com.

The Iron Bulldogge
18 Wheels of Horror; Big Time Books 2015

Red Moon
Fantastic Tales of Terror: History's Darkest Secrets;
Crystal Lake Publishing 2018

The Forest that Howls
Drive-In Creature Feature; Evil Jester Press 2016

Human, Trafficking
18 Wheels of Science Fiction; Big Time Books 2018

Almost Heaven
Appalachian Undead; Apex Book Company 2013

Life on Afterlife's Terms (previously unpublished)

Choking Hazard
Winter Horror Days; Omnium Gatherum 2015

City of Emerald Ash
Endless Apocalypse: Short Stories, Flame Tree Press 2018

The Ballad of Easton Tucker, the Last Man Out (or, Eat Shit and Die)
Hard Sentences, Broken River Books 2017

Ingénue
Solarcide presents: Nova Parade; 2013

Matilda Hits Rock Bottom
Colored Chalk Magazine

Spitfire
Colored Chalk Magazine

White (previously unpublished)

Tidal
In Search of a City: Los Angeles in 1,000 Words; Thunderdome Press 2012

One Shot: God Only Knows
The Booked. Anthology; VON Media 2013

All characters and locations appearing in this book are fictitious. Any resemblance to real persons in is purely coincidental.

<u>**NOVELS FROM THE AUTHOR**</u>

ANGEL FALLS

MISS MASSACRE'S GUIDE TO MURDER AND VENGEANCE

www.ingramcontent.com/pod-product-compliance
Lightning Source LLC
Chambersburg PA
CBHW021121110726
47900CB00007B/2280